D1386018

Wives of the East Wind

Liu Hong

headline
review

First published in Great Britain in 2007
by HEADLINE REVIEW
An imprint of HEADLINE PUBLISHING GROUP

First published in paperback in Great Britain in 2007
by HEADLINE REVIEW
An imprint of HEADLINE PUBLISHING GROUP

1

Cataloguing in Publication Data is available from the British Library

ISBN 978 0 7553 0605 3 (B format)
ISBN 978 0 7553 4473 4 (A format)

Typeset in Meridien by Avon DataSet Ltd,
Bidford-on-Avon, Warwickshire

Printed and bound in Great Britain by Clays Ltd, St Ives plc

Headline's policy is to use papers that are natural, renewable and
recyclable products and made from wood grown in sustainable
forests. The logging and manufacturing processes are expected to
conform to the environmental regulations of the country of origin.

HEADLINE PUBLISHING GROUP
An Hachette Livre UK Company
338 Euston Road
London NW1 3BH

www.headline.co.uk
www.hodderheadline.com

This book is dedicated to my family,
in China and England

Chinese Names

In Chinese the family name comes first, followed by a one- or two-syllable given name. People who know each other well will address each other with given names only; when the given name has only one syllable it is usually repeated, like Zhenzhen. Lao, meaning old, and Xiao, meaning young, are both terms of endearment and are usually placed in front of the family name to show affection, for example Lao Gao and Lao Cui. On formal occasions the full name will be used, for instance Gao Yutang, Xu Zhen and Lin Zhiying.

Prologue

A cheerful young truck driver takes pity on me, and stops to pick me up. I climb in slowly, and thank him. I hadn't been able to flag down a taxi, I explain.

'How on earth did you get here?' he asks, concerned.

'I walked.'

He gives me a puzzled look, and starts the engine.

I turn to take a final look at the factory. The sign, the building, the people, all are new. This young man must be one of the workers, I saw him driving out of the gate. I would have liked to linger longer, to take in how much it had all changed, but the security guards were already hovering close, eyeing me suspiciously.

The driver has a gentle face, I feel safe with him. There is something about him that reminds me of the young Zhiying.

'I don't usually see old women stranded in the middle of nowhere, all on their own,' he says, intrigued. 'You sound like a local, but you don't live here, do you? What are you doing here?'

'Trying to find . . . people I used to know.'

'And have you had any luck?'

I nod but say nothing. I can't tell him I was looking for ghosts, ghosts of my youth. I close my eyes and breathe in the satisfyingly pungent smell of the engine as the truck trundles through the suburbs I had once known so well: hitching a lift in a truck had felt like the most natural thing in the world, but so much had changed since I had last done so. A picture forms in my mind: the red gates of the East Wind factory, wide open to admit a stream of singing youth on bicycles. I am walking down the grand central boulevard of the complex, bordered on either side with flowers and trees, past the many workshops from which I hear loud metallic clangs and the hum of industrial ovens mingled with the low, rhythmic chanting of the workers. The walls of the workshops are decorated as always with red flags and posters of workers with bright smiles. In the distance, newly completed trucks stand in line, gleaming proudly in the sun. Beside the trucks I glimpse all the familiar faces: Zhiying, Lao Gao, Lao Cui . . .

The loud trill of a mobile phone brings me back to the present. I open my eyes and ask if he likes working at the factory.

'It's just a job. I'm on a short-term contract and this is only my second week.'

My people had given the best years of their lives to East Wind.

We are at the city centre. Noise, traffic, people. 'Where would you like to be dropped?' he asks me.

'By the river, please.'

He stops by the ticket office for boat trips, and helps me down, hesitating a little. I wave him off: 'I'll be fine now, my hotel is just around the corner.'

Finally I am by the river, surrounded by tourists from all over the country. On the quay the last boat is calling its passengers and everyone surges on, leaving me alone on the bank. The boatman shouts at me to get on, taking me for a tourist. I shake my head, fearing to speak. Though I have lived abroad for almost twenty years, as soon as I open my mouth, he'll know I'm a local. I don't want to answer any more questions today.

It is getting dark, the tide is coming in. A chilly wind blows, and I shiver. This was where we last met, Zhenzhen and I. I see her face now: it was calm, although pearls of sweat were forming on her forehead . . .

I look beyond the darkness, into the river, where a thin mist is rising. Suddenly, I seem to hear a sharp cry – is she calling to me? In all the years we knew each other, Zhenzhen and I could never agree which of us had cried out first the moment Xiao Tao was born, on the day we met. That was the first time I saw blood on her hands, and it was mine.

Part I:
Xiao Tao, North China, 1960s

1

When our spoons touched in the bowl, we dared to meet each other's eyes. Zhiying must have seen me frown. 'Is everything all right?' he asked, concerned, his head nearly touching mine. I could smell soap-powder on his clean but worn and faded green army jacket.

I nodded emphatically, unable to stop my teeth chattering – the ice-cream had chilled me but I was shaking with nerves anyway. 'I ate it too fast,' I said, smiling, 'so I've got a headache now.'

I couldn't remember the last time I'd eaten out. Such luxury was only possible now because I was dating an employee of the East Wind factory, the largest in town. Zhiying seemed nervous, too: his hands reached out as if to touch my forehead and smooth away the pain, but then he withdrew them. 'Perhaps I should have taken you to Lao Tang's next door. They do hot soup . . .'

His awkwardness steadied me. 'I'm all right now,' I said, and stood up. 'Come on – you said you were going to show me the factory.'

His bike was parked outside the ice-cream parlour, along with a dozen others, distinguished only by the small cushion on the parcel rack. I sat on it, and marvelled at his thoughtfulness. 'Are you ready? Hold tight,' he said, and I gripped the back of his seat. As he pedalled out of the city centre I noticed a hint of green on the willows beside the road and realised that spring was on its way.

For a long time after we left the Big Sand river, I couldn't see anything but a vast expanse of wilderness, broken only by a newly laid railtrack. Hat Hill, under which our city lay, loomed large, its shadow darkening half of the wasteland beneath it. There was a kind of bleak beauty about the scene, and I was moved by the emptiness. But where was the factory?

'Are we there yet?' I asked, a little impatient.

'Nearly,' he panted.

'Tell me more about Lao Gao.' Zhiying had been enthusing about his leader while we ate.

'Lao Gao . . .' Zhiying slowed. 'Where to begin?'

'How did he win the medal?'

'He and his platoon were positioned in a strategic valley as part of a major ambush. The enemies rained a shower of shells on them – you know how cowardly the Americans were, never wanting to risk their lives. One landed on Lao Gao and set him on fire. Instead of rolling over to the stream that was nearby, he remained motionless, thus saving the lives of his comrades and ensuring the military plan remained secret . . .'

'What a heroic, selfless man he must be!' I exclaimed.

Zhiying turned and beamed at me, still pedalling along. 'He's our inspiration. We're lucky to have him.'

I'd heard a low hum ever since we'd crossed the river and now it was getting louder. A gust of wind brought with it a pungent mix of machine oil and a faint peal of laughter. Round the bend of the road an extraordinary sight greeted my eyes: on the left-hand side two giant wooden poles were set far apart, supporting an arch with 'East Wind' written on it in red and gold paint, and adorned with red silk flowers. When the wind blew, little red flags flapped like waving hands. Beyond, I glimpsed a wide asphalt road, and a collection of brick bungalows that gleamed in the last light of the setting sun.

Zhiying braked and got off the bike, wiping the sweat from his face. 'East Wind, the biggest producer of trucks in China.'

Much later I learned that he had been boasting. East Wind was perhaps the tenth largest in our country. Still, to me it was huge. There had always been a truck factory in town, owned and run by the Japanese during their occupation of north-east China. Mother had spoken of passing the grounds and shivering at the sight of the Alsatians with which the Japanese had patrol-led them. After they were driven out the factory was razed to the ground during the civil war, and although there had been talk of reviving it when the new China was established, the American invasion of North Korea had led to postponement – our town was right on the border. A neighbour of Mother's had visited relatives in this part of the countryside and told us the place was riddled with bomb craters. Even after the war ended – some years ago now – unexploded missiles meant the area had been unsafe for some time. Now, though, it had been transformed.

'Welcome to East Wind.' Zhiying beamed, taking my hand – forgetting himself.

Inside throngs of young workers streamed in and out of workshops with wide metal doors, laughing and chatting.

They wore shabby old clothes, but wherever I looked I was met with a smile, and whichever way I turned I heard a hum of singing. No one was idle. The atmosphere was friendly yet busy.

I had wanted to pause and take it all in, but Zhiying hurried me on. 'There's more,' he said, and took me to the end of the road and a sign that said: 'No admittance'. 'There.' In front of me stood a dozen brand new trucks, gleaming with fresh green paint, and across the front 'East Wind' in giant red letters. 'These trucks are made by Chinese hands, our first batch,' Zhiying whispered. 'Next week, they'll be driven through town as part of the celebration . . .'

I peered at him and smiled. He had kept this secret. His work was confidential, he had hinted. He couldn't talk about it as there were still Nationalist and American agents around who might sabotage the factory – indeed, before the Nationalists had retreated south, they had tried to destroy it, to 'leave the Communists an empty shell of a town'.

'It's the workers who make this place, Wenya, and you'll meet everyone at the inauguration party.' Zhiying pointed at a three-storey building just outside the back gate of the factory. 'There's to be a banquet there tonight. Lao Gao will be there and you'll meet everyone. The best of China's youth, from all over the country.'

And Zhiying was one of them.

I had known him since childhood – we had been classmates at school. Then he had been an unassuming boy, wearing patched but clean clothes with quiet dignity. He had seemed old for his age and I had watched him play basketball during breaks with the other boys. However, it was not until after we had left that we became friends, sharing our plans for the future. I felt an instant bond with him.

He had gone to Harbin, a big city further north, to study engineering, and I had gone to our local college of medicine. From time to time I thought of Zhiying, but I was preoccupied with my future – and with other boys – until we met one day by chance in the street, at a time when my mother was trying to match me with the son of a pharmacist. My shyness had made her fear I might never marry. I laughed at Zhiying's jokes and he seemed pleased to see me. When I told him I'd moved house he looked relieved: 'So that's why you never wrote back! I'd thought . . .'

'You sent me letters?' I was excited. Nobody had written to me before. He smiled and said it was probably better that I didn't read them now.

That night, I went home giggling and red-cheeked. I'd recently qualified as a doctor and was about to start at the local hospital, an exciting yet daunting prospect. Mother's attempt at matchmaking had added to my anxiety. Zhiying had made me feel light-hearted again.

It was getting late when we left the factory and headed for the building Zhiying had pointed out earlier. This time, I put my hands round his waist when he started to pedal. Instead of heading straight for the living quarters he took little detours – to delay our arrival, perhaps? I let my head rest on his back and watched the giant shadow of Hat Hill creep across the factory. The sun was setting. How delightful it was, I thought, not to have to check the skies for enemy aeroplanes or listen for their engines . . . The war had ended some time before, but it was only then that I realised there would be no more fighting. Perhaps that was the moment when I began to feel attached to the factory: a moment of peace, full of hope for the future.

Zhiying's room was on the second floor, but it seemed to take for ever to get there. We were stopped constantly by young men with maps, sheets of paper and graphs, eager to consult with him. They spoke many different dialects, some of which I had never heard before: I understood just enough from their brief exchanges to grasp that the living quarters were being used as offices until another building was completed. Standing a little behind Zhiying I noticed how relaxed the young men were with each other – but they were taken aback when they saw me, a woman in the single men's quarters.

When we extricated ourselves, Zhiying pointed to a small room at the bottom of the stairs: 'Lao Gao's.'

'Why is he living with the bachelors? Doesn't he have a family?'

Zhiying shook his head. 'He says he's married to the factory. You'll see how committed he is.'

I glanced at the door. Married to the factory? I wondered how old he was.

When we reached the second floor I heard a flute. At first I thought I was imagining it, amid the hubbub of shouts, the banging of chopsticks and the clatter of food bowls. But then I picked out a tune I knew. It held me – then stopped abruptly. 'What's that?' I tugged at Zhiying's sleeve. We had reached his door and his room-mates greeted him as he ushered me in.

'What?' he asked, but the moment had passed.

Later that night, I sat in a noisy echoing hall, lined with

long wooden benches occupied by animated young men, and thought of silent meals at home with Mother. It was flattering to be the centre of attention. The young men now learnt of my friendship with Zhiying. They were eager to talk, polite and attentive.

The moment I entered the building I had been aware of delicious cooking smells and felt almost weak with hunger. Occasionally in my childhood I had been indulged, perhaps during Spring Festival or Moon Festival, but since I'd been an adult there had been rationing, though with Mother's careful planning we'd always got by. I soon realised that things were different here. We were served a feast: the pheasants had been shot that morning on Hat Hill, and the fish caught in the river. Amid the banging of spoons and chopsticks on aluminium food boxes, the conversation drifted to technical topics, but as the night wore on I heard Lao Gao's name more and more frequently, spoken with the mix of reverence and familiarity that Zhiying had shown when he talked about him. Two chairs at the head of the long table were conspicuously empty. Was one for him?

When we had nearly finished eating, we were plunged into darkness. We were all used to power cuts and Zhiying whispered, 'I'll go and fetch the candles.'

I sat back and stretched. I thought of the flute I'd heard earlier and wondered which young man was the musician.

Suddenly there were sounds of movement at the door, and through the glass window we saw a faint light, gradually getting brighter. Then we heard footsteps and the young men around me murmured, 'Lao Gao.'

Two figures came in, one holding a big candle, and

13

everybody stood up. The first man, holding the candle, was tall but his face was in shadow so I couldn't see him clearly. The second was short, but his footsteps sounded loudest. When they approached the table, the first tall man bent down to pull out a chair for the other, whom I knew now must be Lao Gao, the war hero. At first glance his face shocked me: it was heavily scarred. I wondered why Zhiying hadn't mentioned it – perhaps he no longer noticed it as he'd known Lao Gao for a while – and whether it had put off potential brides.

The tall young man sat next to Lao Gao. He seemed preoccupied, staring at the candle. When he glanced up his eyes rested on me, and for a moment I was almost afraid. But when he smiled the fear evaporated and I knew why I had been intimidated – Lao Gao was ugly, but his companion was a handsome man.

'Comrades, founders of the East Wind Engine Factory.' As soon as Lao Gao spoke, in the accent of Sichuan, the hall fell quiet. 'As you know, I have come from Beijing, and I have news for you.'

From the corner of my eye I saw Zhiying distributing candles along the table, but I hardly noticed when he came back and sat next to me, so absorbed was I in the contrast between Lao Gao's face, and that of his elegant secretary. It was like staring at a craggy hill, then into a smooth valley. Though I knew it was in the craggy hill that I should be looking for hidden treasure, it was the smooth valley to which my eyes were drawn. I tried to concentrate on Lao Gao's speech.

'. . . so the Soviet Union, our so-called big brother, has withdrawn all its industrial advisers.' Lao Gao's hawk-like eyes surveyed the room, and the faces around me sobered.

As he stood up, his shadow loomed large in the candle-light: 'We – are – on – our – own.'

We had heard rumours that the Russians were to withdraw their support from China, but I was struck by Lao Gao's reference to the Soviet Union. In the past, the talk had been of 'our Soviet elder brothers'. Posters and magazines showed pictures of benignly smiling blond youth. Soviet clothes were fashionable, and singing Soviet revolutionary anthems was one of our favourite pastimes.

'What does this mean?' Lao Gao asked. 'I see you are shocked.' He went on, almost softly, 'Indeed, when Director Zhang from the Ministry of Defence told me the news I was shocked, too. Our friend, our comrade, our elder brother, had deserted us. Director Zhang asked me, "What will happen to East Wind?"'

I remembered what Zhiying had told me earlier about the Soviet advisers at the factory. They were the chief engineers and lived at the best guest-house in town. Every day they were chauffeur-driven to the factory, to direct the construction and other operations. I shot a glance at Zhiying, whose face had paled. His eyes were riveted on Lao Gao, who raised a hand. 'Now, this is what I said to Director Zhang: "A grieving army is sure to win. Why? Because now we've got nothing to lose."

'"How?" I see you asking. This is how. Show me your hands.' The young men looked at each other in bewilderment, then stretched out their hands one by one. Lao Gao stretched out his own. 'I had had no training before I joined the volunteer army in Korea. I came from a poor peasant family in Sichuan. These hands, though strong, were only used to restraining buffalo and holding the plough. But in Korea I learned to use a gun, to mend a car, to sew and cook. Why did I pick up these skills so quickly? I had to. It was a matter of life and death.'

He paused, and I held my breath.

'Now, our nation and our beloved factory are facing a crisis, and you can show your country what you can do for it. Jin Lin can make radios. Yi Jia calculates faster than anyone else. Zhiying draws the best maps . . .' He pointed at each man as he spoke their names. 'You are among the best brains in the country. You must rise to the challenge.'

His hand, high above his head, tightened into a fist. 'You are the future, the hands and brains of the new East Wind, our truck factory. Yes, the Soviet experts were the chief engineers. Yes, our first batch of trucks was made with their help. But must we always rely on outsiders? Are foreigners innately cleverer or stronger than us? *We* drove away the Japanese invaders after eight years of fighting. *We* defeated the Nationalists when they wanted to destroy our new republic. *We* beat the American imperialists with their big guns in Korea. Now we will prove to the world that we can build a new China with our own hands. You can do it – *we* can do it! This is what I said to Director Zhang. At this time next year, we'll present to the nation our own, truly Chinese East Wind trucks!'

He paused and it seemed his eyes took in everyone present. Then he said gently, '*That* was my promise to our leaders. Please don't let me down.'

There was a pause – then applause thundered out. We stood up and cheered, we shook hands with each other, we stamped our feet. Zhiying and I nearly embraced. It was then that Lao Gao spotted me and strode over. My hands were gripped. 'I have heard so much about you,' he said. Now I saw the twinkle in his eyes, and the smile that lit his face gave it an unexpected beauty. I warmed to him. He was nearly twenty years older than most of us but the hair that flopped on to his forehead made him seem younger. Speechless, I could only shake his hand.

I had never met a man like Lao Gao before, and never have since. He made me trust him instantly and completely. From his smile, I sensed that he was a straightforward man, unlike Zhiying, who was shy but pretended not to be. It wasn't a fault – I found it endearing.

When the tall young man emerged from behind Lao Gao I blushed. Lao Gao introduced him and I nodded but couldn't think of anything to say. If Lao Gao put me instantly at ease, Cheng Ming made me feel awkward, as if I knew more about him than I should. I shook his hand, which was cool and light, in contrast with Lao Gao's warmth. In that brief moment of contact I felt the hard pads at the tips of his fingers and my heart quickened. My father had had fingers like that: I realised Cheng Ming must be the flautist I'd heard earlier.

'Is Zhiying looking after you? And these lads?' Lao Gao asked.

'Yes, Lao Gao.' I addressed him as everyone else had, and saw from his smile that he liked it. Emboldened, I continued, 'This is such a good party – I wish it didn't have to end.'

'End? It's only just begun!' Then Lao Gao roared, 'Come on, lads, eat, and drink to your heart's content. The republic needs you to be well fed!' He returned to his seat, followed by Cheng Ming. Loud cheers and conversation resumed, even noisier than before.

'. . . we will catch up with the Soviet Union in three years' time, with the British in less than five and with the

Americans sooner . . .' Amid laughter and cheers we pledged our determination. So what if the Soviet Union had deserted us and we were on our own? As we used to say: 'We are young, we can move mountains. We will show the world.'

I don't remember much more about that evening, other than that towards the end we started singing, mostly Soviet songs: we had made them our own, and saw no reason to stop singing them. 'Night in the Moscow Suburb', 'In the Ukrainian Forest', and 'The Red Blossoms', which was one of my favourites. We sang with passion and righteous anger. We had been wronged, our Soviet elder brothers had deserted us but, like the phoenix, we would rise from the fire to be reborn stronger. My hands hurt from clapping and my voice was hoarse, but still I wanted to sing. The music was the invisible thread that bound us together and I felt I had been embraced into the heart of East Wind.

Lao Gao did not try to stop us but neither did he join in. Already his scarred face was dear to me and spoke to me of his nobility and courage. I saw the affectionate way in which he looked at me and Zhiying, and the glow I felt made me lean closer to Zhiying. The night ended with the song that people still sing in karaoke nowadays:

> 'March, march, march
> Across the river,
> For the sake of peace and homeland,
> We fight the American invaders.'

As we sang all heads were turned to Lao Gao, who nodded and smiled, his hands moving in time to the music.

When Zhiying took me home on his bike he spoke again of Lao Gao: 'You thought his speech was good? You haven't heard him telling stories. He can recite whole chapters from the classics: *San Guo, The Romance of the Three Kingdoms*.' If he was in the mood he told of his years fighting the Americans . . . Every night there was a story. For a war hero he lived modestly, eating in the factory canteen, even though he was entitled to a small kitchen and his own cook. But I shouldn't be fooled by his modesty, Zhiying warned. If you did something wrong you wouldn't escape his attention. Make a mistake in your design and he'd notice it. But he was fair, Zhiying was quick to add. He had high standards for others but even higher ones for himself.

'What about his secretary?' I found myself asking. 'What's he like?'

For a moment Zhiying didn't answer. Then: 'What do you want to know about him? He's just a southerner.' He hesitated. 'From Hang Zhou.' I had to bite my lip to stop myself laughing. 'He plays the flute quite well. Lao Gao likes it,' Zhiying added 'There's going to be a band – the East Wind entertainment dancing troupe. Shame you don't work in the factory. You have a good singing voice.'

As the city lights came into view, Zhiying stopped the bike and turned to me. 'I missed the singing,' he said. 'I missed hearing your voice. Can we sing together now?'

I sang. But our voices sounded thin and reedy, and the songs, drowned by the traffic, seemed wanting. Singing them alone with Zhiying wasn't the same as singing with the others in the canteen . . .

2

I don't remember much about the days between that night and Zhiying's first meeting with Mother. I made many more visits to his living quarters and had many more meals there, but none matched the intensity of the first. What I do remember, vividly, are the railway tracks, which grew longer each time we walked beside them. They were the factory's artery, transporting to it badly needed equipment and fuel. Our country needed trucks, the kind that East Wind would produce, Zhiying told me.

As we strolled past the rail track, Zhiying talked of how, as a child, he had often run several *lis* from his remote village home just to watch the trains. Where they lived, they'd never seen roads, let alone trains, and the sight of them had filled him with excitement. He had decided then to become an engineer so that he could design them. He didn't mind being assigned to a truck factory, he told me, as that, too, meant contributing to the revolutionary cause. We were used to obeying the call of our country; we all relinquished our dreams gladly to the grander vision of a shared, bright future.

It had been my idea that he should meet Mother. She

needed some persuasion. It was strange that she had wanted to rush me into marriage with a man I hardly knew yet was reluctant to meet one I liked. But I was used to her ways. I'd been led to believe that she hated a particular aunt, only to see her crying inconsolably when the woman died; she had been Mother's best friend, I had been informed, with whom she had shared many secrets. What about all the heated arguments I had witnessed? Mother glared at me. 'Mind your own business.'

I remember the day of his first visit well. I saw everything with new eyes, sensitive to the impression it might make on him. Some distant relatives from the countryside had been to visit and had brought with them a present of precious chicken. After we'd eaten it, Mother had boiled the bones for days to get all the goodness out of it. The smell had begun to make me feel sick, but when I complained Mother said coolly that I had never known real hunger. That day, she boiled the bones again, just before Zhiying arrived. I almost died with embarrassment when I opened the door and Zhiying sniffed. I scowled at Mother. 'Here he is,' I said, and she came to the door as if nothing was wrong.

'Come in,' she said. 'I was preparing dinner.'

Zhiying smiled. 'It smells good.' Approval glinted in Mother's eye.

Inside, Zhiying's eyes were drawn to Mother's large collection of framed photos on the walls. In our sparsely furnished house, they were precious treasures. They represented Mother's compensation for her small family, which consisted of herself and me. My father had died more than ten years ago and my little brother in infancy of pneumonia.

When Mother came in with the tea, Zhiying was studying a picture of me aged nine, standing with my parents in front of a tall pavilion. 'I can tell it's you,' he said, then turned to Mother. 'Wenya is so like you, Auntie.'

Mother glanced at the photo. 'She never does her hair properly, I'm afraid. Drink your tea, before it's cold.' She sat on the bed – Zhiying had been invited to sit on the only chair, which we reserved for visitors. Our sitting room was also our bedroom, but Mother had made sure the bedding was packed away in the chest. The bed was bare, with no hint of intimacy.

Zhiying leaned forward and gestured to the handsome young man standing behind Mother. 'That must be Wenya's late father?'

Mother nodded, then looked away. I stepped closer to the photo. I knew it well, partly because it was almost the only photo we had of him. Father was the handsomest man I had ever known, an impression drawn not from memory but from the photo. When I had been young, the house had been full of pictures of him, standing tall, wearing a western suit. I didn't remember him looking so smart in real life – in my memory his clothes had smelt of tobacco, food and the wood we burned in the fireplace.

I drank my tea as Mother and Zhiying chatted. I heard mother sigh when Zhiying told her both his parents had now passed away. She leaned forward and gave him a sympathetic look. I supposed most of the older generation would take to Zhiying – he was so polite and presentable.

'But, Auntie, it can't have been easy for you, bringing up Wenya alone all these years. I admire you,' Zhiying said. Mother smiled.

Emboldened, Zhiying asked, 'Why have you so few photos of your husband?'

Mother stared at the picture, then waved a hand vaguely. 'We lost the rest.' She stood up. 'I must go to check the dinner.'

Zhiying and I exchanged a glance. I noted the sympathy in his eyes. Had Mother told him how often we'd moved house when I was a child? At one point we had been staying with a distant cousin when I was woken one night by Mother's sobbing. I asked her why she was crying, and she told me she had lost all her photographs of Father. She had searched everywhere, but couldn't find them. I had held her heaving shoulders and listened to the night train's lonely whistle.

Mother brought out dinner: coarse rice, chicken broth with carrots and potatoes. The carrots tasted especially good – their sweetness melted in the mouth. I could judge Mother's mood by the flavour of her food. Today I knew she wanted to reassure me. But I was embarrassed – I remembered the pheasant and fish Zhiying and I had eaten in the canteen. How could he enjoy our food after what he was used to?

Later he invited me to an outing with the factory to celebrate May Day – Workers' Day. It would be at Hat Hill, he said, and all of his friends would be there. 'Make sure you're ready by nine o'clock – I'll come on my bike to fetch you.' I nodded and said yes, but I was a bit disappointed: he should have whispered his invitation to me in private. It was not that Mother would object, just that I wanted to feel we had a secret to share.

After dinner Zhiying rose to leave, and lingered at the door. Mother stepped past me and held it open for him, saying repeatedly, 'Go carefully.' Her hands were shaking – it seemed she was more nervous than I was. Zhiying waved and turned away.

It was then that we were plunged into darkness. Even his hurried 'goodbye' seemed swallowed by the night. Mother murmured, 'Power cut again,' and went to fetch a candle, but Zhiying's voice rang out, 'Don't worry, I'll find my way.' I imagined him walking past the other bungalows near ours, built by the Japanese and now occupied by poor city people, like ourselves. The front of each served as storage space and the smell of rotten vegetables and household waste would waft to him as he passed. I prayed he didn't stumble over anything. It was all so different from his clean, cheerful home at the factory. I wanted to run after him, walk with him, shelter him from the squalor until we emerged into his world where poverty and hunger had no place. Standing in the dark, I had a vision of the brand new house that would be ours if we married, with white walls and high ceilings, the floor smooth and shining, a large window with curtains I had made . . .

Mother called and I blushed: could she read my thoughts? I glanced back at her face, lit up by the candle she held. She looked into my eyes. 'A nice young man,' she murmured. I waited nervously, but she said no more.

That night we went to bed early. When I heard even breathing beside me, I let out a long sigh. My eyes moved to the pictures on the wall where, by the moonlight, I could just make out my father's slender figure. I missed him. I thought again of the night the photographs had gone missing. Something I had tried to suppress that night came back to me: the look on Mother's face. It wasn't simply grief – there had been something else . . .

3

May Day was cloudy but that didn't dampen our spirits. Before Zhiying and I became close, I had never given it much thought. It was simply International Labour Day, a day off for the workers, who'd go to parks, riversides and the hills to picnic and party. Now, because of him, I was part of it.

While Zhiying went to deposit the bike I admired the park's giant gate. In its grandness and scale, it reminded me of the gate at the East Wind factory, but it was more colourful and ornate. Two golden dragons spiralled round giant columns, raising their heads to the sky; the tops of the columns were joined by a wooden pole, painted with intricate blossoms. The paint was so new I could smell it. Zhiying pointed to the calligraphy above the blossoms. 'Lao Gao himself wrote that: "East Wind workers' park".'

Mother had been to the park in the past, when it was used almost exclusively by the occupying Japanese – no Chinese were allowed. She was sewing for a Japanese family at the time and was allowed to use the park as a short-cut. She remembered families picnicking there and spoke of cherry blossom so pretty she couldn't believe it was real. In my childhood I had ridden past it once, and glimpsed the wounded, retreating Kuomintang masses – the Nationalist troops had used the park as a temporary field hospital. When they were driven away, the park was a wreck, filled with litter and filth. Now it was being turned into a workers' paradise, one of Lao Gao's many grand designs. As I followed Zhiying around it, he showed me the newly planted trees. Some were already in blossom, but there was much still to be done. However, it was filled with people, and I felt a sense of belonging: this was *our* park. That it was incomplete didn't bother me: the activity around us was uplifting, and Zhiying so attentive. I leaned closer to him, away from Mother's stern stare.

A photo of us was taken at around this time, at the town studio. We were still shy with each other and our hands barely touched. I still have it, in its original frame. You don't see that kind of smile any more, not even in young lovers.

We didn't stay in the park for long – the bright red of the wild flowers blooming on Hat Hill whispered an invitation we couldn't refuse. We hopped through a gap in a half-built wall and on to a path leading upwards.

Hat Hill was part of the Mount Forever White Range, which had given birth to two nations and three rivers. Bitter battles had been fought among its valleys and peaks, blood shed when guerrillas had ambushed the Japanese, and the Communists had defeated the Nationalists. People from outside our city came to marvel at the red flowers, although locals murmured that the blood of the fallen had given them their brilliance.

Bikes were left outside the park gate so we had to carry our food up the hill. When Zhiying offered for the third time to take my bags, I slid them off my shoulders. He tried to carry things for other people too, which pleased me – he was kind to everyone, not only to me.

A group of young men rushed up to us. I knew many of them now, and Zhiying joined them while I caught up with some girls. At first we kept looking for each other and waving, but soon the two groups swept us apart and I lost sight of him. Eventually the girls I was with sat down to rest, but I was eager to rejoin Zhiying and went on.

My feet were sore – for a trip to the mountain, I'd put on a pair of lace-up shoes I didn't often wear. The leather was soft and old, but still they hurt. I felt lost – why hadn't Zhiying waited for me? I wondered, as I wandered into woodland.

The peace there was pleasant. The thick scent of decayed leaves calmed me, and the sounds below were muffled. I thought of Father, and the sentimental old poems about spring that he had recited to me. The beauty of the images formed part of my picture of Father – it reminded me of his love, which I could draw on when I felt sad. I had always kept such thoughts to myself – when Mother had called Father *wenruo shusheng*, 'delicate scholar', it had been with sarcasm: we couldn't afford such a man as the main rice-winner, she had complained, sweeping the floor as he practised his flute.

I sat on a fallen tree. As a child I had worshipped Father, and would close my eyes as he played those mournful, magical tunes. 'Stop it,' Mother said. 'You'll bring back the dead.' She had pressed her hands to her ears. Later, when she had left the room, I would beg him to go on. Those brief but perfect moments bound Father and me together. They took us out of the mundane, everyday world to which Mother insisted on bringing us back.

I stood up to continue walking. Last winter's dead leaves, turning to mud, squelched beneath my feet and a stream sang nearby. I heard the drip of water, though I could not see it. A light rain began to fall, but the trees formed a canopy. In the distance I seemed to hear someone call my name, but I wanted to stay where I was, listening to the rain, remembering my life with Father.

'*Kong shan xin yu hou*. Fresh rain on an empty hill . . .' I murmured, and seemed to see Father nodding.

From the depth of the wood I heard someone moving in my direction. Soon a shadowy figure stood before me, holding a flute. I felt a slight chill at my back. The undergrowth rustled as he approached. It was Cheng Ming. At the same time the voice called my name again, closer now.

I gazed at the flute. '*Er quan yin yue*. Two fountains reflecting the moon,' I said. It was both a request and a question. Cheng Ming stared at me, puzzled.

The voice called again, urgent now. I stepped towards Cheng Ming. 'Play it,' I demanded.

He smiled, licked his lips and swallowed, as Father would have done. 'Two Fountains'. Last time I heard it, Father had cut it short. A job interview, he had said, then changed into a smart suit. He promised to come back and finish the melody. I never saw him again.

Cheng Ming raised his hands, and I was struck once more by his elegance. His eyes were downcast as he prepared to play, reminding me again of Father. He put the flute to his lips and I closed my eyes.

'There you are!'

It was Zhiying's voice, and as he reached me I sighed,

annoyed that I wouldn't hear the whole tune, after all. He leaned on a tree, breathless. 'Wenya, what are you doing here?'

Cheng Ming must have made a sound because Zhiying spun round. 'Who's there?'

'It's me,' said Cheng Ming.

The smile disappeared from Zhiying's face. 'What are *you* doing here?' He frowned.

Cheng Ming smiled as if he hadn't noticed Zhiying's tone. 'It seems Wenya and I got lost in the same part of the wood.'

Zhiying turned to me but said nothing. Still annoyed with him, I asked, 'How do we get out of here?'

Zhiying hesitated then said, 'Follow me.' He started to walk, with me behind him, then Cheng Ming. We didn't speak while we climbed to the top of the steep hill. I felt strange to be walking between the two young men. Though Zhiying and I were going out together, I felt I shared a secret bond with Cheng Ming. When we emerged from the wood and were reunited with the rest of our group, the rain had stopped and the sky was blue.

'Zhiying ran back to the park to look for you,' Lao Gao said, and smiled. 'He thought you'd been kidnapped by Soviet agents.'

Laughter erupted and Zhiying blushed at the teasing, but said nothing. I was struck by the look in his eyes – he cared for me, I realised suddenly, and was touched. I glanced at Cheng Ming and felt the distance between us. What I had with Zhiying was solid and real. The moment of closeness I had experienced with Cheng Ming in the woods had been fleeting, insubstantial.

After we'd eaten our picnic Zhiying and I found a spot

by a tree and sat down. He leaned close to me to point out the factory chimneys and the river that snaked round our city. I could see the grey and brown factory workshops, dull coloured but familiar and welcoming.

It was then that I heard 'Two Fountains'. I turned round but could see only the backs of the clapping youths, who cheered as the flute was played. I knew many of them were from the East Wind entertainment troupe, which was already preparing to enter a citywide competition. Soon a violin and a guitar had joined the flute. I had always considered flute-playing a solitary, meditative occupation, and at first the music sounded strange to me. But gradually I began to enjoy the music, and the way it brought us all together. When the tune ended, Lao Gao's voice said, 'Well done, Cheng Ming – that's my favourite piece.'

My eyes met Zhiying's. Something in them made my heart beat fast. In all the time we had spent together, I'd never seen him so full of longing. I had to look away, but his words held me.

'I really like you, Wenya,' he said. 'When can we marry?'

Ever since that first night, when he had taken me to the factory, I had expected him to propose, but at that moment it was the last thing on my mind. For a second I was silent. Suddenly the group around us burst into applause again, and Cheng Ming bowed, Lao Gao patting his neck. This was the world to which I wanted to belong. Now Zhiying had asked me to join it. 'Whenever you would like us to,' I said.

4

It was only after we had parted, when I walked alone along the short dark lane – I had begged him to drop me off at the top so that Mother's nosy neighbours wouldn't see us – that sadness came over me. As he was getting on to his bike I nearly asked if we could carry on as friends. Marriage seemed such a big step. He was kind and gentle, and I was fond of him, but I was terrified by the prospect of spending the rest of my life with him – sometimes he still seemed a stranger.

Suddenly I was plunged into darkness: another power cut. Mother opened the door before I could knock, holding a candle. As soon as I was inside, she blew it out – to save wax. We talked in the dark, as we did whenever there was no electricity.

'You must be tired,' she said.

'Not really,' I replied, although I was exhausted.

'Did you have fun?'

'Yes.'

'Are you hungry?'

'No.'

'What's happened?'

I turned my face away from her.

'What is it?'

'He asked me to marry him.'

For a long time she said nothing. Then: 'But that's good isn't it? Why are you crying?'

'I don't know what to think, Mother. I don't know him very well.' I hesitated. 'I do like him . . . How was it between you and Father?'

Mother sighed. 'There's something you should know about your father,' she said softly.

I glanced up and saw, in the moonlight, that she was searching for the photo of him on the wall.

'I've thought of telling you many times, but I've always held back. Now I have no choice.'

'I've lied to you. He wasn't run over by a car. Remember I said there was to be no funeral, that I told you you couldn't see his body because it would be too upsetting?' She fixed me with her gaze. 'I didn't see his body, either.'

'You mean he's still alive?'

'No, he's dead.'

'But I don't understand!'

'Shh, not so loud!'

'Soon after the Japanese invaded your father lost his job. For a long time we were very poor, partly because he was reluctant to look for work – with good reason because he would have had to work for the Japanese. We both came from well-to-do families and for a while we managed by selling heirlooms. But after you children arrived things were harder. By then the Japanese had been driven out and the Kuomintang were recruiting. Your father was interested, but I told him the Nationalists had no future and would soon be on their way out. He said he'd only apply for administrative work – he wouldn't join the army.'

I gripped the headboard. 'He joined the Nationalists?'

'Yes, Wenya. Now, please let me finish.' Mother sat closer to me. 'He took office jobs, but they were always short-lived, and with inflation there was never enough money even to cover his travel expenses . . . So one day he went out to another interview and didn't come back. Do you remember? You waited for him till quite late – you wanted him to play something for you on his flute.'

' "Two Fountains".'

'He didn't come back that day. I was so worried, but I didn't want to frighten you, so I made up some excuse about him having to stay overnight for another interview. But the next day someone came with a letter from him saying he'd joined the army. It was far better paid than the other jobs he'd had – he enclosed some money with the note. I was so angry with him and wrote straight away asking him to come home, but he wouldn't . . .' she started to sob '. . . and the next thing I heard he had been killed while retreating with the Kuomintang as the Communists advanced.'

'Father? Killed?' I stared at the photograph in its frame, although I could see only a blur through my tears. 'Father,' I sobbed. The horror of his death was too much for me.

'Ssh.' Mother put a finger to her lips. 'You mustn't tell anyone about this – certainly not your fiancé.'

'Why not?'

'Why do you think? He wouldn't want to marry the daughter of a class enemy who fought the Communists!'

'But I must! I can't lie to him!'

'If you tell him you'll have no future.'

I rose abruptly. 'I'm going out.'

'Wenya, come back!'

But I rushed out of the door. As I ran, I wiped away the tears. I must catch the last bus! I must see Zhiying, and tell him the truth! He was too kind, and too dear to hide the truth from and . . . A thought struck me. Perhaps this was the perfect excuse not to marry him. I had found something good in all the sadness.

But as I sat on the last bus to the factory my mood changed. Zhiying's smiling face flashed into my mind: I saw him helping me onto his bike, carrying the heaviest loads, lookng concerned when the ice-cream had given me a headache, wanting to take away the pain . . . I couldn't lose all of this. I was so confused: at one moment I wasn't sure I wanted to marry him, and at the next I was terrified of losing him. I wanted someone I could lean on – I wanted Zhiying. But would he want to be burdened by such a wife? I prepared myself for the worst.

I got off the bus, then trudged through pouring rain to his building. I ignored the door-keeper, who eyed me curiously through his little window – I knew I should report to him but I didn't care. I went straight up to Zhiying's room on the second floor. On the way I made up my mind to let him go. Then I couldn't damage his prospects. The decision hurt me so much that I thought I might cry when I saw him. Did that mean I truly cared for him?

I had no more time to think – he was at the door, wearing only his underpants. He took one look at me and dashed back into his room. A moment later he emerged again in an inside-out shirt. 'What's wrong?' he whispered and glanced over his shoulder. When he turned back to me I saw panic in his eyes. It was quiet and I realized the whole room was listening. 'Will you come out with me for a minute?' I asked, trying to sound calm.

We stood in the porch under a bulb that cast only a faint glow. The rain still poured down. A tremendous sadness came over me. I was not the person I'd thought I was. I felt stained, different. The door-keeper hovered, keeping his distance. He coughed loudly to remind us that he was there. This might be my last night with Zhiying, I thought. I didn't want to tell him about my father, but I had to. I took a deep breath.

'We can't marry,' I whispered.

'Can't marry?' he repeated, as if he didn't understand what I'd said. 'Why not?' His face was expressionless.

'My father was a Nationalist, a class enemy. He was killed while retreating with the KMT. I didn't know this until just now. Mother told me. I'd thought he died in an accident.' Despite myself I burst into tears, and began to walk away slowly, hoping he would come after me. I took five steps, but he didn't move. I turned abruptly. 'I'm sorry to have misled you,' I shouted.

Suddenly he was beside me. He said something I didn't hear. 'What did you say?'

He smiled. 'Oh, Wenya, thank goodness that's all it is.'

I felt so weak I wanted to sit down. 'You don't mind? You still want to marry me?'

'If you still want to marry me.' He rubbed his hands together. 'I thought you were going to tell me something much worse. I thought you were going to say you cared for someone else . . .'

I pulled him to me. 'Oh, you,' I murmured, blushing to remember my doubts of two hours before. Now all I wanted was to be with Zhiying. The door-keeper coughed again and we sprang apart. When I dared to look, I saw that he had retreated into his room and shut the door. Zhiying and I laughed.

'But . . .' I began, but couldn't go on. I was thinking that as the daughter of a class enemy, I would be an outcast if the truth came out, as would all of my family. Zhiying would lose his post as chief engineer at the factory and the esteem of his peers. He would be despised, pitied and never entrusted with the work he aspired to. It was a big sacrifice for him to make.

'Don't worry, all will be well,' he reassured me, laying his hand on my shoulder. My eyes filled with fresh tears. He wiped them away with his fingers. 'Does anybody else know about this?' he asked gently.

'Only Mother, I think.'

'So let this be a secret between us,' he said. 'We'll talk tomorrow and in the days to come. The important thing is, we're in this together and nothing will come between us.'

Zhiying rode home with me in the rain. It was the wettest day I could remember, but I was warm inside, and rested my hands round his waist. I felt I knew him a hundred times better now.

After the wedding, I asked Mother why she had told me about Father on the day Zhiying proposed. If she had kept the secret for so long, surely it would have been safer not to tell me at all. 'I wanted to make sure Zhiying was truly in love with you, and you with him,' she said matter-of-factly. I was astonished. 'How else would you have been able to tell?' she added.

5

We were married in our new home, in a building designated for married couples, just a few blocks away from Zhiying's old single's quarters. The walls were as white as I'd imagined and the ceiling as high. We opted for a simple, modern wedding with as few as possible of the traditional elements our generation despised. The wrapping-paper on the sweets was red, but that was the only concession we made to custom – that and the red quilts Mother sat up sewing for me on the nights leading up to the wedding, using some cloth from her own marriage quilts. I fell in love with them – the rich red velvet embroidered with yellow blossoms, the white cotton border that highlighted the elegant patterns and the exuberant colour. We bought some essential furniture, like the bed, the bookshelf and the wardrobe, but the quilt made me feel truly married – I loved its luxurious feel, and the link it provided to my old life, with Mother.

Instead of bowing to our ancestors we bowed to the portrait of Chairman Mao, then to each other. Neither Lao Gao nor Cheng Ming was in the crowd of well-wishers – they were in Beijing on business, but Lao Gao had sent a couplet, listing the four Ultimate Happinesses: sweet rain after a long drought; encountering an old friend in a strange land; lighting the blossom candles for the newly wed; and coming top in the scholars' exam. In a note he congratulated us: the candlelit wedding night was the happiest of all, it said. The couplet was written on two scrolls of red paper in his own calligraphy, which took pride of place in the middle of our living room. It was a traditional gesture, but we did not think of it in that way. It had come from Lao Gao, and for us, he could do no wrong.

Our guests stayed late, but not as late as in the old days when everyone hid behind windows to eavesdrop, to tease the newly weds and encourage them out of their shyness. Mother commented wryly that although her own wedding had been much grander – with a fleet of sedans as transport, a band and twenty tables of guests – by the time the formalities had been observed, she was so exhausted she had wanted only to sleep. Ours, though simpler, was more moving, she told me. I had been lucky to find Zhiying, and she wished us a long, happy married life. She held my hands for a long time before she left us.

We were alone. 'It's getting late,' Zhiying said, and switched on the light. For a moment the room seemed too large and we looked at each other, unsure what to do: we were unaccustomed to having so much space to ourselves. In time, I knew, we'd make it our own, but now we were awkward. We'd hardly ever been alone together in a room before – except when we were painting our flat, but that had been different: the room was bare, the windows wide open, and people from the factory would stop to chat. Once or twice we'd brushed each other's hands in passing, surrounded by ladders, brushes and buckets. Somehow those intimacies had been both thrilling and safe, but now . . . As he came towards me I felt nervous. 'It's too hot,' I said, and went to the window. Behind me a formal voice spoke – Zhiying had switched on the radio. 'Jin Lin gave us this,' he said casually. 'He said he assembled it himself. Not bad, eh?' He was flicking through the stations, one after another.

'I'll make dinner,' I said, and went in to the kitchen.

He left me alone while I cooked, and I was glad. The small space was only big enough for one person to move about, and I could relax in it. I surveyed it with pride. I loved the red and white checked curtain I had made for the window, which opened on to the square courtyard from which I could glimpse other women in our block cooking, as I was. The radio was louder now and I wondered if Zhiying had turned it up so that I could hear it, too. I found it reassuring, to tune in and out of the formal voice, which hinted at normality.

I scrutinised the shelf of basic ingredients, moving this and that because I could – at Mother's house I had respected her arrangements and put things back as she wanted them. I wasn't usually superstitious, but today I felt we should eat noodles, which represented longevity, on the first day of our marriage. Eggs, with their spherical shape, stood for togetherness. The noodle dough was bouncy, and I stretched it into long thin strips, then dropped them into the boiling pan. The white dust of the flour creamed the surface of the water, then the noodles swam up like little water dragons.

I put a wok on to heat with some oil in the bottom, then took the eggs out of the basket. Mother had bought

them for me, fresh from the country. I chose three and
saw a thin strand of red on one shell. I winced and my
hands trembled as I cracked it into a bowl. Quickly I
cracked the rest, then beat them with a pair of brand new
chopsticks, the effort calming me. I chopped some spring
onions and a little ginger and mixed them with the eggs. I
saw that the oil in the wok was hot, so I poured in the
mix. My heart lifted. 'Dinner's ready,' I called, then again,
louder, when I heard no reply.

When I emerged from the kitchen with the food, the
table was laid. My hands were trembling again when I
passed Zhiying the bowl. This was the first time I had
cooked for him, but I was nervous because the room was
silent – he had turned off the radio. I sat down and we
started to eat.

My unease grew as the silence continued. Zhiying
would not look at me as he ate, but when he'd finished I
felt I should ask him if he'd like more. He nodded. 'I
would, but you sit down – I can help myself.' He
disappeared into the kitchen and spent a long time there.

When he finally came back, his bowl was still empty. I
stared at him, and he glanced down at his bowl. Then he
dashed back into the kitchen. I couldn't stop myself
giggling. 'Oh, Wenya,' he put the noodles on the table and
came to me, 'stop it!' He was laughing too. He put a hand
on mine, which made me giggle all the more.

'I want you to serve me, wife,' he said, trying to keep a
straight face.

'Feudalist! We're in the new society now! Don't expect
me to wait on you,' I said, pushing the bowl back to him.
The chopsticks in it flew on to the floor.

He bent down to pick up the one that had landed by my

feet, then squatted in front of me and looked up, beaming. 'The noodles taste so much better when you serve me, wife.'

My legs were suddenly weak. I sank back in my chair and he laid his face in my lap. He was murmuring, but I couldn't make out what he was saying. I struggled to get up, but I couldn't move.

'Wenya . . . Wenya . . . my wife.'

He stood up and lifted me. I closed my eyes as he laid me on the bed. I felt his hands on my face, stroking it. At a tiny sound from outside I stiffened. 'The window! Close the window – and draw the curtain!' He was there like an arrow. I sat up and switched off the light.

It was very dark, and I couldn't see him, but I heard his footsteps coming towards me. 'Where are you?' he whispered, and I wriggled forward on the bed, my face tilting to meet his. A sharp blow landed on my cheek and I cried out in pain. 'You hurt me!' Tears sprang into my eyes.

'Oh, no! Where? Show me. I'm so sorry – it's so dark and I can't see anything. Can I switch the light on?'

'No!' I said. 'Come here.'

He came nearer and this time our lips met. He almost suffocated me with his first kiss and I struggled a little – I didn't want him to think I was pushing him away, I just needed to breathe. But the more I struggled, the more he kissed me and the tighter he held me.

'Wenya . . .' he murmured. I took a deep breath. His lips searched for mine again. 'I've heard it hurts a little the first time, but soon it will be all right,' he whispered.

I recoiled – he had used almost the same words that I would use to reassure a child before an injection. He made me want to laugh and scream at the same time. I shut my lips and turned my face away.

'Wenya, it's true – you know it anyway, don't you? After all, you are a doctor.'

I sat up and moved away from him. When I had dreamed of our first night together, I had imagined him taking me in his arms, like the hero in a Russian movie. I switched on the light. The top button of his shirt was undone and his sleeve button had caught on a pillow case – he was trying to disentangle it. He smiled apologetically. I had to suppress the urge to laugh as he freed himself, but I wanted to run away too, from the crushing disappointment. Suddenly I felt exhausted. I sighed.

'Wenya, what's the matter? Is it me? What have I done wrong?'

'What have you done wrong?' I was amazed that he didn't know.

'Yes, tell me – don't look at me like that,' he begged.

I did not know what to say. Eventually he spoke: 'It's late, let's go to sleep.'

Once I could hear Zhiying's light snores I opened my eyes. They moved to Lao Gao's couplet, the words now a cruel joke. My wedding night was a night of shame. Zhiying was not the man for me. How could I have been so wrong? To think that I had married him because of what Mother had told me about Father. Perhaps I had been punished for lying to myself. I had known even as I rushed to him that rainy night that I didn't love him.

6

The famine lifted Zhiying and me temporarily out of our misery. It was the result of the so-called Great Leap Forward which Mao Zedong had initiated in a bid to move China quickly towards an industrial future, and it killed many people, especially in the countryside. Agriculture suffered, and Nature added to the misery with unprecedented droughts or flooding. All over China there were scenes of devastation but the countryside was hit hardest.

Of course, we didn't know then how serious the situation had become, although we couldn't ignore the dwindling of food supplies. As East Wind was a major state industry, its canteen was still adequately stocked, but at the hospital I noticed a sudden increase in the number of puffy-faced patients – malnutrition caused water retention. Eventually the crisis reached such a pitch that doctors were brought from the cities to manage the suffering in the countryside. I received my orders to leave only two weeks after my wedding.

I leaned out of the van window. The road was largely empty, but for a man dozing in a thick blue coat on a horse-drawn cart, clutching a long whip with a red ribbon at the tip – the only bright colour for miles around. Even as we overtook him he didn't look up. I feigned interest in him partly to avoid conversation with my colleagues and the chatty driver.

Zhiying's forlorn face hovered in my mind. I was sure that for both of us my departure was a blessing. With no trace of emotion in my voice, I had told him that I would be away for two months: the hospital was sending me to a remote clinic in Xiliang. I reminded him of the pact we had made: that I must strive to be an exceptional worker to minimise scrutiny, and the chance that my father's status might be discovered. In any case I wanted to work hard. If anything, Zhiying had seemed relieved that I was going. Later that day, when my bags had been packed and the tension had eased a little, we had found time to go to the factory together for Zhiying to play basketball with others who had finished for the day. I watched him throw, dodge, aim and score, but I felt empty: now that I was on the point of leaving I knew how much I would miss him. I began to think of all the things I loved about him . . .

The driver cursed as the road became bumpier – we had left the city behind. My thoughts turned to Mother. I wondered if she knew something was wrong between Zhiying and me, even though when she had asked me how things were, I had said, 'Fine.' Perhaps I had answered quickly – perhaps that was why she had squinted knowingly at me. The look she gave me was accusing, as if I had wronged Zhiying – since our wedding, she and Zhiying had become closer than I liked. I had heard her saying to her neighbour that she had not lost a daughter but gained a son. She said that he had all the qualities she admired in a man: he was attentive and helpful, not full of himself.

Attentive, helpful. Yes, that was Zhiying. And yet on our wedding night he had been neither. I recalled his fumbling attempt at intimacy, the outstretched hands in the darkness and his bewilderment when I had switched on the light. Guilt rose in me. Yes, he had been clumsy, but I had done little to help. Because he was a man, I had expected him to know everything and to guide me. Now I realised he had been as nervous as I, perhaps more so.

We were half-way up a steep hill. Exposed rocks hung over us on one side of the track and a steep drop plummeted on the other. No wonder the driver was quiet – he had to concentrate on what he was doing. The sun streamed through patchy cloud on to dry-looking fields. A bird of prey swirled and dived to an unseen target. The van lurched dangerously to the left, making my colleague and me gasp. As it righted itself, I met Ying's eyes for the first time since the journey had begun. She grinned and, before I could say anything, reached into her bag and brought out an apple. 'Here.' She pushed it into my hand.

I hadn't had one for months. This was the time of year when most of the cabbages and apples we had stored for the winter had run out, but the new crop wasn't ready. I was taken aback by her generosity. 'Go on,' she insisted, then asked teasingly, 'Do you miss him?' I shook my head, then changed my mind and nodded – I didn't want to seem callous. She smiled again – unusual, I thought. In all the time I'd known her – we shared the same office after clinic hours – we'd hardly spoken. That was partly because of her temperament – she was divorced with a young child, and had a sharp tongue. I had always been shy, and since I had discovered the truth of Father's death, I had been even more guarded. I would not have chosen Ying as my companion for two months in a strange place.

The apple was sour, but I ate it to the core, which I pushed out of the window. A cold blast of wind struck me. In the distance, I could see a cluster of low huts. 'That must be Taohua Chun, the Peach Blossom Village,' Ying murmured.

When we stopped there, an eerie quiet greeted us. There was no sound but the howl of the wind, stirring the dust. All the doors of the low mud huts were shut, the narrow streets empty – no children, no cattle. The only sign of life was the bare branches of a few poplars that waved in the wind. The driver frowned. 'It's a strange village that has no barking dogs,' he observed.

'I was told we'd be met by the village head,' said Ying. 'Is anybody here?' she called.

We waited, and called again, but no one came. Ying decided to venture further into the village and soon we were setting up at the clinic, which we had managed to locate. Next to it we found the Peach Blossom village store and poked our heads in. Nothing, except several large empty jars.

Ying was in the middle of sending me and the driver off in search of people when we heard footsteps. Excited, we rushed out.

A man was walking towards us. As he came closer we saw his legs were unsteady, his face puffed and shiny. At a distance he seemed young but he was not. Many of my patients at the hospital had looked like him – lack of protein had caused these typical signs of marasmus.

'You the doctors?' he asked, in a faint, almost feminine voice. Before we could reply he went on, 'We've been waiting for you for three weeks.'

We shook hands. Ying asked him where the patients were. He stared at us blankly. 'Patients?'

She nodded. 'I was hoping you'd take us to them.'

'I know nothing.'

Suspicion grew in me. 'Aren't you the village head?'

He shook his head. 'That's Lao Zhang. He can't come.'

'Why not?'

He hesitated, then pointed to something in the distance. Half-way up the hill we saw several mounds.

'He's dead,' the man sighed.

Ying frowned, then collected herself. 'Well, can you take us to those who are ill?'

'You mean the ones who can't work in the fields? There are so many. But we don't need doctors – we need food. Did you bring any?' He craned his neck to peep into the van.

Ying barred his view. 'This is medicine for the patients,' she said coldly.

The man licked his dry lips. He had glimpsed the buckets of soya milk. Suddenly, he squatted on the ground, held his head in his hands and bellowed like an animal. 'We're starving. There's nothing left to eat – chickens, pigs, even dogs, all gone. So many have died – Uncle Jing, Grandma Yue, and even Yilin, Oh, please, please, save my son, Little Stone . . .'

'You must take us to those who are most at risk,' Ying snapped. 'Tell me who is dying.' The man did not look up. 'Who is dying?' she repeated, then bent down to whisper: 'I know you are upset, but we need your help.' She spoke softly now. 'Will a drink of soya milk help, do you think?'

The man stopped wailing. 'You need to save Granny Tong first. She lives there with her youngest daughter and son-in-law.' He pointed at a pretty hut half-way up the sunny side of the valley. 'Her older children have all married and left home, so she's stayed with the youngest who is expecting a child. There's not enough food for them all, so Granny Tong's starving herself . . . No one can get her to eat.'

Silently Ying went into the clinic and came out with a bottle of soya milk and a packet of biscuits from our own supply. She handed them to the man, who clasped them to him. He began to open the bottle, then stopped as if he'd just woken from a dream. 'My child, Little Stone,' he said. 'Please, may I take these for him?' Ying nodded.

As soon as the man had gone, she said, 'Wenya and I will go up the hill to treat Granny Tong,' and picked up some buckets and bottles. I followed suit. The driver leaned over to help, but she stopped him. 'No, you stay here. Guard the equipment and medicine.'

We staggered up the hill. The house didn't appear to be far away but it never drew closer as we climbed. We followed a rough track that zigzagged through rocks. I gritted my teeth and tried to keep up with Ying, but my feet felt so heavy. I tried not to remember that, apart from the apple, I had had nothing for lunch. What had the driver and Ying had? As far as I could remember she had given him an apple, and eaten one herself.

Within striking distance of the house, we saw a pregnant woman – the daughter. Even before she reached me I saw the grin of welcome on her face. Tall and handsome, she had high cheekbones, and blushed as she introduced herself. Her name was Yun, and she urged us to hurry. She took the bag off my back and set off for the house.

When Yun introduced me to her mother, I saw the family resemblance, although the old woman's cheeks were sunken and sagging. She was awake, but wouldn't open her eyes, although I sensed from her quick, shallow breaths that she was conscious of our presence. Yun whispered, 'Mother, the doctors are here. They'll make you better.' She leaned even closer: 'They have food, enough to feed us for days. Please listen.'

We held our breath and watched as the old woman's hand fluttered, but her eyes remained closed. Gently Ying tapped Yun's shoulder and she moved away. In turns Ying and I listened to Granny Tong's heartbeat, which was weak and irregular as we had expected. I undid the old woman's sleeve and held her arm firmly. Ying administered a glucose injection.

We tiptoed out of the room and into the kitchen where Yun was standing before a pan of boiling water, wiping away tears with the front of her ragged blue top. She produced two bowls and filled them. We took them outside so that the water would cool quickly.

Ying and I sat on two low stools set apart from each other. The sun was setting, bathing the brown huts in warm light. I was struck by the stillness and remembered my father's verses about Tao Yuan, the earthly paradise. There, peach blossoms symbolised good fortune and abundance. In those poems the peasants never toiled: the land yielded readily – one had only to reach out a hand and pick the fruit. But here, in Peach Blossom Village, a mother was dying because she wanted to save her child and her grandchild, and I doubted Yun ate well if her mother did not eat at all. As doctors we could cure illnesses, or try to, but we could not prevent death, especially when someone had lost the will to live.

I turned to meet Yun's eyes. Like any concerned relative, she was searching my face insistently for clues. 'When are you due?' I asked, to divert her attention.

'In the autumn,' she said shyly.

'Your first?'

She nodded. 'What about you?' she asked. 'Do you have children? No – you look so young.'

Ying cut in: 'She's only just got married.'

Yun's eyes widened.

I nodded slowly, and saw confusion cross her face.

'Where is your husband?' Ying asked her. 'It's getting late.'

She smiled. 'I don't expect him to be back until dark. He works in that field.' She pointed down the hill. 'We know there's little point. The drought has lasted so long, and the earth is so dry, but we have to keep trying. The heavens might still have mercy on us.' She opened her hands and tilted her face to the sky.

While Ying and I drank our water Yun went back inside. We heard her moving pots and pans in the kitchen. Her steps sounded weary and I imagined the weight of her baby anchoring her down. I wondered what she would have for dinner. I had seen no sign of food in the small clean kitchen. Was there a secret place where she hid it? It wouldn't have surprised me. The desperate look of the man we had met earlier had told me that when we are hungry, we are not always the noble creatures we had thought. Why should she trust us because we were doctors?

Ying stared at the village below. 'There is light still. We must go back to the clinic to treat more patients.' We told Yun we'd return after dinner, to check on her mother, and when she invited us to stay the night with her we agreed. Anyway, it made sense: we needed to watch the old woman and see that she pulled through.

Back at the clinic, several villagers were waiting, the driver reassuring them that we were on our way. He looked relieved to see us, and we got on with the work in no time, dispensing medicine, giving injections. It was almost a relief to have a few patients to treat for minor ailments among so many starving souls. While I stayed at the clinic, Ying did a few house visits – the villagers had told her that some were too ill to come to the clinic. It was not until she returned after dark that we had our own small dinner of preserved cabbage and rice. Afterwards we worked a few more hours because people were still pouring into the clinic. Eventually the driver stopped us. 'You two are exhausted. You must stop now.' He turned to the few who were still queuing. 'The doctors need to rest. Look at them!'

With a candle to guide us, we clambered up the hill, carrying more soya milk, glucose and medicines for Granny Tong. My legs shook with every step and I cursed myself. We had had dinner only a few hours ago but my stomach was rumbling, and I felt dizzy. Suddenly I fell.

When I came to, there was something in my mouth, something that tasted familiar. I swallowed, enjoying the sweetness. 'Have some more,' Ying demanded.

I opened my eyes and realised it was the soya milk we'd taken for Granny Tong. I clenched my teeth. 'That's for our patient.'

'Does a fit person faint like that? Drink it.' She helped herself to a mouthful. 'See?' She wiped her mouth on her sleeve. 'If we're not strong, how can we help the peasants?'

I closed my eyes and took a deep breath. I was sure she had tasted the milk so that I would drink more, but I couldn't. I struggled to stand up, but slipped and fell again. I felt Ying's arms supporting me. 'I'll run over and let them know we're here – maybe someone'll come to help.' She took the candle and strode off.

I watched her skip away, heavy-set though she was. She disappeared into the house, which was in darkness. I looked at the chimney. No smoke, no food.

I forced myself to sit up and my hand brushed against the bottles of soya milk. Suddenly I was ravenous. I could still taste the sweetness. All was still and dark around me. It would be so easy to reach out . . . My hand touched the open bottle – a mouthful or two wouldn't hurt. Ying was right. I'd fainted, and if I was sick I'd be of no help to the villagers. I picked up the bottle. Just a drop, I told myself, to moisten my throat and give me some strength.

A sound made me put the bottle down quickly. I looked around. Nothing. Ying had been away a long time. A thought occurred to me. She had known I wouldn't drink it in front of her: had she created the perfect opportunity for me to take a few mouthfuls without any shame? My face felt hot, and I stood up to move to a rock, away from the supplies, where I would be more visible in the light of the moon, which was rising now.

Presently a flickering light emerged from the house and I saw Ying followed by someone else. In no time they were with me and I glimpsed the face of a young man, Yun's husband. He nodded, picked up the supplies and we followed him back to the house.

Ying told me to rest in the kitchen, then went to Granny Tong, taking the medicines with her. In the candlelit kitchen I smelt something delicious and peered at a small bamboo steamer on the stove.

Ying tiptoed back and gestured to me that all was well. 'Have you eaten?' she asked Yun.

'Yes, we have,' she replied, too quickly.

I peered once more at the steamer and wondered what was inside it.

Ying put the bottle of soya milk and some biscuits on the kitchen table. 'We've brought you these,' she said.

The young man's eyes brightened, but Yun rose abruptly. 'We have food,' she said, and went to a corner of the kitchen. She came back with a basket and flung off the cloth cover to reveal half a dozen *mantou*, steamed rolls. Even in the candlelight I could see that they were made of fine white flour, not the coarse variety we had been eating in the city. I also saw that they looked stiff and cracked – they had been made some time ago. 'This is what I cook for Mother. You see? We have plenty,' she said, and looked to the young man as if for support.

I stole a glance at the basket sitting beside me on the table, as Yun murmured, 'I got the fine flour from our cousin in the other village – I walked twenty *lis* for it. I made the *mantou* but Mother wouldn't touch them. Said she wasn't hungry. I was angry with her and said I wasn't hungry either.'

I noticed how the young man looked at her, and she stopped talking. There was an awkward silence. Ying picked up the soya milk and the biscuits. 'Drink this and eat these. I'm a doctor and you must do as I say.'

'But—'

'You don't want to be ill and make things harder for us, do you?'

Yun watched us, and her eyes moistened. 'All right,' she said, and reached for the bottle. She sipped, then passed it to the young man.

Suddenly Yun exclaimed, 'I nearly overcooked it.' She rushed to the stove and the steamer. The smell wafting out was almost unbearably delicious now. She took the steamer off the heat and put it in front of me. 'Open it,' she urged. 'Go on.'

Gingerly I took off the lid. A single fat bun sat in it. There was a split in the middle, filled with a large red date. 'We call it the Couples' Bun here. Newlyweds eat it to make sure their marriage lasts.' She smiled apologetically at Ying. 'I have no flour left – and I could only borrow enough for one from the other villagers.'

'Don't worry.' Ying laughed. 'I can't even remember when I got married, it's such a long time ago. It's Wenya who should eat it.'

I picked it up, burning my fingers, and bit into it. It was sweet, soft and melted in my mouth. 'It is made of sweetcorn flour and blossoms, any blossoms, but here, of course, we use peach.' Yun sighed. 'These are last year's, dried.'

She showed us our bedroom opposite Granny Tong's – her door had a poster on it of a fat boy sitting on a giant fish. There were also three smaller red-paper posters of double happiness. I realised this was their bedroom. 'We'll share with Mother. Sleep well,' she said, and tiptoed out.

The bed had been made; the quilt was embroidered with a giant red silk peony and gave the room a curious glamour. Ying and I climbed in and lay down. I was immediately enveloped in a smell that reminded me of Zhiying.

Only fifty-eight more nights, I told myself. Then I'd be home.

7

Nearly two months later, we came back to a changed city. I had looked forward to the familiar buzzing scene, only to be greeted with empty streets and weary people. The pagoda trees were in bloom, but only a few flowers were left on the tallest branches, gently waving in the wind, as other-worldly as the spirit-calling flags at a funeral. The trees' bark had been stripped off. Were people so desperate for food now that they ate it? I wondered how Mother had fared, and Ying's daughter, whom she had left with her own mother, and the driver's sick wife. New concerns wrenched us all from our patients in the countryside – Granny Tong had pulled through and waved us goodbye among other tearful villagers as we drove away, leaving with them the supplies we had brought with us.

As we passed through the suburb and I glimpsed the East Wind factory, whose flags waved proudly above its sign board, my thoughts turned to Zhiying. He wouldn't have starved – the factory bosses would have made sure of that – but how would he receive me? More familiar scenes unfolded in front of me: the park, the traffic . . . I had missed it all while I had been in the countryside but now I was reminded of how I had felt when I left. And soon I would see Zhiying. Over the last few weeks something inside me had changed, putting things into perspective. I had missed him desperately – but I needed to see him to find out how I really felt about our marriage.

A man holding a packet of dumplings came out of a restaurant. As I watched, mouth watering, a child of about twelve swept out of nowhere, snatched the dumplings and, instead of running away, started to cram them into his mouth. The man pounced on him and pummelled his back, but the boy continued to shovel the food into his mouth.

We went straight into work at the hospital, and found that the wards, too, were unnervingly quiet, with none of the usual banter between doctors, nurses and patients. In the afternoon a man was rushed in with food poisoning. He was unconscious, and weak from dehydration, but though I resuscitated him several times, I couldn't save him. From his wife and sister, I learned that he had eaten poisonous grasses. 'He was desperate for food,' they muttered.

That afternoon I saw the cart in which the body had been carried through the hospital to the mortuary. I dropped my eyes and hurried on. But when I got back to my office, the image of the dead man, his feet barely covered by the white sheet, remained in my mind, although Ying was chatting and laughing as usual. I stopped her mid-sentence – I'd left something at the lab, I said, and needed to retrieve it. Soon I was back on the path to the mortuary. It was covered with cinders, which crunched berneath my feet. The mortuary was a place we avoided, but today I needed to see it.

When I got there, I was greeted with a sight I had not expected: a pagoda tree leaning against the wall of the mortuary, draped with white blossoms. I thought of the bare trees I'd seen on the way back into town. Why had this one been spared? The blossom floated on a gust of wind, and the answer came to me: the tree must feed on the spirits of the departed. Perhaps that was why it looked so healthy – and why it had been left untouched.

A worker pushed an empty cart out of the mortuary, and I stepped back to let him pass. The blossoms hung still on the branches now. I realised I was hungry, and thought of the bun Yun had made. I could make something with these blossoms . . .

I took off my shoes, then my hospital gown, and climbed the tree with ease. Before I knew it, I was on the ground again, my arms full. I stuffed the fragrant blossoms into the pockets of my white gown, then put it back on. Then I walked back along the cinder path.

When I got back to the office, Ying asked me if I was all right. I said yes, but she pushed me on to the examination couch. 'You look so pale – are you sure you're okay?' she asked. I didn't answer, so she injected me with glucose and told me to go home. All of the doctors were used to staff fainting from starvation and automatically administered glucose.

The bus wasn't crowded – it was mid-afternoon, so I found a seat. I tried to concentrate on the view from the window but I felt as if I was in a dream. Familiar scenes flashed past, making me feel dizzy and sick. Instead, I stared at the horizon where the big chimneys stood, puffing smoke.

When I got off the bus it was raining, and somehow this

made me happy – I had always loved the freshness of the first drops on my face.

In the flat I flung off my gown, and put on my slippers. I walked around my home, and saw that it had been well looked after during my absence: the floor had been washed that morning, and so had the table Zhiying had made from some discarded wood at the factory. I took the blossom out of my pockets and spread it, bruised and yellow, on the kitchen counter. Its fresh, wet fragrance filled the air and the petals were smooth and cool. With a rolling-pin I crushed them, watching them bruise and disintegrate. From the shelf I took down a clearly labelled, nearly empty bag of sweetcorn flour. Zhiying's neat writing on the label made me pause briefly. Then I put the flour and the blossoms into a bowl, and with some water, kneaded it into a paste, and divided it into buns.

The water was hot when I put the buns into the steamer and covered them with a lid. While I waited for them to cook I went to the bed, lay down and closed my eyes. I needed a rest, but I couldn't relax: the smell of the flowers intensified as the buns steamed. I thought of Zhiying, a stranger, yet so familiar. I wanted him with me now, but he wouldn't be back for some time. What to do? I got up and prowled around the room. At the end of the bed I found one of his shirts, picked it up and held it to my face.

The steamer hissed, and I ran to the kitchen to turn off the cooker. The smell of the buns ensnared me. I couldn't wait for him. I had to eat now.

I lifted the lid. The steam moistened my face. I grabbed a hot bun, and tossed it from one hand to the other.

The first burned my throat but the second was

delicious. Half-way into the third I remembered I had only made three.

I sat down, sobered, still hungry. I had starved in the countryside, I thought as I circled listlessly. I remembered Yun's words, as I ate the Couples' Bun, watched by three starving people. 'You only eat those once in your life,' she had said, 'when you're newly married.' Now I'd had three more, would they bring bad luck?

A bicycle bell made me look up hopefully, but then I remembered that on Monday he was home even later than usual because he played basketball for the factory.

Somehow I was back in bed. I lay on my side, and closed my eyes. The hunger gnawed.

When the door opened I didn't stir. 'Don't turn the light on,' I said. 'I'm here.' He came in, smelling of sweat, oil and something else. I stretched out my hands, which he took, and drew him to me. We kissed. I pulled his hand to where I'd wanted it – the den where the hunger beast lay. I heard a quick gasp, like a cry and suddenly we clasped together like one.

Later, we showed each other the scratches on our bodies and laughed. They must have hurt, when we made them, but we had felt no pain. That was the night on which Xiao Tao, our son, was conceived.

8

The day after I had learned I was pregnant, Ying slipped into the office holding a cardboard box. I smelt formaldehyde, and knew she had been to an anatomy class. As well as treating patients, we both taught at the medical school attached to the hospital. 'There,' she said. 'For you and the little one.'

Something moved inside the box, and I realised what it was. 'But . . . you know I don't like rabbit meat.'

'Oh, come on – you need to eat properly now.' She put the box on my table and I peeped through the hole in a corner. I saw long fluffy ears and downy white fur. 'It's so pretty,' I said.

'Is it? I didn't look at it. They told me they could spare this one so I grabbed it before anyone else did. Thought you could do with some extra protein.' She left the room.

I peered through the hole in the box again. 'Lucky me,' I murmured. The rabbit's nose twitched. I opened the box, reached in and stroked the soft fur. I put the lid back on and placed the box on the floor by my desk, my feet on the lid. For the rest of the day I felt the rabbit hopping

65

from one corner to another, distracting me. The tissue samples I studied under the microscope, which usually absorbed me, were colourful but meaningless patterns. Instead of analysing and diagnosing, I thought about the past month when I had discovered what it was to be married. I had been late for work, and the first to go home. Several times Ying had caught me daydreaming.

'You were singing,' she said once.

'Was I?' I blushed, putting my hand to my mouth.

'I used to when I was first married. A reunion after a long separation is often better than the wedding night.'

I blushed again.

It was hard to tear myself away from our flat. Even as I was on my way to work I missed my cosy nest, which meant so much to me now, because I shared it with Zhiying. It was no longer spotlessly clean. We were not half as keen to sweep and tidy it as we were. Occasionally he used my comb and I liked the way our hairs entwined in it. He loved brushing my hair at night – 'Do it quickly, or just cut it off,' I'd say, but he continued to smooth out the tangles. Our intense closeness frightened me sometimes, but when I burst into tears Zhiying held me until I was soothed. Our new intimacy taught him to be bold and me to be gentle. I had once heard a character in a movie say 'First marry, then fall in love.' That was what happened between Zhiying and me.

When I walked into the courtyard outside our flat, carrying the rabbit in its box, I saw Mother's silhouette in the kitchen and heard her voice, unusually cheerful. Something told me she knew about my pregnancy.

When I opened the door she was beaming in the way

she did when I had done particularly well at school. She wouldn't say, 'congratulations,' I knew, and she was not one for small-talk. She grabbed the rabbit's ears and held him up. 'I know how to make a rabbit stew and that's just what you need, Wenya.'

Zhiying took the rabbit from her and put him gently on the floor. He shivered, and I noticed how small he was. He hopped forward a pace. Mother stood with her arms folded and frowned. 'It's a bit skinny,' she said. 'Not much meat on it.'

Zhiying squatted and reached out a hand, which the rabbit sniffed. Then he smoothed its ears. 'They say rabbit tastes like chicken,' Mother said.

'I don't eat chickens, or rabbits, or any other meat,' I said. 'I don't like it.'

'But you do—'

'No!' I stormed out to the kitchen and slammed the door.

From the living room I heard Zhiying's soft murmur, then a long silence, broken by a few short words from Mother.

I took a deep breath and opened the kitchen door. Mother's back was towards me.

'We'll have to keep the rabbit for a while to fatten it up.' Zhiying looked me in the eyes. 'For now, where shall we put him?' He went over to the space opposite the kitchen door where the roof slanted down, leaving a triangular area where we stored sacks of rice. 'Here,' he pointed, 'if I clear those out and make a little door, we could keep him—'

'Little White is his name,' I said.

'– keep Little White there. What does a rabbit eat?'

'Anything you eat, he'll take food from you,' Mother said.

'Grass,' I added. 'They eat grass.'

In the end Mother was right. Little White ate all our leftovers. There was little grass for him – the earth was barren because the drought still dragged on.

I started to feel sick, and Mother announced joyfully that I was *hai xi* – 'fearing the happiness'. Soon I was vomiting three times a day, but still wanted to eat all the time. She would stand over me as I rinsed my mouth, pat my back, and say, 'Good! It means the baby is staying with you.'

Suddenly the baby was the least of my concerns. The sickness was as brutal as my insatiable hunger. Three meals a day were not enough. I wanted food all the time – but no meat.

Mother thought differently. I overheard her talking about me with a neighbour: 'A boy, of course,' she said proudly. 'She craves meat, a sure sign she's having a boy.' I didn't confront her about the lie, partly because I was confused. The elders said boys made you crave meat, and girls, fruit and vegetables. But did I want a boy or a girl? I had no idea

I was reminded of how stubborn Mother could be. In my childhood she had ignored my dislike of tomatoes, and deliberately cooked them so I had no choice but to eat them. Now she would bring a meat dish whenever she visited. Though the amounts were small, I knew they were more than her ration allowed. Where was she getting it all from? Neighbours? The black market? But she couldn't force it on me. She came most days, bringing favourite dishes of my childhood – chicken cutlets with peanuts, beef preserved in soy sauce and brown sugar, or marinated pork spare ribs. Zhiying ate most of them – lately even the factory canteen had been affected by the shortages, and we couldn't let food go to waste. The meat was never greasy or stringy; Zhiying told me it was tender and delicious, just as I used to like it. But not any more.

One day, Mother didn't come. She didn't come the next day either, or the day after.

9

For three days we lived on rice and preserved cabbage – the only vegetable available at that time of year. The saltiness I had grown up with comforted me and settled my stomach. But at meal times Zhiying was sullen, tapping his chopsticks when he had finished, as if he was waiting for something else. Mother's meat dishes, no doubt. I kept silent. I was relieved to be hostage no longer to her food.

But as the days went by and Zhiying's tapping grew louder, I felt her absence keenly. The empty chair Zhiying put out each evening in anticipation of her arrival became a question mark and was hard to ignore. I must have offended her deeply, I thought. Mother was not a woman for hugs and kisses – instead she showed her love in cooking. By rejecting her food, I had insulted her culinary skill, and her affection. Besides, I had grown used to her daily visits and her absence left a void. In those early days of my pregnancy, I had come to rely on her experience and advice. Would I be a good mother? Would the baby be healthy? Would I be able to love him or her? I never asked those questions outright, of course, but Mother sensed them from my half-finished sentences and managed to dispel my fears.

By the time I'd gathered courage to look for her a week had passed. As I stood outside her door, wondering why she didn't answer my knock, a voice said, 'She's not in.'

I whirled round. It was the old widower who lived next door.

'Been gone for three days,' he went on. 'Said she was going to the countryside to look for something. Didn't she tell you?'

I shook my head.

'Tell me,' he moved closer, 'have you married a butcher?'

'Why?' I was surprised by his strange question.

'Because her house always smells of meat. I don't know anyone else who can afford so much.'

I could only shake my head again.

'Well, we all have the same ration – two *liang* of pork per month. Where does she get it all?' He scrutinised me. Suddenly he laughed. 'Sorry, child, I don't begrudge your mother her good fortune – I'm just curious. Keep it to yourself, if you must.'

As if I knew. I peered through my mother's window. All I could see were dried corn cobs lined up by the window – empty of corn. When they were crisp they'd be ground into flour. That was one of our staples now, and I hated it. It was not the odd taste so much as the sweetcorn scent that lingered. Lately, even this was hard to come by. I decided to leave, and had just turned the corner when I saw Mother striding down the lane. For a moment I was stirred by the triumph in her eyes. She couldn't walk fast, with her small bound feet, and now her speed made her wobble. When she spotted me she tried to cover the basket she was carrying, then changed her mind. 'What are you doing here?' she called. 'Why aren't you resting at home? Go into the house – don't catch a chill!'

Inside, she moved the basket to the window where the light streamed in. I leaned forward to examine the leaves, fanning out flat like green petals. They were called *song xiacao*, Mother explained. They appeared after the spring rains and were as elusive as the famed *lingzhi* – a herb that was reputed to have magical healing powers. The local peasants knew about them, Mother said, and it was with their guidance that she had found these.

'How far did you go?'

'Oh, only thirty *li*. I hitched a ride on a lorry,' she said.

I swallowed: thirty *li*? At her age? In a lorry? But I knew better than to make a fuss.

'They look like spinach.' I picked up a leaf. Spinach was my favourite vegetable, and I knew now why she had gathered these.

'How did you know about it?' I asked.

'Herbs are a poor man's friend. I have your father to thank for that lesson.'

'Father?' I repeated stupidly, my eyes moving to the photo on the wall. 'What did he know about herbs?'

Mother smiled. 'Oh, nothing – it's less a question of what he taught me, and more of what I picked up because he wasn't there.'

I watched her face intently. Since her revelation that he had been a Nationalist, we hadn't mentioned him, and I had thought, from her silence, that she had wanted to forget about him. But now . . . She sat down with the basket in front of her. Despite a lengthy trip away from home, and whatever hardships she had encountered, her hair was smooth and her back straight. Suddenly I wanted to know what it had been like to look after two young children on her own through war and famine. She had never talked to me about those years.

It seemed as if she knew what was in my mind. She turned to me and from that angle all her wrinkles seemed to disappear. I stared into young eyes.

'The hardest bit . . .' She stopped. She gazed into a corner of the room, one hand on the leaves, her head supported by the other. I thought she wasn't going to say any more but then she sat up and her eyes hardened. '. . . was to watch helplessly as you starved.'

I felt a chill creep up my spine. The room was quiet. Even the lane outside was still.

'Da Tao, your little brother, died of hunger. I had so little food for myself that my milk dried up. That was when I cursed Zhou Chen and . . . wished him dead.'

So Da Tao had died of hunger. 'But you always said pneumonia had taken him!' I exclaimed.

'If I hadn't had to wean him so early, he'd have been strong enough to fight it. I wished your father dead,' Mother repeated. She swallowed. 'I called myself the living widow. "Is he alive? Is he dead? I just want to know," I said to myself. I waited and waited . . . Then I pulled myself together, went out and begged. I, the wife and daughter of a respectable family, *begged*!' She glared at me.

It was as though I had become a child again. I remembered moments like this, when she'd suddenly been angry. But then her fury had been directed at me, for small wrong-doings I now knew had not warranted such outbursts. Today I had discovered what they had really been about.

She sighed. 'It got easier as I practised,' she said. 'Once or twice I sent you to do it while I watched.'

I put my hands to my burning cheeks.

'You won't remember it,' Mother said.

It was not only the begging I didn't remember – as far as I knew I'd never been hungry. We'd been poor but had never gone without. Her lip curled, and I saw what should have been obvious: like Granny Tong in Peach Blossom Village, I didn't remember hunger because Mother had starved and humiliated herself. My throat felt tight.

'I waited outside restaurants, people's houses, my palms open, back bent but ready to run if they set the dogs on me. The smell from those houses . . . I remember a plate of freshly made tofu, hardly touched. At first you wouldn't eat it, then I tasted it and realised it had no salt. So we went home, added some, with soy sauce, and you . . .' She smiled.

'But Father – I thought you were going to tell me something about him.'

Her eyes narrowed. 'Where was he when I needed him most? When the Japanese came and everybody ran for their lives, when the baby was dying and we had no money for a doctor? When the man who owned the silk shop offered to buy me as a concubine for what it would cost to save Da Tao's life?'

For a moment we stared at each other. Then she dropped her eyes and murmured, 'Never marry a flute-player, that's my advice. They haven't even the strength to tie up a chicken when you're starving!'

I turned once more to Father's photo. Mother's words

made me look at him anew. I'd always taken him to be an affectionate, sensitive and caring man, but now I saw something more: his abandonment of us. But, even so, it was hard to think ill of him. His flute-playing had been beautiful, and nothing Mother said could change that.

I went to the window and flung it open, nearly hitting someone standing too close to it outside. It was the widower. 'What on earth are you doing there?' I exclaimed.

'Just passing,' he said, and backed away. I leaned out and retched, then breathed in deeply – the fresh air was reviving. When I turned back, Mother was bending over the sink, washing the leaves. 'You're staying for dinner tonight.' Her voice sounded normal again.

'I'd better go home,' I murmured, 'and let Zhiying know that you're all right. He's been worried.'

She stiffened, but still she didn't turn to me. 'You go.'

10

'Make sure you stand in the shade,' Mother chided as I stepped off the path and under the apricot blossom. 'But not in a draught!' She pulled me back into shelter. I laughed but obeyed.

At last the sickness had abated. I began to eat properly, to Mother's delight. She was dropping in regularly again with her meat dishes. Now I could eat them, which pleased her. She was so pleased, in fact, that she even brought treats for Little White: apple cores, the ends of carrots and other titbits. She didn't mention rabbit stew again.

Before the end of the month we'd finished our rations, but I didn't starve: friends and colleagues saved us food. Ying handed me some sweetcorn paste that the peasants from Peach Blossom Village had given her, and neighbours would leave plates of dumplings or stew when they could. When he came in from work, Zhiying brought gifts of baby clothes and blankets. Lao Gao pressed on us his ration of brown sugar, and when I protested he said, 'I don't like it so you should have it. Do you think I'd let your child starve when I have so much to spare?'

Usually Zhiying and I spent Sundays in town, hitching rides with passing traffic. It was mostly lorry drivers who stopped. I would always be invited to sit in the cab, even if someone was already there – they were told to join Zhiying in the back. If the driver couldn't take us all the way to where we were going, we'd catch a bus to the riverside. There we would board a boat to cruise along in the centre of the river. Sometimes we passed a boatload of colourfully dressed Korean children, waving. They sang Chinese songs, mispronouncing the words, which made us laugh, and we would join in.

As my belly grew bigger, Mother became worried – no more bumpy rides in lorries, she said. 'Why don't you two go to the park instead? It's on your doorstep, and you don't want to miss the apricot and plum blossom. Especially now that the park belongs to us and not the Japanese. They've done some spectacular things to it since Lao Gao's been in charge – you *must* go!' Zhiying wasn't interested and at first I protested – I loved our trips outside the factory complex. But Mother was insistent, so she and I went. I showed my East Wind family card proudly, and we walked in. Because the park belonged to the factory it was free to all family members – one of the many benefits Lao Gao had instituted for his workers.

The management had spared no expense in creating a paradise for us. Oddly, though, for someone who admired Lao Gao so much, Zhiying said little about it. What I knew of it, I had heard mostly on the bus, from other passengers, and at the hospital from patients and my colleagues: how expensive rocks had been ordered from the south to build the mountains, and rare plants transported from far-off nurseries to be grown in the glasshouses. Apparently there was a shortage of gardeners now because they had all been recruited for the park.

Now I admired the bridge across the pond and the giant green lotus leaves. The blossom was nearly over, but some remained, pink and delicate. Girls in floral dresses holding umbrellas wandered about like colourful butterflies, and clusters of young men, many in East Wind uniform, strode noisily past us. In the pavilion at the centre of the pond, two older men played chess, an ancient teapot between them. I put a hand on my belly and felt at peace. This was such a beautiful, restful place. I wished Zhiying was with me. My pregnancy had made me bolder in expressing my affection for him, and lately Zhiying had sometimes stolen a kiss from me when he thought no one was looking. 'You're blossoming like a flower,' he had whispered once. I glanced at Mother and saw she looked weary. I suggested we made our way to the bench on the other side of the bridge.

We sat down and Mother closed her eyes. Mine were drawn back to the bridge and a sign I hadn't noticed before: 'Pavilion for Listening to the Flute'. I thought of Cheng Ming and my heart beat a little faster. I laughed at myself, but as I closed my eyes I couldn't dispel the image of him playing his flute for me. I would go for a short walk while Mother slept to shake it off, I decided, and stood up. At that moment, I saw Lao Gao, with Cheng Ming beside him. Lao Gao put a finger to his lips – I understood that I should not disturb Mother. I went across to them so that we could talk without waking her.

'I'm glad to see you here,' Lao Gao said. 'You're looking well.' He cocked his head to one side. So many had paid me compliments lately that I had begun to believe them. In any case, I felt well.

I smiled in acknowledgement and nodded to Cheng Ming. 'Congratulations, Lao Gao, on the park,' I said. 'I've heard so many good things about it, but I'd never dreamed it could be so beautiful, with your calligraphy at the gate, and the blossoms and the bridge.'

'Well, do you know who designed the bridge and chose the plants?' Lao Gao winked. 'It was this young man.' He pointed at Cheng Ming. I smiled again, shyly. If I'd known it was him, I'd have been more circumspect in my praise.

It seemed Cheng Ming sensed my embarrassment. 'Lao Gao overestimates my role, I am afraid,' he said. 'I suggested the bridge to make more of the pond. My real passion is botany. I love plants.'

So the pavilion had been his idea! I blushed to think that there might be some connection between our encounter on Hat Hill and its name.

Lao Gao broke the silence: 'I'm so pleased you've come. Zhiying should have brought you before now.'

'You know him, Lao Gao – he's not one for nature.'

'That's why he should come – to be educated. Oh . . .' Lao Gao had seen that Mother was awake '. . . I want to say hello to your mother. Cheng Ming will enlighten you on botanical matters.'

For a moment neither of us spoke. Then I said, 'I . . . like the pavilion. It has a lovely name – and I appreciated your kindness when we met on Hat Hill. You see, my late father played the flute and . . . what I meant to say was . . . Please, you mustn't think I was being – being . . .' I stuttered and couldn't quite bring myself to say 'forward'.

His smile deepened as he met my eyes. 'Wenya, don't

say any more. I wanted to play for you. I saw nothing wrong in it. Isn't appreciation of beauty the most natural thing in the world? There is no need to apologise. I feel honoured that you asked me. Allow me.' He stepped forward and removed a fallen petal from my shoulder. I was filled with an inexplicable happiness. How sensitive he was, I thought.

When Lao Gao returned with Mother, I was almost sorry. It would have been pleasant to talk more of music, poetry and beauty. But Lao Gao patted my shoulder. 'Come,' he said, 'I want to show you and your mother the glasshouse where we have some rare southern flowers that will delight you both.'

11

Zhiying started to dig the vegetable cellar on Liqiu – the Day of the Establishing of Autumn. Winter is long in our part of China, and he had to store enough of the only three vegetables available – cabbages, carrots and potatoes. We had no fridge, and they were best kept underground. Come autumn, digging cellars was the major occupation of the men in a family. Some of our neighbours had started long before us, but Zhiying had waited – he needed to plan and design it. I asked him what there was to design – didn't you just dig until the hole was big enough? He looked at me as you might a child, but said nothing. In the weeks leading up to Liqiu, he sat beside the bed lamp each night planning our cellar. I lay listening to the soft scratch of his pencil on the paper, watching his idea take shape: 'Vegetable Cellar, to be completed before . . . diameter, length, unit . . .' Usually I would doze off before he had finished.

As soon as he got home each evening, he would start on the cellar. Because of Father's absence, and because we had moved around so much, Mother and I had never had a vegetable cellar. Now, as I watched my husband dig, I felt proud. The cellar meant to me what a garden might mean to others – a symbol of stability.

I watched him measure the ground carefully with string, striding back and forth to check that the lines were straight, and saw the deep frown that meant concentration, rather than anger. Once he saw me and waved.

All he had to show after the first day were footprints. The hole was not half an inch deep. He had chosen the patch beneath our window – it was nearly the size of a small house. 'How are we ever going to finish it?' I asked.

He smiled. 'It's got to be big.' He pointed at my belly. 'We'll have another mouth to feed soon.'

Next, he set up his carpenter's bench in the corridor. He explained that he would need to lay planks over the cellar, once it was dug, as a roof.

Over the next few days, perhaps inspired by Zhiying, neighbours who hadn't yet started began to dig. Soon the land in front of our block resembled a building site. I saw then that there had been no need to worry – the factory lent spades, and we all helped each other. The men did the digging, while the women gathered together to prepare food for all. With my large belly, I was the centre of attention, while Zhiying was teased for his earnestness and the determination with which he worked. I smiled and said nothing. Newly married women had to appear demure, but as I went down to him with a Thermos of hot water or a bowl of rice congee to warm him, I felt all eyes on us.

As the season deepened Zhiying dug frantically to finish before the frost came and the ground hardened. Soon, he was hidden from view, emerging occasionally, like a seal from the waves, for food.

When at last the cellar was ready to be filled, the cabbages were delivered in big yellow lorries and piled up in the courtyard. Zhiying stood with the man from the food-supply department as he counted the cabbages in our pile and checked our ration books. I hovered beside him, amazed by the size of our pile, even though I knew it had to last us the whole winter. Afterwards we wheeled them to the cellar in a barrow. I helped Zhiying to stack them – some of the older women had told me that we must treat the cabbages carefully: the cellar should be cool but not freezing, moist but not damp. When we laid down the last one, we were pinned to each other, back to back. Briefly our hands clasped.

Zhiying pulled me out of the cellar, then knelt down to put on the wooden lid. He locked it, then pushed a rock on top. Side by side we walked through the dusk, backs aching, hands nearly touching. My nose was still full of the scent of cabbages. Our nest was ready. The baby could arrive.

12

On New Year's Eve the factory held a party. Water had been pumped into the dried-up marsh pond next to the bachelors' quarters and had frozen to become a magnificent ice rink. Red and yellow ribbons and flags, on tall wooden poles with a lantern at the top, had been positioned at regular intervals along the bank. The workers were on it in no time – many could not afford proper skating boots, but they enjoyed sliding on the ice in their bulky but soft-soled winter shoes. At first Zhiying and I stood on the edge and watched.

Near the centre I spotted a tall, slender girl dancing with Cheng Ming. She was wearing a rainbow-coloured woolly hat, tilting her head back and laughing. Her face flashed by me and the words 'beautiful as a startled swan' came into my mind.

'That's Lao Gao's new bride,' Zhiying whispered.

'Lao Gao's got married?' I could hardly believe it. Family and Lao Gao didn't go together.

Zhiying nodded. 'They met in Beijing.'

I stared at the couple, now gliding past us, and noticed how Cheng Ming looked at her.

'Remember?' Zhiying went on. 'Lao Gao couldn't be at our wedding because he went to a conference. That was when he met her. They were married in the south about a month ago. She's called Zhenzhen, and she's from Yang Zhou. She can sing, or so they say – a new recruit for the entertainment troupe.'

My eyes were drawn back to Cheng Ming and the girl, weaving in and out of the crowds of other dancers, like a pair of shooting stars on a night sky. When the music stopped, the girl took her hand off Cheng Ming's shoulder to wave. Following her gaze, I spotted Lao Gao standing on the bank wearing a grin; he was looking at Zhenzhen so tenderly. I was touched. It was about time such a kind and brave man had someone to care for him. We all loved him, but he needed someone of his own, as I needed Zhiying. Suddenly, I wished I wasn't pregnant and could dance on the ice with the others. 'Why isn't Lao Gao dancing with her?' I asked.

Zhiying peered at Zhenzhen and Cheng Ming. 'He's being too generous with his bride.'

'Why do you say that? Why shouldn't she dance with other people?'

'It would be better if she didn't dance with *him*.' Zhiying avoided my eyes and I saw, to my surprise, that he was blushing.

'But he's Lao Gao's secretary – he's only being friendly.'

We said no more for a while. Then, suddenly, Zhiying spoke: 'Wenya, when we first knew each other, I thought you felt something for him.'

'Did you?' I asked, trying to keep the shock out of my voice.

He peered down at me. 'Not any more, though, I hope?'

Our eyes met. He looked funny – so serious, with frozen red cheeks and a thick woolly hat.

'Don't be silly!' I tugged at his hand. 'What are we waiting for?' I dragged him to the ice. As my feet touched the slippery surface I felt dull pain shoot through my lower back. I had been experiencing it on and off over the last few weeks, and had put it down to too much standing around the cellar. I hadn't worried about it – the baby wasn't due for another six weeks. The pain faded as we danced to the music. For a while I leaned on Zhiying, rocking gently to the music. Once we bumped into Lao Gao and his wife – even then I didn't see her face because he was holding her close, but she danced with the grace of a deer. Now I felt the pain again, stronger this time. I told Zhiying I needed the washroom. I left him and headed for the bachelors' living quarters, but kept turning back to wave to him at the edge of the pond.

I slowed when I knew he could no longer see me. I thought of Cheng Ming, who was cultured, sensitive and elegant, all qualities I admired – I could see now why Zhiying had wondered. But Zhiying was the man I had married and I cared for him. I tried to shake off my unease as I walked on. A friendly exchange with a young couple I met on the way helped me to feel normal again, and the girl commented on my bump. By the time I reached the living quarters I had nearly forgotten about Cheng Ming.

Then I caught a waft of cigarette smoke, and spotted a familiar shape.

'Wenya,' said Cheng Ming's voice, stopping me in my tracks. 'I saw you earlier.'

'And I saw you,' I said. It felt strange to talk to him – a

man I barely knew yet with whom I felt curiously intimate.

'I was getting to know Zhenzhen. I asked her to join the entertainment troupe. Why didn't you come to say hello?' He stared at me – and I remembered that this was how he had looked at Zhenzhen. What had he been saying to her?

'I . . .' I paused, remembering what Zhiying had said about him. 'You looked busy.' I fought not to catch his eye – I didn't want him to see how he overwhelmed and confused me. 'Excuse me.' I began to walk towards the living quarters. 'I was on my way there.'

As if to himself, he said:

'This night, in the rain, you hear the melody of "Broken Willow",
How can you resist that longing for your old home?'

I turned back and met his eyes. 'A soul-mate,' he said. 'That's all I want. Nothing more. You understand me, I know.'

I stood rooted to the ground, heart pounding.

'Wenya,' he murmured, and came close.

'Soul-mate,' I said, and suddenly I felt as if I had always known Cheng Ming. Our eyes locked, and the night receded. But as he reached down to me, I smelt the spirit he had been drinking. His arm brushed against my belly and I gasped. 'No,' I said, and moved away. I turned sharply and walked on. He didn't follow.

Nothing had changed since my last visit. As I stood by the door-keeper's window, that night flooded back – the night when I had first met Cheng Ming and Lao Gao. With a painful longing, I remembered, too, the day on Hat Hill, the first faint notes of the flute, so melancholy and mysterious, which Zhiying had interrupted. I stood still now, and listened.

Nothing. All I could hear was my own heavy breathing. I closed my eyes and saw Zhiying's face. I felt ashamed. I opened my eyes and stumbled away from the building. Cheng Ming had gone.

When I got back to the pond I searched for Zhiying. Where was he? I called his name. Finally I spotted him at the edge of the ice, looking out for me – and I knew then that I couldn't live without him. I had been so close to forgetting this – to falling for a few lines of poetry and some nonsense about soul-mates. Cheng Ming had been drunk: his words had meant nothing. Suddenly the blood rushed to my face and I ran to my husband. I reached him as 'Red Blossom' began to play.

In Zhiying's arms, I danced. When the song died away, I felt a gush of liquid down my thigh. I gripped Zhiying's hand and he gripped mine. When I had made him understand what was happening, he panicked.

I told him I was fine – but the pain intensified. I crouched on the ground and suddenly people were surrounding me, calling instructions: 'Hot water, warm quilts, disinfectant – pick her up! Get Lao Hang, the factory doctor. We need a stretcher! Please, out of the way!'

I rejected the offer of a jeep to drive me to the hospital – my professional training told me the baby would arrive very soon. I was taken to the door-keeper's room at the bachelors' quarters, and lay on a pile of coats. Two women I didn't know attended to me. I was told Zhiying had gone for the doctor.

I clenched my teeth as each wave crashed over me. Between contractions, I took deep breaths and tried to calm myself. I've attended births, I thought, it's all perfectly straightforward. But this was different – now I was the one in pain.

That night time had no meaning. I fixed my eyes on the crescent moon and concentrated on my breathing. My child was arriving with the new year, nearly two months early. The young woman who was kneeling by me, whose hands I had been gripping, demanded, 'Make a sound! It helps.'

I didn't make a sound. A head midwife had once told me that the mothers who screamed were the ones she hated most.

'Why don't you scream?' the woman asked, and began to encourage me. As I clutched her hands she moaned, and a sound poured from me, a sound I didn't recognise. I lost count of the times she said, 'Breathe in, out, in, out. Here it comes.' At first I was annoyed, but soon I followed her lead and rode the crushing wave that came from within my body.

As I felt the baby's head slide out, I heard a tremendous groan – I wasn't sure from which of us. And as she put my son into my arms, Sister Zhen introduced herself to me.

13

I ached all over and wondered where I was. Then a familiar smell wafted to me and I knew. I opened my eyes and saw the sign for Jing – silence – that hung in all hospital wards. Things fell into place: the birth; a voice saying I was bleeding heavily; Zhiying holding my hand; an ambulance siren . . . the hard voices of the doctors. Was that how I sounded to my patients? Would I die?

But I knew there was something else, something more important, something obvious . . . 'My baby! Where's my baby?'

There was a flurry of activity. Zhiying strode in, followed by a nurse, a small bundle in her arms.

I couldn't sit up so they laid him on my chest. He was much lighter than I'd expected, and his eyes were closed. A shout from the corridor made him jump. His eyes opened, the corner of his mouth twisted and a tiny cry burst out. He sounded more like a piglet than a human but he was my baby.

I froze and turned to Zhiying. So far in his short life, Xiao Tao had been handled more by his father than by me. Zhiying picked him up and began to rock him, but still the baby cried. The nurse rescued us. 'Back to the incubator,' she said, and took Xiao Tao away.

Zhiying sat on the chair beside my bed, holding my hand, the ward quiet now. We were parents, but I'd not expected to feel so numb and detached. I should be ecstatic.

I became aware of prickling in my breasts; and I realised the milk was coming in, ready for the baby. Despite my medical training, when I became a mother myself, I was as helpless as the rest. I felt the pressure of Zhiying's hands and glanced up to meet his eyes; it was the first time since the birth that I had been alone with him. I remembered how he had been bustled out of the delivery room and how a stranger had attended to me in my moment of utmost vulnerability.

'Could you fetch the midwife?' I asked.

'What midwife?' Zhiying frowned.

'The woman who screamed, during the birth.'

For a moment he seemed puzzled. Then he laughed. 'You mean Zhenzhen – she's not a midwife. She's Lao Gao's bride.'

I hadn't seen her face when she was on the ice, and had thought that the woman bellowing instructions at me was a trained midwife. Lao Gao's bride? In my mind's eye I saw Zhenzhen's ethereal figure floating across the pond, but I couldn't match it with the woman whose hands I had gripped. No new bride should be made to assist at a birth.

The next time the nurse brought the baby, she wanted me to feed him. The baby sucked, but I had little milk. Though I knew this was not unusual, I felt frustrated with both myself and the baby. I dared not hold him too tightly, in case I crushed him.

I felt useless.

14

From the envious looks of the other new mothers I realised how lucky I was to be driven home in the jeep Lao Gao had sent for me. Most went home with the baby on the back of their husband's bike. 'Of course, she's an East Wind wife,' I heard one say to another. Zhiying helped me to my feet, wrapped in a blanket; Xiao Tao was in his arms. The wind cut through the thick blanket as if it were paper. The driver introduced himself as Lao Cui and I climbed in. He covered me with another blanket – 'Lao Gao said to make sure you don't catch a chill' – and Zhiying handed me our son.

I held Xiao Tao close. I had had a battle to leave the hospital. Because he was premature, and I had bled so much, I had been advised to stay another week – but I was sure we'd recover better at home. I won, but only because I convinced them that, as a fellow doctor, I knew how to look after myself and my child.

Mother stood at the door of our flat, wearing her best jumper. She took the baby from Zhiying and held out her other hand to shake the driver's. She glanced at me, 'You're back,' then turned away. I stepped past her and sat on the bed, exhausted. The flat looked different, but I couldn't tell why. For a while it seemed full – the driver had come in for tea. When he rose to leave, Mother walked him to the door and called after him, 'Go carefully.' I remembered she was to stay.

For a whole month I was to remain in bed and she would look after me, observing the centuries' old tradition. During those thirty days, I was not to drink cold liquid or open the windows. I was to get off the bed only when it was absolutely necessary, and Mother would wait on me hand and foot.

When she came back into the room, having seen off Lao Cui, she took Xiao Tao from me without a word and started to walk him about. I was annoyed. I lay down, turned my back and refused to talk to her. Later, Xiao Tao began to whimper and wouldn't settle. I stretched out my hands for him several times, but she said, 'He's all right.' Eventually, when he was crying inconsolably, she sighed. 'I suppose he wants a feed,' she said, and handed him back to me.

Under Mother's scrutiny I undid my buttons, desperate to appear calm. My nipples hurt, but I was determined this feed would go well, if only to show her I could do it. She remained close, watching over my shoulder. 'I wonder if he's getting enough milk,' she said, and tickled his little toes. 'Suck harder.'

Zhiying could see I was getting upset, and, to distract her, he said that he, too, was starving. They left me to struggle with Xiao Tao, who tried to suck, failed and tried again.

A little later, Mother brought out our dinner. She and Zhiying were to have cabbage stir-fried with potatoes, but she put a bowl of suspicious looking soup in front of me. 'Drink this,' she urged.

Used to obeying her, I sipped and nearly spat it out. 'There's no salt!' I exclaimed.

Mother nodded. 'You mustn't have any – you'll make less milk.'

She had combined pigs' trotters with red dates – a traditional dish for nursing mothers – she had gone to great lengths to get hold of the ingredients, then spent a long time preparing the soup. 'Come on, drink it.' She stood over me, her voice gentler. I took a deep breath. Dates and pork – separately they were rare and expensive treats, but to serve them together . . . The very thought of it made me feel sick. I knew, though, that for Xiao Tao's sake I had to get used to it – my family had saved up to supply me with nourishing food and I couldn't let them down.

15

At the end of the first month we invited Lao Gao and Zhenzhen to help us celebrate. It was our way of thanking them for their help and presents, and also of welcoming them as our next-door neighbours. Now that Lao Gao was married he was entitled to leave the bachelors' quarters for a family apartment. Zhiying had helped them move in.

I had to exchange a few words with Zhenzhen through the open door – during the month's rest, outsiders were not encouraged to come in for fear of bringing germs with them. She was warm and pleasant, and did not refer to our previous intimacy as I had feared she might. I liked her soft southern accent, which often echoed round the family complex.

I asked Zhiying why she was at home so much and he told me that her work and personal files had yet to be transferred from her unit in the south. An application had been made for her to work in the propaganda department at the factory, and it was hoped that she would eventually lead the entertainment troupe. At the moment, though, she was without a job.

I fed Xiao Tao before our guests arrived – he was taking more milk now, but gaining little weight. I had put on my best red winter jacket but feeding had made me sweat so I took it off and washed myself again. When the knock came at the door I checked myself in the mirror, feeling nervous – I had seen hardly anybody apart from Zhiying and Mother for nearly a month. I didn't like the face I saw in the mirror – I looked old and something else . . . I didn't have time to identify it before Zhiying opened the door. I heard Lao Gao's hearty greeting – 'How he's grown! He's just like his father!' When he came in, he lowered his voice and said to me, 'There! I always told you you'd have a boy, didn't I?' I recalled no such conversation but I nodded anyway.

Mother smiled. 'That's what I said, too, but she never believed me.'

Lao Gao took Xiao Tao from her. 'Well, we two could have taught the young ones something, couldn't we?' He winked at her and smiled down at the baby.

Fond though I was of Lao Gao, I had had enough of everyone's obsession with boys. When Zhenzhen stepped up to my side, I almost expected her to say the same thing, but she surprised me. 'Are you really pleased it's a boy?' she asked softly. 'I'd be just as happy with a girl.'

Nobody had ever said such a thing to me. At last, I thought, I had found someone I could really talk to. 'How do you like it here?' I asked. 'Are you used to our food yet?'

She hesitated a little before she said, 'Yes.'

Lao Gao had overheard my question. 'What are we having today? I can smell something good already.'

At this Mother summoned me to the kitchen. We had made pork and cabbage dumplings, a traditional feast on such occasions, and had used up the whole month's meat ration. When the dumplings were in the boiling pan Mother sent me back to the sitting room to entertain the guests, but suddenly I was shy. Zhiying knew them well, but their laughter seemed to exclude me. Unnoticed, I went back to the kitchen.

The dumplings were well received. Lao Gao especially made appreciative noises and kept turning to Zhenzhen. 'Good, isn't it? Try another with the sauce.' It was almost as if he was the host, not us. But we smiled – he was forgiven because he was a newlywed and his enthusiasm for Mother's food was endearing.

It was plain that Lao Gao was besotted with Zhenzhen. With her, he was relaxed and playful. Instead of giving orders he told jokes. Zhiying and I exchanged a glance. This wasn't the Lao Gao we knew. Zhenzhen must have bewitched him. I watched her as she gave him a wide infectious smile, elbows on the table, face framed in her hands. Her sparkling eyes seemed to urge him on with more tales. She was plainly devoted to him. I was so intrigued by her that I only caught half of the conversation, until Cheng Ming's name came up: '. . . so I said to the lad he must take Zhenzhen out more, while I'm in this busy period.'

'I'm fine, really. I can darn his socks,' Zhenzhen joked.

'She can come to play with Xiao Tao,' Mother said.

'I'd be delighted to,' Zhenzhen said, and beamed at my baby.

'It'd be wonderful if you could keep her company,' Lao Gao said. 'I'd give Cheng Ming more leave from work to be with Zhenzhen, but I don't like to do it too often.'

'So don't – really, Lao Gao. You know it's wrong. I can't believe you of all people . . .' Zhenzhen eyed him with a mock-accusation. 'I'll go for walks with Wenya, too,' she added.

'Of course.' I nodded, thrilled at the prospect of being away from Mother for a while.

When they rose to go, it was nearly midnight.

'That was the best meal I've had for ages,' Lao Gao said to Mother. 'Real north-eastern cuisine, Zhenzhen. We're so lucky.'

'Dumplings are a northern speciality.' Mother smiled. 'But I'm sure you eat far more interesting things in the south.'

'Actually our dumplings—'

Before Zhenzhen was able to finish her sentence, Lao Gao cut her off. 'The northern dumplings are delicious, and Sister Wen,' he turned to Mother again, 'I'd swear to heaven yours are the most delicious of all.'

'It was a shame we couldn't offer you something more interesting.' Mother protested modestly. 'I'm sure you're used to better things.' Lao Gao was a high-level cadre, who was entitled to superior rations.

Our visitors looked embarrassed.

Zhiying said quickly, 'Where do you store your vegetables? I'm not sure you have a cellar. Do say if you need help.'

'That's very kind of you.' Lao Gao smiled sheepishly. 'We've been advised about the lack of winter vegetables – but we didn't want to store lots of food we wouldn't eat.' He glanced at Zhenzhen. 'We shall be all right. We have no children and we can eat at the factory canteen . . .'

When our visitors had gone, Mother turned for the kitchen. 'Southerners have no idea.' She rolled her eyes. Of what, she never said.

16

Although I had responded enthusiastically to Zhenzhen's suggestion of a walk, I didn't take it too seriously – she was the factory director's wife and had the secretary for company. Why should she want to go out with me? But one morning not long after their visit, Zhenzhen knocked and asked me to go out with her. 'That would be lovely,' I said, and went to fetch my coat. She stretched out her hands for Xiao Tao, who was in Mother's arms. 'I'll carry him,' she said.

'You mean to take him too?' Mother held on to him.

'Of course! Fresh air will do him good.' Zhenzhen smiled, and pinched his cheek gently. 'Come for a walk with Auntie Zhenzhen!'

Just before she had arrived Mother and I had been arguing about that. At forty days old, Xiao Tao hadn't been out of the flat. The nearest he'd got to the outside world was being held at the window for some fresh air. The season was not right for him, Mother had insisted. The wintry wind would make him ill.

'Here's his coat, Auntie. Let me put it on – you hold him. There, that's done. Doesn't he look snug?' Zhenzhen turned to me: 'The weather forecast said the sun will be out most of the day, but you never know. I told Lao Gao I'd be back in time to cook him dinner – he's busy with new staff. He was pleased when I said I was going out with you. "Give the baby a kiss from me," he said.' She leaned over to Xiao Tao.

I saw Mother's hands loosen at the mention of Lao Gao. His approval meant more than anything else Zhenzhen could have said.

Zhenzhen was already in the corridor, Xiao Tao in her arms. She stamped her feet. 'Come on – don't make the baby wait.'

I had been cooped up with Xiao Tao for so long that everything seemed too large and vivid. There were few people about as, although it was sunny, the wind was biting. Those we passed huddled inside their winter overalls, their backs hunched. The crisp air excited me – it was as if I saw and experienced everything from Xiao Tao's point of view. The first flood of spring rain had washed away the grime of winter. I peered at Zhenzhen beside me. Her clothes – a loose cotton jacket over a woolly top – were too thin but she didn't seem cold.

As soon as we were out of Mother's sight, she took off Xiao Tao's heavy coat. 'A bit of sun,' she said, 'is what he needs,' and Xiao Tao, who had stopped whimpering as soon as we were outside, squeezed his eyes shut in its warm light and yawned. Zhenzhen grinned. 'That's more like it.' She cradled him close to her, wrapping him inside her own coat. I hung back. For all my excitement I, like Mother, wasn't used to the idea of a walk in winter.

We headed for a path that ran parallel to the workers'

park up Hat Hill. From the way she strode ahead without looking left or right at crossroads where several tracks joined, it was plain she had done this many times before. I asked her if she had been this way with Cheng Ming. She nodded and said that was why she knew this path so well. 'And with Lao Gao?'

'You must be joking! He works so hard, he never has a full weekend with me. I'm sure I see more of his secretary than I do of him.'

'Do you mind that?'

'No, of course not. Cheng Ming's like a younger brother. He knows so much and makes me laugh . . .' She smiled, and I realised that she was closer in age to Cheng Ming than to Lao Gao. I remembered the last time I had seen them together, leaving the flat one weekend when Lao Gao was away: they had stood shoulder to shoulder, two tall figures, and as she locked the door he had leaned forward to whisper in her ear. She had giggled, which made him laugh, and it was then that he'd turned and seen me. I had smiled and he waved – it was as if the episode on the night of Xiao Tao's birth had never happened. Now my heart lifted: the encounter by the marsh hadn't meant anything to him. With that wave he had dismissed it – he wanted us both to forget it. I shouldn't judge him harshly for one drunken incident. Anyway, Lao Gao trusted him, so I should be pleased that he made Zhenzhen happy. I hurried to catch up with her.

It grew windier the higher we went. Xiao Tao burrowed deeper inside Zhenzhen's jacket. An old woman passed us briskly, then glanced back and pointed at Xiao Tao. 'What kind of mother are you?' she said to Zhenzhen. 'Your son will die of cold.'

'But she's the mother,' Zhiying pointed at me, 'and she's quite happy . . .'

The woman glowered at her. 'Then you make a fine pair,' she sneered and stalked off.

Zhenzhen and I burst into uncontrollable giggles. The old woman's rebuff had reminded me of my battle with Mother, and made our escape all the more thrilling. I'd spent so long indoors that I'd become as obsessed she was with Xiao Tao's health – his frailty made us terrified carers. Now, for the first time since I had become a mother, I felt joyful. Cautiously, I let myself relax.

As we marched on I noticed fresh patches of bare earth along the path, which I knew had been dug by desperate people looking for edible plants. As a nursing mother, I had been given the lion's share of our food, but Zhiying and Mother were often hungry. I slowed down, hoping to spot some. We crossed a deep ditch that ran parallel to the rough track and I saw from the lack of footprints that nobody had ventured so far into the wood. There was a large expanse of uninterrupted green, and I bent down to a clump of *song xiacao*. I smoothed the underside of a leaf and was reassured by the rough edges, like tiny teeth.

'*Pei.*' Zhen grimaced.

'What?'

'Watch out.' She gestured at a fresh animal dropping near my hand.

I fingered the leaves again. 'This is *song xiacao* – you can eat it.' I expected her to be as excited as I was. But she said nothing. For a moment I debated whether to pick it now or wait for the leaves to grow a little, then bent to the task.

Zhenzhen stepped away. 'Surely it's not worth . . .'

'Of course it's worth it. People are starving,' I said.

'I know.' She glanced disdainfully at the droppings, then turned away.

Did she know this was how the rest of us lived? You were grateful for any food you found, whether you liked it or not. I had to swallow the funny-tasting soup Mother made for me because Xiao Tao's life depended on it. She used *song xiacao* not because she thought it was a culinary delight but because she wanted to pass on a basic survival tip. Did Zhenzhen know any of this? I doubted she'd ever experienced hunger as we had. The gulf between us grew. I remembered Lao Gao's numerous offers of food and help, and how grateful I had been to receive them. But his gifts had emphasised that he and Zhenzhen had far more than they could ever eat. Now, I felt insulted by their generosity. My cheeks were hot with humiliation when I saw I had no choice but to continue to accept because there was Xiao Tao.

I strode up to her and tapped her shoulder. When she turned I stretched out my hands. 'Can I have him back?' I asked. Still asleep, he didn't stir as I breathed in his milky smell. I started down the hill, but she stepped in front of me. 'Wenya, wait – what's the matter?'

'I want to go home,' I said coldly.

'What have I done? You're angry with me – is it because of that plant?'

'The edible plant,' I said pointedly.

Her chest was heaving, and I saw that she was trying to control herself: 'I'm sorry,' she said. 'Perhaps I was insensitive. But . . . you're a good friend and I didn't want to pretend. I was disgusted at the idea of eating—'

'I'm flattered you consider me a friend, Zhenzhen, but we're different—'

'How? Because I'm married to the factory director? I've never thought of it in those terms. You're my friend. It's as simple as that.'

'We starve, you don't. We dig cellars like the rest of the factory, and you eat whenever you feel like it. Do you think I would eat this plant if I had a choice? And you tell me we're the same.' I stepped past her and went on down the hill.

The sun dimmed and I glimpsed the tops of the chimneys with their spiralling smoke. Ahead of us lay the sprawling factory workshops, not a beautiful sight but I loved it anyway. A train hooted in the distance, and I heard Zhenzhen coming up behind me. When she had caught up, she said, a bit out of breath, 'I'm not meant to tell you this – Lao Gao wants it kept secret – but . . . I don't want you to think us heartless. He has been sending his extra cadre's rations to a sick retired factory worker whose family needs it far more than we do. We live on my ration.'

'Zhenzhen!'

'We're fine, Wenya. I need very little and Lao Gao . . . as he said, he often eats at the factory . . . so . . .' She smiled at me.

I was speechless with shame.

She stepped close to me. 'Promise you won't tell anybody else – not even Zhiying. Lao Gao would be furious with me.'

I nodded slowly.

'Spring would be the best time . . . The hill's full of blossoms.' she murmured.

What did she mean? I saw, from her dreamy look, that she wasn't talking about this hill. 'One day, Wenya,' she continued, 'I'll take you to my hometown. One day you'll know that I'm not as spoiled as you think, though I can be a bit thoughtless. Please forgive me.'

Xiao Tao coughed and stirred. We bent down to him and our gloved hands touched. Zhenzhen took the clump of leaves from my hand. 'How do you cook it?' she said.

'I've never had to,' I confessed. 'Mother knows what to do with it.'

At the grocery shop outside our block we saw two people forming a queue. 'Look,' Zhenzhen whispered. A large lorry was parked nearby. As we watched, the engine was switched off, a man jumped down and went to the back. He slipped off the backboard and I glimpsed small dark green bundles. We hurried closer. 'Spinach!' Zhenzhen's eyes gleamed. We stared at each other. Then, without a word, I ran. 'Give him to me so you can run faster!' she shouted.

I stopped, about to hand over Xiao Tao, then had another idea. 'No. You run home for the ration books. Mother knows where ours is. I'll wait in the queue,' I called back.

I was fifth in the line. Spinach and omelette soup with ginger, or spinach fried with garlic?

As the person in front of me was being served, I heard a yelp, swung round and saw Zhenzhen running towards me. A few steps short of the queue she fell over, but struggled to her feet and limped the rest of the way to me.

That night we had spinach and omelette soup. It was the first time we had eaten any green vegetables other than cabbage for a long time. Earlier, when I was washing the spinach, I had come across the clump of *song xiacao*, mixed up with the spinach. I paused only briefly before I gave it to Little White. It was edible, but now I remembered its bitter aftertaste – that was why it was not considered a vegetable. Spinach was for humans, *song xiacao* for animals. It was not simply a matter of taste; but of dignity.

'Zhenzhen is giving you ideas,' Zhiying accused me later, when I explained. Laughing, I agreed.

I kept her secret, but always made sure that Mother sent some of any special food we cooked next door to the Gaos.

17

Getting on to the bus was the easy bit, and Xiao Tao enjoyed the rocking as we drove along, and the admiring looks he got from fellow passengers. He thrived on attention. The fat woman who had helped me on now prodded his cheeks. 'So, where are you off to, my boy? Going to see Granny?'

I told her this was my first day back at work since his birth and that I was taking Xiao Tao to the nursery.

'You'll miss him, then,' she said.

I nodded. I didn't want to talk. I had just had a battle at home with Mother, who was very against him going to the nursery. But the woman wouldn't give up.

'Why can't he stay at home? Can't your mother or mother-in-law look after him?'

'My mother-in-law's dead and my mother has been looking after him, but now . . . in spring, her asthma . . .'

The woman appeared to be satisfied, but before she got off she said, 'They'll never look after him as well as your mother – you've got to watch them.'

I wished I'd never spoken to her. With just a few words, she had unsettled my resolve. I had tried hard to convince

Mother that the hospital nursery had a very good reputation, that it was renowned for good hygiene and professional care, and that all the other mothers had told me they were very satisfied with it. What was more, I could feed him during breaks, which I couldn't if I left him at home – it was at least an hour's journey each way. It was this that finally persuaded Mother. Xiao Tao was barely four months old and was still dependent on my milk.

I buried my face in his blanket in case anybody else felt like chatting. It was strange going to work holding a baby, and painful to think that soon I would hand him to a stranger – well, not a complete stranger: I had met the staff a couple of times and they were perfectly nice people. It was just that, having established a routine with him, I was reluctant to enter a new phase.

It was only when I stepped on to the cinder path that I remembered something: that to get to the nursery I had to pass the mortuary. Last summer, I had climbed the tree in front of me to harvest the blossoms and make those buns. I had always felt there had been a link between them and Xiao Tao's conception. I didn't look up as I walked past, but held Xiao Tao tightly. A girl of about twenty took him from me and ushered me out. I heard him crying as I turned the corner and saw that the pagoda tree was in blossom again. As the wind blew, the clusters stirred. Suddenly I felt fearful, and it was all I could do to stop myself rushing back to the nursery and grabbing Xiao Tao from the girl's hands.

That day Xiao Tao wouldn't feed properly. It didn't help that since my break I had been asked to take on more teaching in the medical school next door. Even the short walk round the corner took fifteen minutes off my lunch-hour and I was breathless with dashing from one place to the next. After only three days, my healed nipples cracked and became infected. Xiao Tao wailed, his cries tugging at my heart. But I bit my lip and persevered.

After a week I gave up. 'You win,' I said to Mother as I got home, clutching Xiao Tao. 'He can stay with you.'

18

For a week or so, things seemed to work well. In the morning, after a feed, I'd express what little milk I had left for Mother to mix with rice paste for Xiao Tao. At lunchtime the factory would send a car to bring Mother to the hospital with him so that I could feed him – Lao Gao arranged it at Zhenzhen's bidding. Then I'd express a little milk for Mother to mix with more rice paste. It wasn't ideal, but we struggled through, and Xiao Tao seemed to gain weight.

It wasn't long before the routine was upset. Mother had a bout of asthma when the weather changed, and I felt guilty each time she braved the cold wind to bring Xiao Tao to me, even in the car that Lao Gao was still sending. I wanted to feed my child, but I didn't want Mother to suffer. The only solution was to give up feeding him myself.

'Let me bring Xiao Tao to you,' Zhenzhen volunteered, when I confided in her. 'And I can help your mother with him, too.'

'You?'

She nodded. 'I still have no job.' When she had last

enquired at the factory personnel department she had been told her file transfer was still not complete, and that it was likely to take at least another month. She watched my face closely. 'It'll give me something to do with my day.' She added, 'And, anyway, when I need to, I can always ask your mother for advice.'

'What will you do with him?' I asked, curious. Apart from bringing him to the hospital, Mother preferred Xiao Tao to stay indoors, even though the weather was warmer. Spring was a bad time to be out, she insisted, even worse than winter, because germs were breeding.

Zhenzhen winked. 'Well, on still, warm days, we'll go out for walks, and on windy days there's always my flat.'

Their flat was large and spacious. I remembered the first time I had gone into it. I had expected it to be bigger than ours, but I hadn't reckoned on it being so bare, which made it seem even larger. On the sunny day we visited, I had been drawn to the south-facing window, which made the room feel warm and summery. We had sat there for a long time, Xiao Tao propped up on pillows. It was obvious he liked the light and space as well.

'Don't worry about him,' Zhenzhen said now. 'He'll be fine.'

Looking down at Xiao Tao, who was fast asleep, I felt a pang of jealousy. I didn't see enough of him. When I came home from work, I only had time to eat, feed him, then go to bed. During the night he'd wake up several times for a feed, but then I wasn't in the mood to enjoy his company.

'Let me think about it,' I said slowly. There was Mother to persuade, and she would surely object.

Surprisingly, she approved. The Gaos were good people,

she informed me, and although Zhenzhen was not yet a mother, she would make a perfect one when the time came. 'And she's obviously fond of the baby,' Mother declared.

Summer came and the food shortage intensified. Rations grew scarce, but I was happy.

Everything went like clockwork: Mother scavenged so that we had enough to eat, Lao Gao made sure that either Zhenzhen or Mother, as her health improved, brought Xiao Tao for his feeds when I was at work, and Xiao Tao was healthy. He started to gain weight, much to everyone's delight. Children were the flowers of the motherland, Lao Gao had said, and it was their blooming that assured us of hope for the future. Now was the hardest part, he had reminded us in one of his speeches at the factory. The world had stood still to watch us – the Soviet revisionists in particular were waiting to see us fall but by tightening our belts, being determined and helping each other, we'd show them all what the Chinese people were made of.

And within Lao Gao's charmed circle the four of us – Zhenzhen, Cheng Ming, Zhiying and I – were drawn to him like flowers to the sun. Recently we had seen much more of Cheng Ming, mostly at weekends when Lao Gao had to work. Lao Gao sent his driver, Lao Cui, to take us on outings, sometimes with Mother too, and it was on these trips that we forged a deeper bond. Even Zhiying was prepared to give Cheng Ming a chance – he didn't disappoint. The more time I spent with him, the more I realized why Zhenzhen and Lao Gao had been so disarmed – Cheng Ming was impossible to dislike. He was courteous to Mother, affectionate with Zhenzhen, brotherly to Zhiying and so gentle with Xiao Tao – I caught sight of him holding the baby and it struck me that he was as tender with him as a woman would have been. It was his gentleness, more than anything, that won me over. He always kept a slight distance between us, and he never brought his flute. In time I found it easier to put the New Year episode out of my mind. But it was not until I heard a startling revelation that I could relax in his presence, and trust him as implicitly as our neighbours did.

As part of its welfare programme for the workers, the factory arranged for them to have annual check-ups at my hospital. I wasn't involved in the examinations, but I had to help with filling in and checking forms. When I chanced upon Cheng Ming's, I noticed he had written nothing under 'next of kin'. Later that day, I met Lao Gao outside our flats and asked about Cheng Ming's origins. I explained that I had come across his form and asked if Cheng Ming was an orphan.

'That's right,' Lao Gao said, 'and that was how we met. I was in Beijing one winter, and was on my way to a meeting when my car stopped – there was a boy lying half frozen in front of it. I told the driver to take him to the nearest hospital, and after the meeting I went to check on the lad. He practically glued himself to me. Said he'd never leave me – and he never has.'

'So you saved his life!' I gasped.

'Well, anybody would have stopped to help him. But I suppose after that we had a bond . . . He's always going on about repaying his debt and defending me to the last drop of blood.' He chuckled, but I knew he was touched. 'He's like a younger brother to me and he's never let me down.

I'm very fond of him.' He paused and smiled. 'As I am of Zhiying. You must know that.' I blushed. But Lao Gao laughed: 'They're different from each other but both clever kids. You like Cheng Ming, no? Anybody would. Such a quick learner – you show him something once, and the next time he'll do it better than you can. Anything, you name it – flute, singing, dancing. He's good at art, too.'

I smiled, and made to go into my flat, but Lao Gao hadn't finished. 'That's why I like him to spend time with Zhenzhen. They get on so well, don't you think?'

'Oh, yes,' I agreed, with conviction. I felt so relieved to know the true nature of the relationship between Lao Gao and Cheng Ming. One had saved the other's life. There could be no stronger bond.

19

How could I ever forget that trip to the pond? I examined every minute, every expression, every shaft of light that penetrated the gaps between the leaves on the trees in minute detail for a long time afterwards. I revisited it in my memory so often that it had become like a film I'd watched over and over again. The sounds I'd heard but ignored, the gestures I'd seen but misunderstood ... On the surface nothing remarkable had happened. It was yet another happy day when a group of young men and women had set out in search of fun. There was plenty of laughter, bantering and singing: Chinese songs with marching tunes, and Soviet songs for the sentimental moments to which we were prone during those outings to the wood, a stream or the top of a hill.

Indeed, at the end of the day I remembered thinking that it had been one of the nicest days I'd ever spent with my closest friends. Seen with the benefit of hindsight, everyone was on their best behaviour. It was as though they knew that this image of them would be engraved on my mind: Zhiying was his most considerate self, Cheng Ming exquisitely sensitive, Zhenzhen so natural, relaxed and beautiful, and Lao Gao, our leader, the soul that bound us together.

It was just another of the days out that Lao Gao loved to arrange, except that that hot, oppressive Sunday was Zhenzhen's birthday. Having promised that he would be there for once, on that of all days, Lao Gao had to disappear at the last minute to a meeting. When he had knocked on our door to invite us, I wasn't keen – the idea was to go swimming, but I couldn't swim and was afraid of water. But you must come, Lao Gao had insisted. Zhenzhen had been brought up near water and had missed it all the time she'd been here. Cheng Ming had discovered a secluded pond and she was so excited about it. He couldn't go, but Zhiying, Cheng Ming and I must – he didn't want her to be disappointed. He begged and cajoled and bullied in the way that only Lao Gao could. And, of course, we agreed.

Once we were in the car, the four of us, we soon became noisy, gesticulating and shouting, to Lao Cui's disapproval. On those trips, it took little to make us laugh – even though our rations had been reduced because food was even scarcer . . . We needed those trips as an escape from the bleakness of everyday reality, measuring rice in tiny quantities, foraging for edible plants, and queueing endlessly for precious seasonal vegetables. During an outing we'd use up a large amount of our rations, which meant less food for the rest of the month – this was partly why Mother was so against the trips, and although she couldn't utter a bad word about the Gaos, she had berated me a few times.

Physically, I had recovered from Xiao Tao's birth and the sleepless nights. I was young, which helped, I suppose, and had a group of close friends. When I watched Zhenzhen with Xiao Tao, so careful, yet so relaxed, I found it hard to believe she wasn't a mother herself.

That day Zhiying and Cheng Ming, sitting at the front, were arguing about the plot of a Russian novel. We were used to Lao Gao's absences, but we always pleaded with him to come. He was older than we were, though, and Zhenzhen was noticeably less formal when he wasn't around – some would have considered her disrespectful when she was with him, but I was sure that for him it was part of her charm, as it was for us. However, when he wasn't with us, we could talk more freely. He was a dear elder brother, but he was also Zhiying's boss.

On those outings, we shared our dreams for the future. Young and idealistic as we were, they were bound up with the fortunes of our country. We'd be richer, we'd be stronger as a nation, we imagined, but exactly what the future held was beyond us – except that there would be enough food and clothing. But didn't Communism mean more than that? For me it was about warmth and optimism, being part of a group of people united by their ideals, a sense of belonging.

We drove up Hat Hill until we came to a path I didn't know. The jeep entered a dense wood, where a rough track had been. The air grew swiftly cooler. Soon we couldn't drive any further, so Lao Cui stopped and we got out with our picnic. I clutched the pot of green bean soup Mother had made and walked beside Zhenzhen, who was carrying Xiao Tao. Cheng Ming and Lao Cui, with the chairs and the rest of the food, had gone ahead. Whistling to himself, Zhiying brought up the rear with the bulky picnic table, which Zhenzhen had insisted on bringing.

Everybody seemed at ease, Zhiying and I used to enjoying the same privilege as the Gaos. A pavilion near the water attracts the moonlight first, I thought. It was pure luck that we had found each other.

Ahead, a small rockface marked a cliff. Zhenzhen pointed at it. 'The walks we usually do, if we carried on, we'd come to it. The pond is just below it. I was going to bring you here and surprise you one day.'

When I first set eyes on the pond, I stood stock still. I had been feeling hot and sticky all day, but suddenly I felt a chill. The pond was beautiful and still, an emerald oasis, a haze hovering above the surface. But I had a powerful sense that I'd been there before.

Zhenzhen brought me back to earth. 'I so wanted Lao Gao to be here,' she whispered, and held Xiao Tao closer. 'I'd thought, today of all days, he might have made time.'

I felt at a loss for the right thing to say. She had been so cheerful that I hadn't realized his absence meant so much to her. 'Come on, Zhenzhen,' I put an arm round her, 'you know how busy he is. I'm sure he'd have come if it was at all possible. Zhiying said that this time central-government leaders called him in . . .'

Before I could finish my sentence she was smiling again. 'Don't worry, Wenya. I'm fine now. I'm going to enjoy myself, Lao Gao or no Lao Gao. First, though, let's hand over this bundle.' She went to Zhiying and gave Xiao Tao to him, then came back to me and told me to get changed. I protested that I couldn't swim, but she said she'd teach me in no time at all.

She climbed up on a big rock, perched on top of the pond and jumped right in. I heard a shriek of joy. The pond's smooth surface was shattered. Then she popped up, shaking her hair off her face, splashing and laughing. Her voice carried across to me: 'Come on!'

How I gathered enough courage to jump I didn't know. Zhiying and Cheng Ming cheered me on, which helped, and Lao Cui said I wouldn't dare, but I knew, as I held my breath and leaped into the air, that my trust in Zhenzhen had persuaded me to do it. I had learned to rely on her and Lao Gao's judgement, sometimes more than my own. I tried to enjoy feeling cool as Zhenzhen held me and taught me how to move my arms and legs in the water. I might not learn to swim in one go, she assured me, but I'd been very brave to jump in.

Once I was out of the pond, Zhiying put a towel round me, while Cheng Ming passed me a mug of hot water. I got dressed quickly and sat down to watch Cheng Ming brushing mud off some mushrooms with a clean white handkerchief. 'Where did they come from?' I asked.

'The woods.'

'Are you sure they're edible?' Zhiying looked suspicious.

Cheng Ming stopped what he was doing and regarded him quizzically, then smiled. 'Well, if you don't trust me, don't eat them. I'm afraid you'll miss out on something delicious, though.'

While we ate our green bean soup, then the preserved pork, Cheng Ming lit a fire and put a pan on it. He took a lump of lard out of a small plastic bag, and melted it in the pan. I could smell it as it heated. Into it he threw some slender green shoots, then the mushrooms. A delicious scent filled our nostrils. Lao Cui, who had been sitting at a distance, smoking, got up and came over. 'That's meat,' he said.

'No, it isn't.' Cheng Ming grinned.

'No, it isn't,' Zhiying echoed. 'It's wild mushrooms. Eat them at your own risk.'

Lao Cui remained where he was. 'Well, I'd rather be a happy ghost than a hungry one. Give me some.'

Cheng Ming smiled and put some into his bowl. Lao Cui tasted them, and sighed. 'Mmmm.'

Then Cheng Ming turned to me, his eyes gleaming. 'Well?'

I glanced at Zhiying, who was standing a little away from us, with Xiao Tao in his arms. 'Don't risk it,' he said. 'You've got Xiao Tao to think of.'

I looked at Cheng Ming and shook my head. He was starting to eat with the cooking chopsticks, plainly savouring the taste. Suddenly the smell was too much for me and I leaned towards the pan. 'Want to try some?' he asked, in a low voice.

I nodded, and he passed me the chopsticks. It was delicious. My fear disappeared. 'But what are the green shoots?' I asked.

'Wild garlic,' he said, and helped himself to another mouthful.

'What are you eating?' Slippery, eyes sparkling, Zhenzhen was standing in front of us. 'A banquet in my absence – is that how you treat a friend? I want some now.' She closed her eyes.

Cheng Ming picked out the juiciest mushroom with his chopsticks and put them into her mouth. She breathed out deeply. 'Ooh, what is it? Don't tell me you've used your ration to buy . . . duck? Goose?'

We laughed, and she opened her eyes.

'It's wild mushrooms, Zhenzhen! You should have

checked first . . .' Zhiying's voice floated to us – he was sitting a little further away, probably trying to lull Xiao Tao to sleep.

'Really?' Zhenzhen looked at Cheng Ming, who nodded, without a hint of apology. She frowned, then ran her fingers through his hair. 'Oh, you clever kid! Did you find them in the wood?'

He nodded, gazing up at her like a faithful dog.

She rubbed his hair again. 'There must be something you can't do?'

Cheng Ming would have done anything for her. I saw that from the look he gave her. But we were all a bit in love with Lao Gao and her.

I sat apart from the rest to feed Xiao Tao. Zhenzhen was wrapped in a towel, getting dressed. I heard her curse: 'Damn, I can't zip up my dress – can you help me?'

'Come here and turn round.' I held Xiao Tao with one hand and fastened it, then went on feeding him. She sat down next to me, smoothing her hair, watching Xiao Tao. 'He's happy.' She sighed. I didn't miss her envious expression. The question I had wanted to ask for some time slipped out of my mouth: 'Why aren't you two having children yet?'

The normal question to a newlywed would have been: 'When are you going to have children?'

She bent down to pick up her socks as if she hadn't heard me, so I asked again. This time, she looked at me, stony-faced. 'I've heard that northerners are direct,' she said slowly, 'but I'd never imagined they'd be quite so impertinent.'

I bit my lip and blushed. Of course, it was none of my business, and I'd upset her. Suddenly she grinned. 'It's all right, Nosy, I don't mind telling you. We've tried, but nothing's happened.'

'You've seen a doctor?'

She shook her head. I thought of Lao Gao's scars. It was said that as well as his burns he had been hit several times by American bullets. I wondered if his fertility had been affected.

She was pensive now, eyes on the pond, and I felt guilty. I'd made her sad on her birthday. 'Thank you for the dip,' I said, trying to change the subject.

She nodded absent-mindedly. 'You're right,' she said. 'He's not getting any younger. Really, we spend so little time together, sometimes I do wonder . . .' Her cheeks were hot. 'I'd die for him, I really would. I worship him.'

For a moment we were distracted by Zhiying and Cheng Ming arguing again about the Russian novel.

'I'm so lucky, though,' she whispered, and somehow I knew that she was talking about her friends. 'Come,' I said, rising with Xiao Tao in my arms. 'Let's go and join the boys.'

At our approach they stopped arguing. We called Lao Cui over, and presented Zhenzhen with her birthday surprise: six peaches. It would have been traditional to give noodles, but we weren't superstitious. In any case, she would prefer the delicious summer fruit, we were sure. Cheng Ming had got hold of them, though we had no idea how. She insisted we shared them with her, so we did, leaving one each for Mother and Lao Gao.

As I ate slices of peach, it seemed I couldn't be happier. What more could I possibly ask? Well, perhaps an improvement in the weather. That afternoon it was hard to ignore. A thunderclap heralded a storm. At first we didn't mind, but when the rain began to pour down we gathered our things and made for the jeep. Xiao Tao was crying – he didn't like the rain or the sudden bangs. Holding him I was fearful too – what if one of the trees near us was struck by lightning? I tried to keep the rain off his face and comfort him – 'Nearly there, we're nearly there . . .'

But the wood had darkened, disorienting us, and it took us a long time, after a few wrong turns, to locate the jeep, parked under a pine tree. We hopped in, cursing loudly but cheerfully now that we were safe.

But not for long. The jeep got stuck in a deep ditch full of mud that had accumulated with the downpour. First Zhiying and Cheng Ming, then I and even Zhenzhen had to leave Xiao Tao and get out to push while Lao Cui revved the engine. To no avail: the four of us were not strong enough to ease it free. We began to despair.

'We need another man,' Lao Cui said.

Zhenzhen scowled. 'I don't believe it. Let's try once more.'

'Sssh.' Cheng Ming had been staring into the wood. 'I can hear engines,' he hissed.

Another jeep drove straight to us at tremendous speed and stopped in front of our stranded vehicle. Out jumped a familiar figure. 'Lao Gao!' Zhenzhen yelped, and ran to her smiling husband.

Standing shoulder to shoulder with us, Lao Gao and the other driver helped us to get our jeep out in one push. As we congratulated ourselves, the rain stopped and the sky cleared. Xiao Tao stopped crying and gazed up at the beautiful bridge in the sky – a rainbow. Once again Lao Gao had proved himself our leader and saviour. At his bidding we returned to the pond to enjoy the rest of the day.

I didn't go in this time, but sat watching Zhenzhen and Lao Gao in the middle of the water, like two dolphins. To my surprise, I found myself humming 'Night in the Moscow Suburb'. Lao Cui and the other driver were nodding to the rhythm. Encouraged, I sang the words: '. . . the person of my heart sits next to me, silently looking at me. I wish from now on, neither of us will forget . . .' Cheng Ming joined in, but when I turned to him, his eyes were on the two people in the water.

Soon Zhenzhen returned to us with Lao Gao. 'Singing those Soviet revisionist songs again!' he teased. We sang louder. Soviet songs they might have been, but they were full of emotion. We often sang Chinese songs – all the time, in rallies and competitions – but the softer Russian melodies were somehow better suited to our mood then.

When Lao Gao sank down next to me I asked how he had managed to get away.

'I told them it's my wife's birthday, the first since we were married. I'd have bolted anyway, even if they hadn't granted their permission, but they were very understanding,' he said, his eyes on his wife, who was still singing. 'I wanted to surprise her, but I was held up. Now I must go and say hello to our little fellow there.' He got up and went over to where Zhiying sat with Xiao Tao. My eyes followed him as he leaned over my son, grasping his waving arms and lifting him out of the protective shelter Zhiying had made with his legs. I saw that he would make a perfect father. Despite what Zhenzhen had said, they hadn't been married for long and time might surprise them.

I glanced up at the clear blue sky. The rainbow had faded, but Lao Gao's arrival, and the change in the weather, had brought our day to the perfect ending.

Later, as I watched Lao Gao eat his peach next to Zhenzhen, I realised I had been neglecting Zhiying. I snuggled up to him. 'Why don't you join us?'

'I can't sing, you know that. And I don't like those songs – all that sentiment.'

I knew that wasn't true – he usually enjoyed the music – but I wouldn't let him cloud my mood. I leaned over to Xiao Tao. 'How is our boy?'

'He's been sleeping like a little pig.' He smiled.

I noticed that Xiao Tao was not where I had last seen him. There was nothing strange in that – either Lao Cui or Zhiying might have moved him. In time, though, I regretted that I hadn't asked, and had failed to stress to Zhiying that, at seven and a half months Xiao Tao was on the verge of crawling.

20

'Teacher Wenya! Teacher Wenya!' One of my students was calling me.

I rubbed my eyes and put a hand to my aching head. 'What is it?'

'The driver wants to know if you want us to press on or stop for refreshments.'

I shook my head to clear it and looked out of the window to see where we were, then turned back to the student. 'Tell him to press on – we need to get there before dark.'

The driver gestured to show that he understood and the van sped up. I sat back, my thoughts returning to home and to those I had left behind. This trip to the clinic in the countryside was untimely – I had been enjoying the company of my friends, and Xiao Tao had settled into his new routine. I had managed to carry on feeding him, thanks to Mother and Zhenzhen. But this was a two-month trip, which meant giving up. I'd had no choice: the famine had deepened in the countryside and there was now a severe shortage of experienced doctors to lead medical students in treating basic illnesses. All doctors were told to be ready to go to the countryside at short notice; some at my hospital had been twice already. The leaders had been considerate in not sending me when I was pregnant, but Xiao Tao was more than six months old now and could be weaned. And the truth about my father's death hung over me, reminding me that I had to be better than the best and atone secretly for his crime.

It was hard to leave Zhiying and our cosy home, hard to wave goodbye to friends. But it was hardest of all to leave Xiao Tao, who hadn't even cried when I'd waved goodbye to him that morning. Would he forget me or understand somehow that I would come back? My breasts tingled, as they always did when I thought of him – reminding me that I was still producing milk. A feeling like grief came over me, and I fixed my eyes on the view, resolving to be positive. I told myself I was going away to save lives.

All I could see from the window was dust. The two students whispered to each other, respectful of my seniority. Little did they know that despite my confident appearance, I was nervous. Last time I had depended on Ying – and not just on the medical front. There would surely be life and death decisions to make, and I wasn't sure that I could be as quick in establishing priorities as Ying had been.

I thought of the brief I had been given: we were to be based in Peach Blossom Village again. The reports from doctors who'd been in neighbouring villages were alarming: the death rate had soared after a short reprieve in the spring, with many infant deaths. There were even rumours that the hungry had eaten their neighbours' children . . .

As the familiar hills appeared on the horizon, I found

myself thinking back to those days before Xiao Tao had been conceived. I had once found the half-eaten body of a baby beside a mud hut. It had been savaged by wild dogs . . . The self-sacrifice and dignity of people like Yun had raised our spirits, but now I wondered what had become of her. Her child must have been born – it should be three or four months older than Xiao Tao. Had Granny Tong survived?

As last time, we'd been told that someone would be on the look-out for us but in the village no one was about. Now I knew what to do. I led the way to the accountant's home – I remembered it from my last visit. An efficient, able man, he had helped us draw up a list of villagers in need of emergency attention. I was relieved to find him at home, thinner and weaker, but still sharp. Between us we worked out a plan and before long I was sending the students to different houses, loaded with medicines and food.

It was while I was treating a malnourished two-year-old with a severe chest infection that I realized the extent of the devastation these people faced. I insisted that I would try my best to save the child's life, but all the mother wanted me to do was give her something to eat. 'Anything,' she said, her eyes twinkling oddly. 'Let my daughter eat before she dies,' she begged, 'so that her soul will not be wandering as a hungry ghost at the crossroads.'

After forcing an injection on the child, I left my biscuit ration on the bed.

As I felt my way along the dark, rough track, I suddenly realized that that was only the second house I'd visited where I'd seen a young child. At my last visit there had been several toddlers in the village . . .

It was with a heavy heart that I made my way to Yun's home. In the courtyard I paused and looked beyond the village to the graveyard. The mounds there had tripled since my last visit and I wondered which of the new ones was Granny Tong's.

I had been sad to hear of her death from the accountant but he had also told me that Yun's husband had left home, which, according to him, made hers one of the luckier families in the village. Some had been wiped out. 'The old and the weak have died. The strong and able have gone to other counties and provinces seeking work, Yun's husband among them. And that's good. So long as people are alive, there's hope. They're young, their family will not be wiped out.'

'But of course!' I had exclaimed. 'They have the child – what is it? A boy, a girl? Surely he or she . . .?' Something in his eyes made me stop.

'Yes, she is alive, but . . .' At this he'd shaken his head and told me to go and see Yun.

All sorts of things went through my mind during the climb to her house. The conclusion I drew was that the baby was ill or disabled. *But she is alive.* I clung to that comforting thought. Granny Tong had not died in vain.

Someone must have warned her I was coming, as I found Yun waiting for me on a low stool in the dark kitchen, with a small bowl of hot water. As I stepped inside, I saw that she'd aged: last time we'd met, she'd had a smooth girl's face, and stood tall, even as she carried a baby inside her and attended to her sick mother. The woman standing in front of me now was middle-aged, her face dark and wrinkled. The biggest change, though, was in her eyes: their light had dimmed. Last time she had looked into mine. Now she avoided them, though her face showed she was pleased to see me.

'I'm sorry,' I said, gesturing at her armband.

'Mother didn't survive,' she said flatly.

'I'm sorry,' I said again.

Yun shook her head. 'Don't be – she was old, and we were grateful that she lived as long as she did. She didn't suffer. You and Sister Ying did everything you could.'

At least the baby had survived. I turned my eyes to the picture of the boy and the giant fish, now torn and blackened with cooking smoke. 'I've brought food,' I said, dropping a sack of rice on the floor. Her eyes twinkled briefly, then darkened again. She remained on her stool, motionless.

'Where is the baby?' I asked, unable to stop myself.

She didn't move, but her shoulders tensed.

'Is something wrong? Can I see her?'

'Didn't they tell you?'

'I've heard nothing.'

She stirred, putting her hand on the dusty stove as if to support herself. 'I'm not the only one who's done this.'

'Done what?'

'She's gone.'

'Gone? With her father?'

'So you know about that.'

'Did she go with him?'

She stood up suddenly. 'I gave her away.'

'You did *what*?' I also stood up. 'To whom?'

'She'd only have died of hunger if she'd stayed here. I gave her to a southerner who came looking for a child. They didn't mind her being a girl. She's lucky they chose her. I'm her mother, so I know best.'

'But . . .'

'Please,' her voice cracked, 'don't ask any more. She's gone away. I shall never see my baby again!' She ran out of the door, heaving with sobs.

I went after her, but the darkness had swallowed her and I could hear nothing. The night was quiet, but for the whine of mosquitoes. I thought of the little girl I had never met – would never meet. My breasts hurt. At least I still had Xiao Tao. I wondered how long ago Yun had given her baby away – at birth or when she was a few weeks old.

Yun didn't come back.

Sunlight filtered through the trees, touching my face. My vision was blurred. I smelt decaying leaves, summer flowers and damp. Then I saw the pond, vapour rising above it. Something was pulling me towards it, even though my instinct had been to run away from it. But I was too hot to care. A voice called softly, and something rose to the surface. I screamed—

I sat bolt upright, heart racing. Gradually I calmed myself, puzzled by the dream. It must have been brought on by Yun's heartache. Last time I had been here, we had been able to help and our treatments had made a difference. Then there had been hope – now that hope was dashed, and I wanted to run away from the suffering. It was not medicine the peasants needed, it was food.

I tried to sleep but longed for morning, for light – to go home and see Xiao Tao's little face. I felt so far away from my baby.

21

We left Peach Blossom Village earlier than we had intended. I told the driver I'd be responsible for the consequences. Sitting in the van speeding back to the city, I thought of Xiao Tao. He had had a few bouts of colic and seemed thin when I'd left – it was not unusual, the doctor had said, in babies who had started to take solids. Wait a few weeks, he said. Now five weeks had passed, five long, hard weeks. I had moved from Yun's house to the village accountant's. His wife told me that Yun had left the village on the night she had disappeared leaving word with a relative that she had gone to search for her lost daughter. She was still young, the accountant's wife said to comfort me; she was sure Yun and her husband would have another baby.

As I rushed through the courtyard to my flat I couldn't quite believe I was home. I ran breathlessly up the stairs longing to hold and kiss my baby.

Unusually the door was locked and no one was in. I searched for my key, packed deep inside my suitcase. I wondered where everyone was. It was Monday, so Zhiying and Lao Gao would be at work. But Mother or

Zhenzhen should be at home – this was when Mother took her nap.

I opened the door and noticed a strange smell. The flat was a mess – it was as if they had all left in a hurry, Xiao Tao's clothes lay everywhere – I snatched up a little vest and sniffed. How I'd missed his smell! Then I gathered up his shoes, hats, tops and shorts, and sorted them, puzzling over the chaos.

In the kitchen the sink was filled with dirty bowls. They couldn't have been here for at least two days. Had Mother taken them to the countryside to forage? In this hot weather? But Zhiying would have stayed at home – he had to work . . . and he would never leave crockery unwashed. I went round the flat looking for clues, but found none.

I spent a few hours tidying and cleaning, then decided to go to the factory. Zhiying would be there and would tell me everything. Just then I heard footsteps approaching. They stopped in front of the flat and I opened the door. Zhiying was standing in front of me. He looked blank, as if he didn't recognise me. 'You're back,' he said, in a hoarse whisper.

'Zhiying!' I tried to control my panic. His appearance frightened me – he hadn't shaved for days.

Instead of answering, he stared at the vest of Xiao Tao's I still clutched. 'So you know.'

'Know what? Where is everyone? Where's Mother? Has she taken Xiao Tao out.'

'Your mother's gone . . . home,' he said.

'And Xiao Tao's with her?'

'Xiao Tao . . .' He fell to the floor and grasped a leg of Xiao Tao's cot. He gave a strange muffled groan. I stared at him and began to tremble. I saw once more the haunted look on Yun's face when she told me she had given away her baby.

'Where is Xiao Tao? Mother's taken him away, hasn't she? Hasn't she?' I whispered.

Zhiying raised his face. He spoke softly but I heard every word as clearly as if he had shouted: 'He's dead. He drowned in the pond. Wenya, our baby's gone.'

'What did you say?' My voice sounded distant.

'Last week we went to the pond again and . . . Zhenzhen was with him, but . . . Wenya, it was nobody's fault. We all thought we were watching him, but some-how . . .'

I had a sense of *déjà vu*. I was back in Peach Blossom Village. Another casualty, a child dead, my student reported wearily.

But this time it was my Xiao Tao.

Part II:
No Name Child, Autumn,
the same year

1

T he lorry's here,' Zhiying said.

I had seen it arrive and even recognised the driver, but I didn't stir.

'We have five more kilos of cabbages than the others.' He paused at the door. 'Lao Gao arranged it . . .' he offered, timidly.

'How many times do I have to tell you? I don't want to hear his name.'

Zhiying was silent – however sharp I was with him, he never complained.

I listened to his footsteps echoing down the empty corridor. Every day when I came in from work, I looked forward to his return, but as soon as he appeared I retreated to my safe, silent world in the kitchen. I cooked food for which I had no appetite, but which involved a lot of preparation: stir-fried potatoes, which I peeled methodically; coarse rice, full of little stones and sometimes mouse droppings that took time to pick out. Some days all I said to him was 'Hungry?' He would nod and I would say, 'The food is on the table.' I ate only so that I could carry on. Little White grew fat on the leftovers.

I glimpsed Zhiying in the courtyard, gesturing, and the lorry backing towards the cellar. I saw the driver and Zhiying disappearing inside, and imagined them filling the dark empty hole with cabbages. It seemed only yesterday that Zhiying and I had filled it in anticipation of Xiao Tao's arrival. I missed his little body in my arms, which seemed to have lost their purpose. I felt numb. I had hardly noticed the presence of much more red in the streets, the endlessly shrieking loudspeakers, and the way people greeted each other now with Chairman Mao's sayings. Walking to the bus stop, I dodged past hordes of Red Guards stopping people to test them on the Chairman's *Red Book*. Once I was stopped by a boy of no more than seven. As I looked at him, I wondered whether Xiao Tao would have been like him had he lived to that age. Something about me must have frightened him for he let me go and ran back to his friends, shouting, 'She's mad!'

Zhiying returned with the driver, who nodded but didn't speak. I recognised him as one of those who had come after Xiao Tao's death to offer condolences.

We were bereaved parents and the factory wanted to take us under its wing. I could see that Zhiying was grateful for the attention and support. He'd offer the women tea and the men cigarettes, then accompany them out to the courtyard when they left. But I read malice in their sympathy, and felt jealous of the fat woman from the propaganda department who had teenage daughters, and of the man in the design department who had a new baby. I said no to the visits. The factory was no longer our family. The loss of Xiao Tao had severed my link with it.

Alone in the empty flat after work, I was haunted by

the sound of his cry. I welcomed it – I wouldn't let him go. I kept all his things: his bathing bowl, his spoons, his tiger-face hat, his tiny shoes – which still smelt of him. I couldn't bear to wash them.

The driver rose and politely refused Zhiying's offer of another cup of tea, then walked to the door. Zhiying spent a long time seeing him off, their voices echoing down the empty corridor. It had been quiet on this floor since the Gaos had moved out, but that suited me. I let my mind drift to their big empty flat . . .

They had moved after I shut them out. I forbade Zhiying to open the door when Zhenzhen knocked. After a while she stopped trying. The sight of Lao Gao's jeep took me to the pond, where I would replay the scene as Zhiying had described it to me. I blamed everyone: Zhiying, for trusting a childless couple to look after our baby; Mother, for being old and useless; Zhenzhen, as a capable friend, for her negligence. But, above all, I blamed myself. I was sure that if I had been there we would still have had Xiao Tao.

Zhiying came back and sat down next to me.

'Dinner's on the stove,' I said.

Without a word he went to the kitchen. He was used to dining alone now – I only ate when I was hungry, usually in the middle of the night. As Zhiying ate silently on his own at the sitting-room table, I moved to the window. The wind had blown the leaves off the two rows of willow trees in the middle of the complex. When Xiao Tao was alive I had sometimes come back early from work to stand at the window and watch Mother and Zhenzhen walking home along the path between the trees. I had run down to them, grabbed Xiao Tao from Zhenzhen and clutched him to my chest. Now the path was empty, except for an old man.

I glanced back into the room. Zhiying had finished and was staring at his bowl. 'How was it?' I asked, not because I was interested but because I couldn't think of anything else to say.

'You forgot to put any salt in again,' he said. Then, as if to make amends, he added, 'But your mother always uses too much.'

It had been nearly three months since she had gone back to her own house, but he still wasn't used to my cooking.

2

The new neighbours didn't move in until the winter. They made a mess – each time they and their helpers came up from outside they brought mud and dust with them, which Zhiying swept away – and they were noisy. I resented their heavy footsteps, their loud talk and laughter. In contrast to the Gaos, they had a lot of stuff. It took them a whole week to move in. Then there was the endless round of meals to thank the helpers. Never once did they come to introduce themselves to us. I learned from Zhiying that the man, Yang Lian, was the chairman of the trade union, a powerful man, second only to Lao Gao at the factory. I'd glimpsed them through the window, both tall and heavyset, she with an annoyingly constant giggle. They had two teenage sons, who resembled them in height and weight.

On the sixth night of their parties, I said to Zhiying, 'I can't take it any longer.'

He held my hands in the dark and whispered, 'Please, Wenya, it won't last. They're just moving in.'

'You don't dare say anything because he's an official,' I said coldly.

'Wenya, we've got to live with them . . .'

I'd married a coward. 'I'll give them a week, and after that . . .'

On Sunday the banging continued into the evening. After dinner Zhiying sat listening to the radio. 'How can you hear anything?' I asked.

Zhiying moved his chair closer to the radio. I stared at the clock on the wall: nine o'clock. For the next half-hour I watched the hands. Then I stood up.

After six loud knocks she opened the door, smelling of wine and food. I noticed her toes: they spread from out of her slippers like fat caterpillars. She looked down at me. 'Yes?'

I pointed at the big clock in their hall, facing me. 'It's nine thirty.'

'Yes?'

'We want to sleep,' I said. The room behind her was cluttered, just as I had imagined. All sign of the Gaos had gone. But before I could work out whether I was pleased or not, I heard laughter from the centre of the room. 'Who is it?' someone shouted.

The woman giggled. 'Next door, saying she wants to sleep.'

Her husband emerged, hiccuping, holding playing cards. He saw me and paused. Then he smiled. 'Oh, our new neighbour, would you like to come in?'

'No, thanks. I've come to complain about the noise you're making. It's disturbing us. My husband doesn't sleep well.'

'Doesn't he?' The smile disappeared from his face.

'What do you expect us to do? Ban visitors from our home just because your husband's an insomniac?' she shouted.

'They're very noisy.'

'It is not a dog's business to catch mice, mind your own business!' She reached for the door.

I set a foot on the threshold. 'If you dare—'

An arm grabbed me from behind. Zhiying said, 'Wenya, don't!' I struggled, but his grip was surprisingly strong. 'We don't want any trouble,' he said to the woman. 'Let's all be good neighbours . . .'

'Good neighbours? Oh, I see.' She raised an eyebrow. 'Well, of course, I know you loved stroking the Gao's horses' bottoms—'

My hand shot out before I knew what it wanted to do. The slap shocked me as well as her. She clutched her cheek. 'You bitch!' She lunged at me and grabbed my hair. The men leaped to separate us. 'I curse you! You will have no descendants!'

'Say that again.' I grasped her throat.

'You—'

This time her husband slapped her. 'Stop this! Get back inside.'

I stood facing the man. 'If this noise doesn't stop from tomorrow,' I said, 'I'll come and smash up your flat. I mean it. After all,' I stared into his eyes, 'I have no descendants.'

In the dead quiet of that night, we still couldn't sleep. My scalp hurt from where the woman had pulled my hair.

'Wenya.'

'Yes?'

'You shouldn't have—'

'Why not?'

'Yang Lian is the chairman of the trade union.'

'So what?'

'They say he's aiming to be the next director of the factory.'

'Why? What's happened to Lao Gao?'

'Don't you remember? I'm sure I told you.' He paused. 'Why did you think the Gaos moved out?'

'Because they felt too guilty to face us.'

After a brief silence, he said quietly, 'Maybe so. But . . . did you know Lao Gao is under investigation?'

'For what?'

'For his role in the Korean war. There's been a big poster letter saying he's a traitor, not a hero. The Gaos were investigated and sent to a Party school in Wei County, about forty *lis* from here. Someone's gone to Lao Gao's hometown and other provinces to continue the investigation there.'

Now I remembered that Zhiying had mentioned something about the Gaos but, like much that he said these days, I hadn't registered it. I had simply been relieved not to see them daily and be reminded of my pain. I suspected even Zhiying was secretly relieved – their guilt was his too.

'Cheng Ming's been affected as well,' Zhiying continued. 'He's no longer Lao Gao's secretary. They say he hasn't got a job at all.'

That was news. I thought briefly of his pale face, smiling up to me as he passed me the mushrooms. The memory of those innocent times hurt, too. After a long while Zhiying spoke again: 'We all hope for the best – nobody believes the accusations. I think everyone wants Lao Gao to be exonerated.'

I turned on to my side. Lao Gao had been decorated

with a National First Class Gold Medal – what could possibly happen to him? And what difference would any of it make to me? It would not bring back Xiao Tao.

3

'How many have we made?' Mother glanced at the wooden chopping board, which was piled with dumplings. Even though she was frail now, her hand on the dough was firmer than mine so all her dumplings stood up, while mine lay flat. It was for this reason that I was only allowed to make the dough – she stuffed the dumplings. I had a bigger kitchen and a better rolling-pin, but she had been adamant that we come to her for the Spring Festival.

We had made the dumplings in the sitting room on her large table. I glimpsed the falling snow through the window – it covered the clutter in the shabby lane. Though it was evening, the sky was full of a pale light. I heard children playing, their little shrieks of joy. 'How many?' Mother asked again impatiently.

I counted. 'Eighty-six.'

'That's enough,' Mother said, breathing heavily. I put them on to a tray and took it to the kitchen, where she would boil them.

In the sitting room Zhiying had wiped the table and put out bowls and chopsticks. I took a duster to wipe the windows, doors and other surfaces. It seemed to me that not only Mother but the room had shrunk. When I had first come in the general air of neglect had shocked me – she used to be so house-proud. During the last few months since she'd returned to her home, Zhiying had come once in a while to fix things, but it was obvious she needed help with the cleaning. At least I didn't feel Xiao Tao's presence here. I fetched a chair and stood on it to wipe the photo frames on the wall. At this height, I was level with Father's eyes. For a while I held his gaze.

A thud came from the kitchen, then a groan. As Zhiying and I rushed in, Mother was struggling to her feet, the dumplings scattered across the floor. Zhiying helped her up while I picked up the dumplings, then rinsed them under the tap. Breathing heavily in Zhiying's arms, Mother instructed, 'We'll eat the dirty ones. Put them on the big plate, there.'

'What do you mean, Mother? Aren't we going to eat them all anyway?'

She gestured at a pretty blue plate on the sideboard. 'I was putting those out for Xiao Tao, all twelve, but my hands aren't steady.'

Zhiying bent down to her. 'Move your arms and legs – does it hurt anywhere?'

Mother said she couldn't move anything. Zhiying flashed a glance at me. 'Come,' he said, 'let's get you to bed.'

She lay down and I massaged her legs gently. Nothing was broken, but her breathing bothered me, and with spring coming, her asthma would get worse.

'He'd have teeth by now,' she murmured. I kept silent. Xiao Tao's death had hit Mother hard: it was unnatural for 'white hairs' to say farewell to 'black hairs', she had told me, when a neighbour had lost her grandson.

When we started to eat, the dumplings were nearly cold. Xiao Tao's blue plate was next to mine. Mother turned the dumplings every so often with her chopsticks to make sure they didn't stick. Suddenly I was angry. Why had she had to mention Xiao Tao when I had almost succeeded in not thinking about him for an evening? I got up to fetch some water to drink and – crash! The photo had fallen off the wall in its frame, shattering the glass. Mother winced.

'Don't worry.' Zhiying rushed to it. 'You probably didn't put it back properly after you cleaned it. It just needs new glass – the photo's fine.' He was picking up the pieces. I went to get the brush and dust pan.

When I came back Mother was at the table, gazing at the photo of Father. 'That was a sign.'

'What are you talking about?' I asked.

'Your father wants me to join him.'

'Father?'

'He won't leave me alone. He talks to me all the time. He says he's sorry about Xiao Tao.'

'Father never knew Xiao Tao,' I snapped.

A look of confusion flipped across her face. 'But of course he did! He left soon after Xiao Tao's birth. When Xiao Tao died of pneumonia, I wrote to him about it . . .'

Surely she meant Da Tao, my infant brother. I tried to sound calm: 'Mother, would you like a drink?' I motioned to Zhiying, who went to the kitchen.

Mother grabbed my hand. 'He's a nice young man,' she said earnestly. 'I hope he's going to marry you.'

'Mother, we are married!'

'But . . .' She trailed off and closed her eyes.

The frame had left a square mark on the wall. Zhiying stooped down to measure the photo. I told him not to put it back. The picture was a liability. Although Father wasn't wearing the uniform of the Nationalists in it, someone might recognise him and, in view of what was happening now, we'd better be cautious. The 'movement' to 'expose class enemies' had reached white-heat stage, according to the newspapers, and some were so desperate to fill their quotas of 'reactionaries' that they would stop at nothing. I knew that what Father had done would fit neatly into their profile of a what a reactionary was . . .

Snow flakes were still falling when we left Mother's. A lonely snowman stood at the end of the lane. When we walked past him my plastic bag of dumplings caught against his outstretched twiggy arms. I tugged it free and waved to Mother, whose face was at the window. We turned off the lane and on to the main road. It was slippery underfoot and I held on to Zhiying, my other gloved hand clutching the bag of dumplings, which were already turning hard. Would Xiao Tao have had teeth now?

White steam came out of Zhiying's mouth as he said, 'I think Mother should come and live with us again.'

4

'Another.' Ying sighed as she came into the office. 'I can't see his face properly, it's so swollen.' She slumped into her chair.

She didn't need to explain. I knew that by 'another' she meant a 'reactionary', a 'rightist' or other 'undesirable'. They were coming into the casualty department in alarmingly large numbers now, blood streaming down their faces, broken bones, open wounds on their necks where ropes had chafed in . . . Many had internal bleeding – one or two had died. As doctors, it was our job to treat them without comment, but I wanted to scream, 'Didn't Chairman Mao say we must fight with reason, not arms? Even if these people are class enemies . . .' but I held my tongue. I knew my opinion would be considered bourgeois, dangerous, wrong. I watched Ying gulp some cold tea, then go out again. I was only in Casualty once a week. Ying had to be there three times.

I left the office briefly to fetch a tissue sample. On the short walk from the office to the clinic, I had to flatten myself against the wall to let a bloodied man pass, dragged by two bored-looking Red Guards. Several doors away Dr

Li was looking on with pity. But as we caught each other's eye we looked away again – everybody knew what was going on, but no one dared talk about it.

I carried on walking, keeping close to the wall, ignoring the layers of black and white posters pasted on it. Some even trailed down from the ceiling. I was reminded of the spirits' room, in which traditional family funerals took place. But the words on these strips of paper were daggers, not offerings. I didn't bother to read any – I knew what they were about: lately it had not been only the 'practising reactionaries' who were humiliated in mass rallies. Last week a colleague's overseas background had been exposed. As he had bent double in front of us, his hands behind his back, his head forced down by the two young men behind him, I shivered. If the truth about my father's death was ever revealed, I would be treated like the man on the stage. After such meetings I wondered what I should do – to confess would put my mind at rest but the thought of what might happen to Zhiying held me back. The radio and the slogans in the street called for 'frank confession leading to lenient treatment'. But many who had confessed were forced afterwards to further incriminate themselves, admitting to things that were not true. I'd lost Xiao Tao and had only an ailing mother and Zhiying now. I must keep my secret at all costs. I thought of the bare wall in Mother's house and was relieved that I had been prepared for this. We had advised her to burn any old letters. She had cursed my father – even in death he was causing her trouble.

As I walked past Casualty I saw the two Red Guards I'd passed earlier, standing at either side of the treatment-room door. Their severe expressions reminded me of the two fierce gods that people used to have at their front doors to frighten away evil spirits. But those gods were handsome, bearded and armoured; the two young men were fidgety, smooth-faced and held bamboo sticks draped with red ribbons. They were barely twenty. What about the man they had escorted in? Was Ying treating him? As I watched, the door of the treatment room opened and Ying strode out, looking anxious. Seeing me she looked relieved, 'Wenya, quick, can you stand in for me? I've got a man needing oxygen urgently and Xiao Wang is nowhere to be seen.' Before I could answer she shouted, 'The other patient's inside, just needs redressing . . .' and tore away.

The patient had his back to me when I opened the door. He turned, and though blood-stained faces no longer shocked me, his made me drop my eyes. I walked to the table to read the notes: 'Glasses embedded in face, removed; wound needs a new dressing. Eyes bruised. Left leg X-rayed, fibula broken; splint required. Internal bleeding suspected.' I glanced at his face. Some of the old dressing was stuck to his skin with caked blood. 'I'll have to take this off,' I said. 'I'm afraid it might hurt a bit.'

'As long as you're all right, Wenya,' he said gently.

The accent was familiar. I looked into the man's eyes. 'Lao Gao?'

'I'm afraid so.'

My hands trembled as I removed the bandage, and blood seeped again from the wound. I went for a fresh cloth and the door was pushed open. One of the young men looked in. He caught sight of Lao Gao's face, and disappeared.

'Zhiying well?' Lao Gao asked.

I didn't answer.

He sighed. 'I know you hate us, Wenya, and I don't blame you. I just want to say . . .'

The other young man poked his head in. 'Hurry up, Doctor. He's needed this afternoon and we haven't had lunch yet.'

As he slammed the door Lao Gao turned to me. 'Wenya, be firm and quick. It really doesn't hurt.'

I finished tearing off the old dressing. Lao Gao sat silently, hardly stirring. My trembling hand brushed the scar on his neck – a bullet was still embedded there, an American bullet from Korea. It was considered too dangerous to remove – he had shown us the X-ray of it, the dark solid shadow of the bullet pointing down to his heart like an exclamation mark. Once upon a time it had been a badge of honour, a proof of his courage and invincibility – to escape alive was *mingda*, 'great luck'. Why had his luck run out now?

I was just finishing putting the new dressing on when both young men burst into the room. 'Time's up,' one said. 'Come on.' He grabbed hold of Lao Gao.

'I'm ready,' Lao Gao said, attempting to rise.

'Wait,' I said. 'He can't go anywhere. This patient needs to be in hospital.'

The Red Guards looked at each other. 'But . . . our orders were for him to be treated and taken back.'

'You won't be able to do much with him if his infection develops. You'll have to suffer the consequences if you don't follow a doctor's instructions,' I said calmly.

They looked at each other again, then at Lao Gao, who was silent. 'What . . . sort of infection?' The older of the two glared at me.

'Further tests are needed for a firm diagnosis, but I suspect typhoid and I wouldn't like you to catch it,' I said, and saw him wince.

'How . . . will you guarantee that he won't run away?' he asked, after a few moments' silence.

'I won't need to. His leg's broken,' I said.

The young man scratched his head. 'It's true – we had to drag him here.' He turned to the other. 'Let's go and have lunch, then consult our leaders.' He glanced back at Lao Gao with contempt. 'I suppose we'll just have to leave him here.' Then he glared at me. 'Remember – he's in your charge.'

I waited till their heavy footsteps had faded down the corridor. 'Can you try to walk?' I asked, and searched around for something he could use as a walking stick.

'Why, Wenya?' Lao Gao gave me a smile that seemed out of place.

'Turn right at the corridor and follow it through the double door to the cinder path. Walk past the mortuary and the big pagoda tree. There is a side door that will lead you back on to the street. You haven't much time – go.'

He didn't stir.

'What are you waiting for?'

He shook his head and the smile remained, irritating me now.

'They're going to take you back to the rally and beat you up again.'

'Let them. I've had worse,' he said. 'Anyway, if I run, it'll prove to them I'm guilty. And I'm not.'

'It doesn't matter what you think. You're guilty if they say so.'

He stopped smiling and his eyes narrowed. 'So, you

think I should run away like a coward and let them blacken my name? Are you on their side, too? Do you think I'm a traitor?'

'I . . .' I stuttered.

'I can't bear it if the people I trust think I could betray friends.' He spoke slowly, and with difficulty. I could tell he was in pain. 'Did you ever doubt my innocence? Did Zhiying?'

For the first time since I came in, I met his eyes: bloodshot and surrounded by scratches. But I knew it was not the physical pain that hurt him now. I was overwhelmed by helplessness and fear. 'Lao Gao,' my voice quivered, 'I believe you are innocent.'

I saw a flicker of light in his eyes, and he stepped forward as if to take my hand, but the pain in his leg made him wobble. I caught him before he fell and helped him back to the chair. I scolded myself – how could I have encouraged him to walk? He was not even able to stand. 'Wenya, you don't know what that means to me,' he murmured. A teardrop fell on to my hand but I pretended not to see it.

After a pause, I wrote in the log that he should be transferred to a ward, where at least he might get some rest and medical attention.

'Rescue those who are dying, assist those who are wounded, practise revolutionary humanitarianism,' urged Chairman Mao's words, painted in red along the walls at the front of my hospital – I walked past them daily on my way in and out. That day, leaving work, they hurt my eyes.

5

'But are you sure you're all right?' I asked, for the fourth time, as Zhiying turned away from me. He moved to the furthest corner of the bed, curling up like a child. 'Perhaps you have a temperature. Tell me exactly how you feel.'

Suddenly he sat up. 'All right. I'm fine. I'm not ill.'

'Then why did you say . . .?' He'd asked me to send word through our neighbour downstairs that he was sick and needed to take the day off work. I had been trying to find out what was the matter.

'I don't want to go in today. We're having a criticism meeting,' he muttered.

'About whom?'

There was a pause. 'Can't you guess?'

Mother, who had been watching us closely, whispered, 'Lao Gao?'

Zhiying nodded and turned away again.

Mother murmured to herself, then said loudly, 'But I don't understand. How can they do these things without evidence? I thought you said they sent someone to conduct an investigation. Surely they need to wait for the report.' She sat on the bed next to Zhiying. 'Not that they'll find anything wrong with that good man.'

'Mother, things are different nowadays. You don't have to go through the formalities. Every work unit has a revolutionary committee, whose role is to expose class enemies, historical reactionaries, members of the Kuomintang and such,' Zhiying said impatiently.

Mother's hand shook at the mention of the Kuomintang. She shot a glance at me and stood up to put the carrot peel she was holding into Little White's food bowl. On her way to the kitchen she said, 'I thought I'd been through a lot, but these times shock me. Even the Kuomintang, corrupt as they were, would have a proper court and put people on trial. To condemn someone because of what someone else says in a big poster . . .'

'Mother, please! Not so loud.' Zhiying got off the bed, his face pale. 'You'll be in big trouble if anybody hears you talking like that.' He glanced from her to me. 'This meeting doesn't necessarily mean that Lao Gao will be condemned – China's vice chairman, Liu Shao Qi, stood in front of the Red Guards and criticised himself. It's a . . . form of re-education.'

'Re-education indeed!' Mother said indignantly. 'The Kuomintang—'

'Mother, please, not that word!' Zhiying and I shouted simultaneously.

'All right, all right. I know when I'm not welcome . . .' She went into the kitchen.

'Mother!' I ran after her, but she slammed the door on me. I turned to Zhiying: 'You should have been more patient with her.'

'She should try to remember who she is,' he said sullenly.

'So, we're the family members of a Nationalist traitor. Are you afraid? Do you want to separate? You're welcome to leave.' I said, my voice trembling.

'Wenya, that's not what I meant and you know it.'

'What did you mean then, talking to Mother like that? You know very well she's old and confused and—' I broke down.

Alarmed, Zhiying came to me. 'Wenya,' he said, 'I'm so sorry. I'm just scared, that's all. Things don't look good for Lao Gao and I can't bear the thought of anybody else getting into trouble.' He gestured to next door. Yang Lian was the head of the revolutionary committee now, in charge of Lao Gao's case. I understood Zhiying's fear.

'How bad is it? Surely they have no evidence of . . .' I met his eyes.

Slowly he shook his head. 'Nothing concrete yet, and they're still waiting for the special researcher who'll bring the investigation report. But things are in such chaos I worry they might condemn Lao Gao without evidence.'

'Can't you do anything?'

'Several of us have written poster letters of our own, protesting Lao Gao's innocence. That's all we can do. One of the revolutionary committee members is an old comrade of Lao Gao's and we pinned our hopes on him . . . But that man,' he mouthed 'next door', 'is keen to be director of the factory, and will be only too pleased to get rid of Lao Gao.'

I looked past him to the rush of bicycles going to the factory outside the window. The thought of Lao Gao being criticised there was bizarre. 'How is Zhenzhen taking it?'

'We've no news of her, other than that she isn't accused of anything – yet.'

He came to stand close to me, watching the streams of bicycles. Then, suddenly, he buried his face in my shoulders. 'I know it's cowardly to stay here rather than going in to defend Lao Gao, but I – I can't face seeing him suffer. Oh, Wenya. I don't know what to do.'

I'd seen the consequences of these mass meetings many times at the hospital. I'd also seen the Red Guards beating up supposed 'class enemies' on street corners. I'd hurried past, trying to ignore them, taking small comfort from the fact that I didn't know the unfortunates who had attracted their attention. But Lao Gao . . . A sentence I'd heard often on the radio over the past months or so flipped into my mind: '*Zaluan gong, Jian fa* – "Smash the police, and the legal system!"' It was something the Red Guards had been chanting, which, like many of their slogans, hadn't registered with me at first, but now I could see it was becoming reality. How long would the madness continue? I'd never given much thought to courts and police before, but now they were being 'smashed' and I wanted them back. I longed for the opportunity to prove to the world that Lao Gao was innocent.

I tried to sound positive. 'All is not lost,' I said. 'The special investigator might bring good news.'

6

Mother didn't come to greet me when I opened the door. The room was dark and she was huddled in a corner, holding her chest. 'What's happened?' I squatted next to her.

It took her a while to tell me.

It was all to do with Little White. Since she had moved back to be with us, Mother had looked after our rabbit with great enthusiasm. But lately she'd been letting him out for his 'exercise' too often. It must be hard for him to be confined to such a small space, so dark and lonely, she had said, and I had often come home to find her stroking him and talking to him. As the weather grew warmer, she had taken to letting him out in the sitting room to enjoy the sun.

She had let him out as usual this afternoon and was answering the door when he escaped. The two boys next door were back from school and had found Little White much more interesting than the ball they'd been kicking.

'They're just children . . .' Later on, when Zhiying came back and heard what had happened, he had tried to pacify me.

'Children? They're beasts! No – beasts have feelings.' Mother's voice trembled.

'Perhaps they're not used to animals,' Zhiying said weakly.

'That's no way to treat any creature. They'd have kicked him to death if I hadn't—' She couldn't continue.

I stood up and put on my shoes.

'Where are you going?'

'Next door. Those boys need to be taught a lesson.'

Zhiying held me back. 'Let it go,' he hissed. 'We won't let Little White out again.'

'But they insulted Mother! Look at her!'

'You can't go – not this time.' Zhiying stood in front of the door, his arms outstretched to bar my way.

'Let me pass,' I said slowly.

'Wenya, think! It's not worth making a fuss. I know you're upset, but it's not wise to – Little White is only a—'

'Only a rabbit?' I trembled with rage. 'You heartless man. You—' I caught sight of a photo of Xiao Tao lying on the table. 'You give me back my son then! Give me Xiao Tao! You can do whatever you like then. Come on!' I beat his chest with my fists.

He stood there motionless, and however hard I pummelled him, he didn't move. But instead of soothing me, he made me even angrier. 'You're so cold,' I wailed. 'I don't know how you can live this life – cold and heartless . . .'

Suddenly he grabbed my hands. 'You'll never forgive me, will you, Wenya? I'd die happily if it would bring our son back. Tell me what you want me to do – jump over a cliff? Kill the neighbours? Just say it!'

I was quiet. Zhiying was normally restrained. His outburst had shocked me.

Then I heard Mother's voice, weak but firm: 'Stop it, you two. Stop it. Come here.'

We went to her. 'No one mentions Xiao Tao's name now,' she said, 'not in front of me. Wenya, stop treating Zhiying like that. He doesn't deserve it.'

'Mother . . .'

'Zhiying's right,' she continued. 'It's us who will lose out. Don't you see the signs outside about no pets in residential areas? Don't you remember what happened to Lao Lin's dog?' It had been beaten to death by a group of vigilantes. Our neighbours might report us and send in the hygiene committee. Mother began to cough, her face red. We waited till she stopped. She sighed, 'It's all my fault. I should have been more careful. There's only one solution. Move Little White to my old house. One of you will have to go and feed him there. We have to do it soon, without anyone noticing,' Mother said decisively.

7

On the night Little White was well enough to travel we put him into a box. Zhiying listened for sounds from next door, then picked it up and left. Mother and I sat listening to the pitter-patter of the rain.

'It's for the best,' I said to Mother. She nodded, expressionless. We stared at each other, saying silently the words we couldn't bring ourselves to say aloud. It was unlikely she'd see much of Little White now – she rarely left our flat, and her home was damp and cold, bad for her asthma. She went to bed early.

Waiting for Zhiying's return, I thought of the long days ahead. Mother would have no company when Zhiying and I were at work. I had thought she was asleep, but when Zhiying's soft footsteps stopped outside our flat, her voice rang out: 'Is he all right?'

Zhiying, just through the door, whispered, 'Everything's fine.'

After a bout of coughing, Mother settled for the night.

I turned on to my side and Zhiying's hand reached for mine. I curled up, ignoring him – and not for the first time.

'Thank God she's asleep,' he whispered.

'Yes.'

'Wenya . . .' His hand crept up my thigh.

'I want to sleep,' I said.

He felt for my hand and held it tight. 'Wenya, Wenya.' Now his face was close to mine.

'I don't feel like it.'

'I know what you're thinking of.'

'You have no idea.'

'We can make another – it's Mother's idea, too.'

Was it my imagination or was Mother's snoring really louder? I listened carefully and didn't talk. For a long time Zhiying was silent, too. With a sigh he let go of my hand. He sat up. 'I was going to tell you about Lao Gao.'

I waited. Earlier in the evening, I had told him that Lao Gao had been taken away again, now that his leg and face were nearly healed. I had been to the ward almost daily to check on his progress without seeing him. The nurses said he was cheerful, which brightened the atmosphere, but he was also stubborn. 'You'd think he was a doctor himself, the way he has an opinion about everything,' one had said, with a smile. The sudden appearance of several Red Guards had caused considerable distress to the other patients and the nurses, who had grown to like him. They had tried hopelessly to resist the guards.

'Bad news?' I asked.

His lips were close to my ear. 'You said Lao Gao had been taken out of the hospital.'

'Yes.'

'Do you know why?'

I thought I could guess.

'The special investigator's come back,' Zhiying said.

My heart sank.

'He was unable to find any evidence to incriminate him.'

'That's good news, then!' I exclaimed.

'I haven't finished.'

'Go on.'

'There has been another anonymous letter, which might or might not be from the same person who wrote the first.'

'No!' I sat up.

'Sssh – Mother!' he warned. 'Someone wants Lao Gao dead.'

'How can you be so sure?' I whispered.

'The accusations in the letter are obviously pure fabrication: that he had been captured by the Americans and released because he'd signed a letter to denounce the Party, that as a condition of his release he gave them information about his army units ... Lao Gao has a comrade in arms who swore that through all the years in Korea they'd never been parted, let alone been captured, so it's all lies. If only someone would listen to this man ... But what I'm really worried about, Wenya, is that so much of what is written on the big posters and in those letters are things that only a few people close to Lao Gao would know. Things that Lao Gao said and did that, taken out of context, condemn him.'

'You think someone bears him a grudge and wants to frame him?' I asked incredulously. The Gaos were a generous couple, and though Lao Gao could be severe when he discovered wrong-doing, he was always fair. The factory was his life and the workers his family – how could anybody betray him? People who were close to him? Us?

Zhenzhen? Cheng Ming? The drivers? No, it wasn't possible. Apart from our affection for Lao Gao, what would any of us gain from denouncing him? If Lao Gao went, Zhiying, I, Zhenzhen and Cheng Ming, his favourites, would go down with him. One of the drivers? Lao Cui? There could be no doubt of our devotion to him, and now was the time, more than ever, that we should rally round and fight for him. Suddenly I thought of Cheng Ming. How was he faring? I hadn't had news of him for a long time.

'What is Cheng Ming doing?' I whispered.

'After his demotion he was given only menial work. They say he seems depressed, that he rarely picks up his flute now,' Zhiying replied. I waited for more but he didn't go on.

I thought he had gone to sleep, but he took my hand again. 'I'm so scared,' he whispered. 'I feel as if I'm walking on thin ice. What's happening? Oh, Wenya I feel so lonely – I have nothing to hold on to, but you.'

I took him in my arms and held him tight. 'It'll be all right,' I said, rocking him as I had once rocked Xiao Tao. His fear alarmed me. Ever since the night when I had told him about Father, he had been my rock. Now I knew I had to be strong for him – for all of us.

8

I made sure the front door was locked, then drew the curtains. It wasn't quite dark yet, but neither would a curtain arouse suspicion. We had grown experienced in these matters: neighbours had drawn the curtains too early during the day, causing over-vigilant Red Guards to burst in and investigate. It didn't matter that they'd only wanted an early night, the Red Guards smashed the furniture and turned the house upside-down when they failed to find anything incriminating.

A scrabbling sound came from the kitchen – Little White was impatient for his dinner. I rushed to him with the food – last night's left-over carrots and potatoes. Afterwards he licked my hand. I didn't often see him now. Usually Zhiying came over, although occasionally Mother was able to make the trip, now that the weather was getting warmer.

I went back to the sitting room and spotted her slippers under the bed. She had used my spare pair when she came to live with us, but for her hospital stay I felt she would want her own. I picked them up and put them into the bag I'd brought with me. Although she had indicated that all she needed was Father's photo and her reading glasses, I thought she might like these, too. I doubted she'd ever come here again.

The room smelled musty. The large chest had survived all our moves – it had been more of a constant in our lives than the numerous houses we had called home. It was old-fashioned but of good quality, and would have lasted for ever had it not been shunted about so much. The linen chest was dented where I had knocked it with a chair, in my eagerness to help Mother lay the table. She had not scolded me for my carelessness, but later, I had seen her running her hands over the dent. The cupboard had been part of her dowry and she had insisted on taking it everywhere with her, in spite of its size. I could see why she was so fond of it: it was beautiful – dark red wood with four doors, each decorated with ceramic peaches, grapes and flowers. As a child I had taken out the bedding, climbed in through one door and crawled out of another. Once I stayed there all day until the door opened from the outside to reveal my father, whom I hadn't seen for some time.

I gazed down at the small peach-wood stool by the bed. As a child, it was always my preferred seat. I would sit on it to listen to Father playing his flute, or to read, listening to Mother in the kitchen, the smell of food making my mouth water. I'd sat on it the first time Zhiying had visited while Mother and he were chatting.

I glanced up at the empty wall and the space where the photo had hung. I remembered Mother's request. She hadn't told me where she'd hidden the photos, though. 'Photos?' I'd asked. 'I thought you'd lost them.' She'd shaken her head.

Behind the bookshelf, under the mattress, in the folds of the bedding? I unlocked and emptied all the drawers, but I found nothing. I sat on the bed and tried to think as Mother would. I walked to the small table with the mirror above it at which she had sat to brush her hair. I stared past my reflected face and saw, facing the wall where the photo had been, Mother's Model Family Hygiene Certificate, which was exactly the same size as the old frame. It had been there for as long as I remembered, but now something made me look at it again. From this angle, it seemed suspiciously thick. I fetched the stool, stood on it and took the framed certificate off the wall. Carefully I unscrewed the back, and out came the photos, not only the one I remembered of Father in his suit, but the ones I had thought lost.

I sat down with them on my knee, and took out the biggest. I saw myself, my brother, Father and Mother beneath an archway entwined with artificial vines. I had no recollection of this picture being taken. I was wearing a knee-length skirt, my chin close to my collar-bone, trying to hide my face. My mother sat holding Da Tao. Father was standing with one hand resting on the arch, the other on Mother's shoulder. It was a slightly awkward pose and I could almost hear the photographer calling instructions to him. Father wasn't as tall as I had remembered – about the same height as Zhiying, perhaps even shorter. He wore a western suit and a pair of glasses; his thick black hair was brushed back with a central parting. He smiled, but didn't show his teeth, looking pleased with himself. Mother wore a traditional *qipao*, her shapely legs bent demurely to one side, her head leaning towards Father. Their expressions emphasised the gulf between them. Mother's gaze was fixed on the camera, his was distant, as if he was lost in a different world.

I put the photo down, and picked up another, then another, almost greedily. Once upon a time they had been kept in an album, Mother's treasure. If I was especially well behaved, I might be allowed to look at it, and she would point out this and that, then stare at a particular aunt or uncle and sigh. I tried to follow her gaze but knew it went further than I could grasp, back through the years before I was born. Suddenly I knew why she had sent me for these. She was dying: she had no material wealth to pass on to me, only these images and memories.

I imagined Father's first meeting with Mother – it had been love at first sight, I knew, from snippets of conversation I had had with her. It had been a happy union for the two Shandong families too, both fairly well-off. They had made their small fortunes buying and selling wood. Father had been well versed in classical poetry and had trained in martial arts and swordsmanship. He had been educated privately at home by tutors and had written poetry, which Mother had admired. They had met at a large family gathering – they were distant cousins. Mother had been a bit of a rebel – she had insisted on going to school in the days when girls were not educated, except in the most progressive families, which hers was not. The crash had come after their marriage, when they had children and the reality of daily life dawned. My father was loving, but not practical.

I stared at Father, smiling handsomely out of the photo, and imagined him holding me as a baby. My heart ached that he hadn't lived to see mine. I had felt hurt for him when Mother vented her anger after he had gone. Then remorse flooded me. I shouldn't think critically of Mother when she was dying. Suddenly I felt sick and weak: soon I would be an orphan.

9

I lost track of time. I insisted on going to work even though the hospital had given me a week off to bury Mother. It felt good to walk briskly and even to run – no one would see me crying. The thunder and rain brought relief too: I needed the downpour to cool me. I was glad I'd missed the bus. Now I wondered why I always struggled to get on with all the other sweaty bodies. The traffic was bad after work, these days, with the parades of so-called criminals and the trucks full of youth sent to the countryside for re-education.

A car screeched past me, reversed, stopped and hooted. It was Lao Cui, Lao Gao's former driver. 'Hop in,' he said, as a flash of lightning lit the sky. I wasn't sure I wanted to – I didn't know if I was up to seeing him. But he'd already opened the door, and rain was splashing on to the seat. I got in.

He shot a glance at the black band on my left arm. 'Your mother?'

I burst into fresh tears. The last few days I had lived in limbo, hardly knowing where I was. His simple words had made me realise that Mother was gone. She never did wear her slippers, but she saw the photos. She'd died clutching one of her and Father beneath a *mei* tree in someone's garden.

'Wenya . . .' Lao Cui passed me a large handkerchief and started the car. For a long time he didn't say anything but drove along at a moderate speed.

When I stopped crying and looked out of the window, I was puzzled to see that we were in an unfamiliar part of town.

He smiled. 'I just want to talk to you. You missed the bus?' he asked.

I nodded and took a deep breath.

'Wenya . . .' He kept his eyes on the road.

'Yes?'

'Tell Zhiying to watch out,' he said.

'Why?' I asked, but I could guess what he was going to say.

'They're trying to get him because of his connection with Lao Gao.'

This wasn't news – I knew that Zhiying had been aware of it. Still, I was grateful for the warning. 'How's Lao Gao?' I asked.

Lao Cui paused before he replied. 'Bad. I hear they've applied to the Central Revolutionary Committee for him to be condemned as a traitor.'

'The Central Revolutionary Committee in Beijing?'

'Lao Gao's important – he holds the National Gold Medal. They can't just do as they like.'

'And what will happen to him if they find him guilty?'

'The worst, I'm afraid.'

I felt dizzy. Lao Gao had cheated death by American bullets and fire, but now he might be shot in peacetime for a crime he hadn't committed. 'Is there anything we can do? Surely you don't believe . . .'

He shook his head. 'Of course not. But they have evidence and witness statements – fabricated, no doubt.'

The car bumped along the potholed road as I digested what he had said.

'Where are you going to?'

It was a moment before he answered. 'Officially, to bring Chairman Yang's aunt to his house for dinner. Unofficially, I'm on my way to Zhenzhen's. It seems to me that the aunt will have to wait – bad traffic.'

'How is Zhenzhen taking it?' I asked.

'She's nearly hysterical, but Lao Gao is calm.'

'Where is he?'

'Being kept under close observation.'

We drove in silence for a while.

Lao Cui stopped the car a few blocks away from my home. Our eyes met, and then he leaned back, one hand extended to me. 'Wenya, be strong, for Zhiying's sake. Be careful. I don't know what will happen now, but Lao Gao might yet come through – he's remained upbeat in spite of everything, and he has well-placed friends in the province and in Beijing . . .'

I got out and said goodbye. The rain had stopped and no one was about. The feeling of safety I had experienced in the car was gone. Now I understood what fear was: it was knowing that someone was innocent of the crime for which they were condemned and that you could do nothing about it. I headed for home. My heart ached with loneliness. There was only one place to go, and that was to Zhiying's arms.

10

My first thought when I woke was that I'd lost something precious. Moonlight poured through the open window and I sat up. My throat was dry. For a moment I was confused. What was that chest doing here? I used to know it well – and the low stool. Of course! They were Mother's and I was a child, surrounded by our furniture.

Then I heard Zhiying breathing next to me and realised. I was in my own home with Mother's furniture. And she had gone for good. Her chest stood where her bed used to be, where Xiao Tao's cot was before that. I remembered finding one of his little socks among Mother's clothes during the day. We'd hardly talked about Xiao Tao when she was alive. She had tried so many times to bring him into our conversations but I had always cut her short. I wished now that I'd let her talk.

I shook Zhiying. Only he knew how I felt. He had thrown himself on to Mother's body, crying as I stood by. If Mother had gained a son when he married me, he had now lost his mother again – they had been so fond of each other. 'Wake up, Zhiying!' I whispered. I couldn't let him sleep, when I was so lonely. When he stirred I put my mouth to his. I wanted to be closer than close – I wanted to hide in him.

As he embraced me, he filled the void that remained after two lives had ended.

Afterwards, in the middle of the night, I got up, tiptoed into the kitchen and turned on the light. All the windows in the house were wide open, but the air was still. I drank some water and caught sight of Little White's empty den. I hadn't been to feed him for two days. Had Zhiying remembered?

I began to cry – not for Mother or Xiao Tao, but for the crushing loneliness that even making love with Zhiying could not overcome. I would do anything to free myself of it.

11

Xiao Tao waved his arms and I reached out to hold him, but my arms were so heavy. 'Help, Zhiying! I can't move!' I shouted, and felt his hands on my forehead.

'You're so hot.' I heard his voice, then felt something in my mouth. I swallowed.

I passed in and out of consciousness. Mother stood by, trying to feed me something foul-tasting that I had to take for Xiao Tao's sake. I resisted: 'I can't take any more, Mother.' And Ying was here, sticking needles into me. Had we just been to Peach Blossom Village? Her face faded as I heard her say, 'I'll be back later.'

Meanwhile, I felt hot. A fire was burning inside me. I seemed to travel freely: I was with Zhenzhen, Cheng Ming and Lao Gao by the pond, eating mushrooms Cheng Ming had picked – I was walking with Zhiying, Xiao Tao in his arms. Finally I'd persuaded him to come to the park with us. Then we bumped into Lao Gao . . .

'He can sing, you know. He's got a really deep voice. But he wouldn't in front of you. He's too shy.' Zhenzhen's voice.

'Lao Gao, singing?' I asked. But it was Cheng Ming I could hear.

'Lao Gao can sing . . .'

'Lao Gao's dead.' Zhiying now. But I could see Lao Gao by the trees, talking to Cheng Ming.

'He hanged himself last night.' Again, Zhiying's voice, but far away.

'Lao Gao hanged himself,' I repeated, and for once I seemed to be in the present. I opened my eyes and saw Zhiying's tears.

'Wenya, I have to leave you for a little while. I must go to Zhenzhen. She needs me – you understand, don't you?'

'I understand,' I said. Then, confused: 'Go to Zhenzhen, of course, go to her. She always needs us when Lao Gao's away.'

And here was Ying again, with her needles.

Since the investigation report had arrived, the campaign to force Lao Gao to confess had intensified. The revolutionary committee knew that, with a wide network of friends and former army colleagues in senior posts, Lao Gao stood a chance of rescue. To prevent that, they wanted him to sign a confession. But, despite torture and threats, he would not. A friendly former colleague had been on the committee and had fended off the worst beatings, but he had been removed from his position. After that Zhenzhen and Lao Gao's friends had been unable to communicate with him. That morning, as Zhenzhen had got ready for work on the farm to which disgraced cadres and their families were sent for reform, she had been summoned to the leader's office and told abruptly that she was to collect Lao Gao's body. Lao Cui went with her, and they were told that Lao Gao had hanged himself with his belt – 'breaking away from the people' were the words they had used to condemn what he had done.

I lay still as Zhiying held my hand. Closing my eyes I seemed to follow him, in Lao Cui's car, to the bungalows Lao Gao had built for retired workers where his tortured body lay. Some brave soul had defied the factory authorities to allow Lao Gao's body to rest there while secret funeral arrangements were made – since he had died a traitor, Lao Gao could not be formally remembered. There would be no official memorial.

In the bungalow a thin woman had stood up slowly. 'I nearly didn't recognise her,' Zhiying said, and I tried hard to see Zhenzhen, grief-stricken, but couldn't. 'I saw Cheng Ming, too. It was good that she had him, although the state he was in, he wasn't much help to her.' Zhiying's voice quavered.

I closed my eyes again. Zhenzhen, Cheng Ming, Zhiying and Lao Gao. A reunion in my absence. The last time we were together a rainbow had appeared, as if to seal our good fortune. Zhenzhen had been holding Xiao Tao, and Lao Gao had been at the heart of it all. We would never be together again. I buried my head in the pillow. This must be a nightmare.

12

On the day I'd come back to myself after the fever, I spotted Zhiying's big yellow army bag bulging with maps and charts on the table. He seemed to have packed with purpose – had he forgotten it? I could walk to the factory and deliver it to him, I told myself, and went to fetch my coat.

I made my way slowly out of the flat, remembering the snippets of news Zhiying told me over the last few weeks. The illness had weakened me, so that however much I wanted to see Zhenzhen and help her through the worst of her grief, I couldn't. I had heard much from Zhiying, though: the farm leaders had given her three days' leave to arrange Lao Gao's cremation, which Zhiying had attended with many other workers. Despite the authorities' cautions, many had worn black armbands as if a close relative had died. When he told me this Zhiying seemed to take heart. There had been a skirmish before the cremation, when the car carrying Lao Gao's body was driven through the factory, between the militia sent to disperse the crowd and the fifty-strong group of workers defending the hearse. If it hadn't been for Cheng Ming there would have been arrests. It seemed he had persuaded the militia chief to leave the procession alone and avoid further clashes between the two sides.

It was strange to be out and about when everybody else was at work. I followed the lane Zhiying cycled along on his way to the factory. It was early afternoon, and the main road was dusty, dry and empty, the asphalt steaming with heat, hot on the soles of my feet. I walked to the main entrance and peered through the gate: it had been a long time since I was inside. Nowadays even the thought of going there was depressing. All the potted plants had gone, in their place big red and black posters had been pasted to the iron railings. They attracted and repelled me: I wanted to know if Zhiying's name appeared in any, but feared to see it. Hesitantly, I hovered at the gate. How could I get Zhiying's bag to him, without meeting anyone I used to know? These days, relationships were a minefield: I had to be careful who I smiled at, and who I ignored.

Two young female workers, probably just off the morning shift, their hair wet from the showers, walked out of the gate and paused in front of a wall where notices were displayed. My eyes followed their fingers and their conversation drifted to my ears.

'. . . political task,' said one, gesticulating at a bright poster.

The other shrugged and said something I couldn't hear. It was obvious she disagreed.

The first girl raised her voice: 'But would you have sung when your husband had just died?'

'They said he was a traitor!'

'Some may think so.'

I kept still, hoping they wouldn't notice me. A bird alighted on the branch of the tree beside me. A breeze blew. I listened.

'You believe what they say? Were you born yesterday? My father says he was a hero . . .'

Their voices became indistinguishable again.

'. . . such a good voice – the duet was lovely.'

'You're just like the others – secretly in love with him because he's so handsome . . .'

A tractor thundered past. They stepped away, then glanced back and saw me. 'Let's go,' one said, and I pretended to look the other way.

When they were out of sight I crossed the road and approached the wall. I saw the poster advertising the latest entertainment: 'Performance – visiting Korean singing group joining our very own East Wind entertainment troupe for a friendly performance at the Bright Light Stadium, with the celebrated duet between Cheng Ming and Xu Zhen. Tickets for sale on Wednesday at the Trade Union Department.'

There was a cartoon of two figures singing into a microphone against a background of actors and actresses dressed in workers' uniforms. The man bore a slight resemblance to Cheng Ming, but the woman was unrecognisable. A sound distracted me – scolding coming from the factory. Through the gap in the railings I saw a man wearing a yellow army top standing on some steps, shouting at a man on the pavement, who was holding a broom. His voice was loud, so that even from a distance I could hear most of what he said.

'. . . a question of attitude. I see you have not repented enough.'

The man with the broom stood still, head bowed. There was something familiar about his back.

Someone came out of the office and spoke to the man in the yellow top, who turned to the man with the broom. 'Sweep the block again, and don't be lazy. Remember, you're not the chief engineer any more!' He went back inside the building. The man with the broom nodded and turned. It was Zhiying. I clasped his bag, stepped back from the rails so he wouldn't see me, and fled.

Somehow I ended up on the railway track, parallel to the factory. I remembered walking along it with Zhiying when it was being laid and he had told me of his childhood ambition to became an engineer. It had long been fulfilled, and we had never done the walk since. The track led ultimately to North Korea, not to Beijing as we had originally believed. A heavily loaded freight train stole up beside me, and for some time we moved almost at the same speed. Eventually it pulled ahead and I saw I had reached the wilderness at the edge of the factory. A few more workshops had been built there, but the rough ground remained. Lao Gao had once quoted the sayings of Chairman Mao – 'Humans will surely defeat nature.' The look on his face then had convinced me that we were invincible.

But Lao Gao was dead, Zhiying had been humiliated, Cheng Ming and Zhenzhen were about to be made to sing against their will. This factory had once symbolised our hope for the future, our youthful dreams: now it was a place of humiliation and dread. Why did the republic persecute its best brains? How could the factory destroy the hands that had built it?

I began to feel as though I would never get home.

Cheng Ming and Zhenzhen performing together? A few weeks ago Zhiying had said that Zhenzhen had been transferred from the farm back to the factory, but he hadn't said her new position was in the entertainment troupe. How could they make her sing so soon after Lao Gao's death?

A wave of nausea washed over me and I hurried to the flat, trying to suppress the urge to vomit, only to discover that I couldn't find my key. I sat outside until Zhiying came home and found me. I gestured to the army bag and tried to explain. 'I came to see you . . .'

He took me in his arms. 'I'm fine, Wenya, I won't let them hurt me,' he said.

13

Although we wore long raincoats that covered us from head to toe, by the time Zhiying had cycled us to the Bright Light Stadium in the centre of town we were soaked. Not that we minded the rain, and neither did the streams of other people arriving by bike and on foot. Anticipation hung in the air, as though an important announcement was about to be made. We saw a few people from the factory, but the stadium was the biggest local venue and the audience had come from everywhere.

Zhiying's face was expressionless – we were past caring what anyone might think and wore our black mourning bands. They raised eyebrows but few gave us a second glance.

I had been to shows like this a few times before. With Mother I had watched Peking operas, and after I had married Zhiying I had come here once to watch acrobats. As a factory employee, Zhiying could have got the tickets at a discount, but in the light of what had happened recently he had been to the central ticket office so that we could sit away from the factory crowds and avoid suspicion.

Our seats were high up in the stadium so we could see everything on the stage, but the figures were small so we were unable to make out the faces clearly.

The Korean singers came on first: a soprano soloist, Korean folk music, a chorus, a children's dance, Korean revolutionary songs and a big, bosomy woman singing strange translations of Chinese songs. The programme announcer was a well-known figure, a retired singer with a booming voice. 'Next,' he announced, 'the famed duet from the East Wind entertainment troupe! We welcome Comrades Cheng Ming and Xu Zhen.'

I glanced at Zhiying's pale face and clasped his hand hard. Since I had seen the posters, we had argued about what lay behind this extraordinary event. I convinced Zhiying that Cheng Ming must have persuaded Zhenzhen to sing – he was protecting her so that she wouldn't get into trouble for refusing a political task. Now that Lao Gao had gone, his first instinct would be to take care of her, as he had so often in the past. But Zhiying was not convinced.

'They could have refused,' he said.

'How?' I asked. She was so vulnerable now.

'She might have pretended she was ill!' he said.

Now I knew that however they had reached the decision to perform, it could not have been easy for them. I was fearful for Zhenzhen – she might break down on stage. I watched Zhiying redden, and wondered if we should leave. Then the figures of our friends appeared on stage. For a minute they stood looking at the audience, then she turned to him, and he responded with a nod. From where I sat I couldn't distinguish their expressions, but she seemed unsteady, which told me she was

struggling. Zhiying had told me she had been malnourished on the farm and that it was only since she'd come
back to the factory that she had begun to recover her
health.

The hall quietened and I heard her voice. 'We're
honoured to be here . . .'

It was lower than I remembered, but still held the
familiar mixture of north and south, soft but with the hint
of an edge. Instantly I was transported to happier days,
and wanted more.

'How can she do this, with Lao Gao barely cold?'
Zhiying whispered angrily, grief and fury in his eyes.

He began to stand up, but I pulled him to me.
'Listen . . .'

'I'd like to give you a song in memory of my late
husband. He taught me this folk song, which he learned
when he was serving in Korea during the war. He was a
war hero . . .'

I felt my back freeze, and saw Cheng Ming step away
from her.

She started to sing, unaccompanied, her voice soft and
intimate.

Cheng Ming was rooted to the spot, and did nothing to
stop her. Did she know what she was doing in singing Lao
Gao's praises so openly, defying the committees who had
condemned him as a traitor? It would have been much
easier to pretend she was ill, as Zhiying had said. But this
was Zhenzhen, always so honest. Suddenly a tiny spark of
brightness lit within me, but at the same time I was
gripped with fear and concern.

Another voice joined Zhenzhen's – the tall Korean
woman who had sung Chinese songs was back on the

stage. She took Zhenzhen's hand and raised it above their heads. Together they sang a finale. The applause was deafening.

The announcer ran on to the stage. 'What a finale!' Then he was lost for words.

We lingered by the door until nearly everybody had gone. When the vast hall was empty, I touched Zhiying's shoulder.

'We'll wait a bit longer,' he said. 'I want to be sure she's all right.'

The Korean singers drove past in a coach, waving, and still we waited. The rain had stopped and the air was cooler. A police van sped round the corner, siren wailing, as Cheng Ming and Zhenzhen emerged. She spotted us and stared.

Zhiying and I watched helplessly as the police bundled them into the van.

14

'You saw her?'

Zhiying shook his head, then nodded.

'Well, did you or didn't you?' I said impatiently.

Zhiying motioned to the door and lowered his voice. 'They wouldn't let her out of the room so I talked to her through a hole at the detention centre.'

'What did she say? How is she?' I asked.

'She said she's fine.'

I wanted to scream at him – 'Of course she says she's fine! But is she *really*? What are they going to do to her?'

The sight of the chicken soup I had made for her sitting on our table filled me with renewed fury. 'Why didn't you give her that? You'll have to go back now.' There was little I could do for her, but I had wanted her at least to have something nice to eat.

'Oh, Wenya, they wouldn't let her have it, and anyway, it's not food she needs most.' Then he whispered, 'I managed to give her the photo.'

It had been my idea. It was one of her and Lao Gao, taken in the early days of their romance – I had come across it when I was sorting through Mother's and our pictures.

As Zhiying staggered wearily towards the kitchen, I remembered what would happen tomorrow: Zhiying had to read out his letter of self-criticism, after Lao Cui had read his. The meeting wouldn't be on the scale of those Lao Gao had endured but he would have to stand for two full hours in front of all the engineers at the factory, who would tell their former manager exactly what they thought of him. Zhiying had spent the whole week drafting his letter. We had laboured hard over it as he had wanted it to be a true assessment of his work. He refused to make accusations about Lao Gao, but was prepared to admit his own errors and even the level of his political consciousness. 'Will it help?' I asked now.

'I doubt it. But I must tell the truth – nothing but the truth.'

As we lay in bed we heard the usual drunken laughter from next door. They were celebrating now that Yang Lian had finally become the director of the factory. Zhiying clenched his fists. 'We'll settle the score one day,' he said. 'Lao Gao will not have died in vain.'

15

What a relief it was not to think, not to feel. One second, two . . . I had been there for no more than five seconds when an elbow jabbed mine. I wouldn't budge. I'd waited so long for this shower but instead of washing I was standing there, letting the water drip off me. One more precious moment, please.

Elbows and shoulders jostled me deliberately. I glared at the woman nearest to me. When I relinquished the shower it wasn't an admission of defeat – I could have scratched her face and made her wait, but I had had enough. I made my way to the big hot pool, which was not as crowded as the showers.

I stood submerged with only my head above the water. It was hot enough, I hoped, to snuff out the tiny life inside me, if the pill I'd taken earlier hadn't done its work. I remembered the foetus I had seen at medical college, but mine would be even smaller: a ball of grief, sorrow and disgust with the world. I hadn't told Zhiying, and didn't want to. He was too preoccupied.

He was adamant that he hadn't been beaten, but there was a long red mark on his neck where the rope had cut

207

into it. They had hung a placard from it: 'The running dog of a traitor,' it had proclaimed in black ink, with two big crosses above the words, showing condemnation. He walked home in it, and once the door had closed I rushed to take it off him and lay him flat, to stretch out his bent back. Then I tried to bathe the angry mark. Now, once a week, I took a bowl of hot water, removed his shirt, dipped a towel into the water and rubbed his back with it, careful to avoid the tender, healing skin on his neck. We had rubbed each other's backs since we were first married, but he was too exhausted now to do it for me.

I stepped out of the hot water and felt lost. All the women around me were in pairs – you don't come to a public bath-house alone. I turned to leave, but a tall woman standing behind me took my arm. 'I've been watching you, sister,' she said. 'I'm on my own too. Shall I do you and then you do me?'

I rested my hands on the wall and closed my eyes. A total stranger would help me relax. I wondered if she, too, had a disgraced husband at home. She was firm but gentle, and massaged away the aches and pains. I moaned with a mixture of pain and pleasure.

Though I wasn't as expert as she, she turned her head to smile encouragingly. I rubbed harder, but I felt as though my energy was draining. What was wrong with me? I tried again, but was soon breathless. I stopped, apologised, and went towards the door, hoping to catch some air. My throat was dry and suddenly the noise of the bathhouse faded . . .

The faces of the women hovering above me were mostly concerned, but a few were unable to disguise their curiosity. I stared back. Then the woman I had been rubbing bent down with a glass. 'Here, drink this.' I gulped it while she held it. Then I struggled to my feet.

She took my locker key from my hand, and went away. Soon she came back with my crumpled clothes and started to dress me. My body felt cramped, damp and hot, and I was desperate to escape the other women's stares – so desperate that I didn't stop to thank my saviour before I ran out into the fresh air.

I sat on the wide step outside, blinking at the sun's brightness. The kindness of strangers . . . Last summer we had been the guests of dear friends, who had driven us to a beautiful cool place where I had learned to swim. 'Try this,' Zhenzhen had said.

'What is it?'

'A southern dumpling.'

'It's . . . sweet.' I took a bite, uncertain.

She had nodded. 'You'll get used to it, and love it.'

I did grow to love it. Her too.

People stepped past me. The woman who had helped me paused briefly. 'Are you all right now?' she asked. I smiled and waved her on. The ticket collector frowned at me, obviously wondering if I should be removed. I didn't care.

I felt something trickle down my thigh.

The pill was working. Although I'd known my period was late, it wasn't until the nausea and vomiting had set in that I had considered I might be pregnant.

A headache came on, suddenly and relentlessly, then a tremendous tiredness. It was an effort to think, to move, so I stood watching the traffic flow indifferently past me, daunted by the prospect of crossing the street. It seemed that I was a little girl once more, holding Mother's hand, trusting her to lead me. The last time I had held her hand I had taken her to the hospital toilet. But Zhiying would hold my hand . . . I remembered him taking it before we crossed a street when we had first met.

These days, coming home from his endless meetings of criticism, Zhiying's eyes were glazed. There were no bloodstains: the wounds were deep inside him. 'Am I really a conceited man, a selfish, stinking intellectual?' he asked, and the only thing I could do was hold him. The helplessness I felt was freezing my heart, and the world was so dark.

In the white light of the sun, I blinked and moved on. The blood was flowing fast now. I shut my eyes and stepped into the traffic, my arms clasping my chest in a vacant embrace. I heard a screech and opened my eyes. The driver of a lorry stuck his head out of his window and cursed: 'You silly woman, do you want to die? Go and find a better place to do it.' I stared at him until someone pulled me away. Then I carried on.

16

Exactly a year ago, on a hot afternoon like this, Zhenzhen, Lao Gao, Cheng Ming and Xiao Tao . . . Xiao Tao was in Zhenzhen's arms, of course, not mine. I was . . . treating a sick patient in Peach Blossom Village. That was when I had experienced the terrifying premonition that made me take that reckless decision to defy orders and bring my students back early from the countryside. A mother's sixth sense. It hadn't saved Xiao Tao, but I heard of his death sooner.

Now, heading into the hills, I was entering another world. First, it was the sound – or absence of it, that quietened my fast steps. There was no noise – no shouting of slogans, no traffic, even. Then I was struck by the colour: not red, not black and white, the colours of the big posters, but green. The damp scent intensified as I went deeper into the woods. But the more silent it seemed, the more I felt the presence of others walking alongside me. Dark shadows seemed to slip past and jump ahead; strange sounds echoed behind me. The woods remembered how they'd parked the jeep by the half-collapsed tree and walked to the pond – I saw them now. I moved close to them, breathed down on Xiao Tao, his face snuggled to Auntie Zhenzhen's chest. I wished he would wake up and look at me.

The sound of twigs cracking underfoot broke the illusion. I cursed. Concentrate, I told myself. The cool of the wood was soothing, and the scents drew me back. Suddenly I was floating in the past – a rushing stream, songs, an intense look on a beautiful young man's face, the willows smoothing my face as I passed, soft spring wind, echoes of laughter: 'But you have too many white hairs already,' giggled Zhenzhen.

'Then you must pluck them out – I want to stay young for you,' replied Lao Gao.

'Perhaps it'd be simpler if I shaved you,' said Lao Cui, and we laughed.

'What will you be Xiao Tao? An engineer like Daddy or a doctor like Mummy?' That was Zhiying's voice. Xiao Tao's answer was a gurgle. And where was I? Listening? Watching? Not when Xiao Tao disappeared into the water for ever.

Exactly a year ago.

They had approached the pond, as I did now. The surface of the green water seemed to tremble – beautiful beyond words. The hush was broken by the song of the insects, their indifferent warning. Here, now, I dared to imagine him in the pond.

'Xiao Tao,' I whispered, and leaned over to touch the water, feeling closer to him – it was as though his spirit lingered here. I closed my eyes. I was with them again in the last few moments of his life. Zhiying and Lao Gao had gone to fetch wood for a fire, and Xiao Tao was asleep – or, at least, that was how he seemed, to everyone including Zhenzhen, who sat beside him. Cheng Ming was coming slowly towards her. Then what had happened? I opened my eyes. Zhiying had never been certain – he knew only that Xiao Tao had slipped into the water while he was in Zhenzhen's care. But now I was there in spirit, and soon I would know.

The sunshine that had filtered through the trees had all but disappeared and the birds sounded mournful. 'Xiao Tao . . .' I was on my knees, dipping my hands into the water, as close as I could get to him. I concentrated hard. I saw him opening his eyes, seeing the blue sky and smiling. I saw how hot he felt, and watched him reach out to touch a patch of damp close by. He wriggled on to his side and saw the water, then started to crawl, for the first time, towards it . . .

A hand touched my shoulder. My head jerked round. It was Zhenzhen. 'Where were you?' I asked. I was still a ghost and Zhenzhen's had come to meet mine.

'He lay next to me, fast asleep. I had thought of moving him, as the sun was quite strong. But Cheng Ming called me. I thought I'd only be gone for a second, and he seemed so fast asleep . . .'

When she cried I knew she wasn't a ghost. I stood up slowly, feeling better somehow for knowing the truth. 'Thank you,' I said.

She watched as I walked slowly round the pond, throwing dumplings into it. I'd made twelve, one for each month since he had drowned last year. The pond wasn't very big, but by the time I had completed the circuit it was getting dark. I had one dumpling left. I glanced up at the trees, the tips of the branches stark against the twilight sky. Zhenzhen and I had found our way back, how long would it be before the others came?

'Have this,' I said to her, and pressed the dumpling into her hand.

She knelt beside the pond, murmured something, then threw in the dumpling. 'Rest in peace . . .' she whispered.

I could barely see her as she came towards me, her yellow dress billowing in the evening breeze. 'I'm sorry about Lao Gao . . .' I said.

'Wenya . . .' She broke down. 'No more memories. Let's live.'

Part III:
Zhenzhen, Spring, 1970s

1

Even before I got dressed that morning I was thinking of Zhenzhen. What would she wear? Would she bring one or two offerings of food to the cemetery? Would she want to go to Xiao Tao's grave first or visit Lao Gao's on her own? Then I chided myself for being so frivolous. I was going to pay my respects to the dead, not enjoy a picnic. It was Zhenzhen's fault that I felt like this. I turned to the window. It was raining – appropriate on Qing Ming, the Day of the Dead.

> On the Day of the Clear and Bright, the day of the
> Dead, rain fell,
> The lonely traveller with a broken heart stopped
> A herdsman to ask the way to the inn.
> 'It is as far as the Apricot Blossom Village,'
> Said the herdsman, pointing to the distance.

Father had introduced me to that poem, but he'd taught me the words without explaining the meaning. For a long time, whenever I thought of the poem, I conjured up a rather romantic picture of a lonely traveller in mourning, suddenly cheered by the idea of a friendly inn. Only later, when I had been bereaved, did I read more into it: instead of being cheered, the traveller had needed more wine to ease his sorrow.

When I had woken that morning it had taken me some time to recognise where I was. I had taken in the spaciousness, and thought I must be in the hotel to which Zhiying had taken me shortly after he had been appointed director of the factory. I had been in awe of its shining newness, worried that I might break or damage something. Soon enough, though, cracks had begun to appear even in these luxurious buildings: their perfection was just a veneer. Like the other hurried projects of that time, they were not built to last.

I remembered as if it had happened yesterday, the moment when we'd learned from Lao Cui of Zhiying's promotion. About three years after Lao Gao's death, the 'movement' had lost impetus, and for a while we enjoyed a relatively peaceful life. After only two years as director, Yang Lian was dismissed from his position. He had never been a popular figure. Zhiying had by then been assigned to work in the factory library, stocktaking and looking after the books. He wanted no more than to live quietly with me, he told me, one Monday after work, as I fetched a bowl of hot water for him to bathe his feet. It was then that Lao Cui knocked on the door. 'Good news, Zhiying,' he said breathlessly, his eyes sparkling. 'I've come to take you to the East Wind director's office.' He explained that the appointment had been made in the personnel department of the provincial government. Later we gathered that there had been an internal power struggle, and that Zhiying had been given the post because neither of the two rival factions would back down, and he was an acceptable compromise because he belonged to neither. We didn't expect him to remain in post for long – he'd do his best, he declared to me, and strive not to let the workers down.

Zhiying was going to work even though it was Sunday. The factory's day off had been changed to Wednesday. In the early days when he had come home – often late – he would look around proudly. His eyes lit up at the sight of the high ceilings, and he'd go into the spare bedrooms so that he could enjoy opening and shutting the doors. Our move was one of the perks of his new job. We were now like the Gaos, though I doubted that they had been afforded such luxury. The flat overlooked the river, with its boats to Korea. In the past I had dreamed of living close to it, but now that we were here, I had almost lost interest.

I still found it hard to grasp that this was my home. In our cramped old room, all I had had to do was reach out for something, but now there were several rooms to search – we had three bedrooms – and sometimes I would forget what I was looking for. Although it was convenient to have a fridge, I missed the large cellar we'd left behind. I'd heard that the family who lived there now used it to store their junk.

I stood by the window but made sure I couldn't be seen from outside – there wouldn't be any visitors yet – they came in droves after work and on the factory's days off.

There were all sorts: wives in tears, sometimes with bruises, men angry and occasionally in tears, quarrelling neighbours, retired workers looking for justice. No problem was too large or too small to bring to Zhiying: a child's football had broken a neighbour's window, the amount the factory should contribute to a worker's funeral, whether the insane son of an employee should be sent to the asylum, the quantity of cabbages the factory grocer should order for the winter now that some families had fridges ... At first it was exciting to see my soft-spoken husband treated like a king dispensing justice. He was always polite, respectful to the elderly and quietly authoritative. He said little and nodded often, but the few words he uttered carried conviction. 'Call a nail a nail, a rivet a rivet,' he'd say. Younger men were harder to pacify; they would return again and again, angrier and angrier. It was my job to soothe them with cups of tea, and some-times the offer of a meal.

I felt the pull of the factory again. It was flattering to be treated with such reverence, and the employees' gratitude was touching. A family would come on their knees to thank Zhiying for making sure they lived in a house rather than a shed with a leaky roof; wives would offer heartfelt thanks when their wayward husbands were prevented from sinking into disgrace. Old women offered words of gratitude for their menfolk's decent burials. All of this Zhiying shared with me, the first lady of the factory. They addressed me as 'Teacher Wenya', a term of respect, affectionate but not familiar. 'When a person obtains the Truth of Tao, his chickens and dogs can go to heaven with him,' says the old proverb, and it seemed that I had benefited in this way from Zhiying's promotion.

There were other visitors, too – those who came with fawning smiles and well-wrapped gifts. They appeared at night and spoke in hushed tones, pressing thick brown envelopes on Zhiying. He never accepted them, although once or twice we found them hidden at the back of the sofa, or by the shoe shelf. Zhiying always returned them. The workers came with presents too, but those did not compare with the others. Once, I found an envelope filled with cash and stopped counting after I had reached five hundred *yuan*.

It was then that I began to dread the visitors. Zhiying would explain that he didn't have the power to give them a house, a job, permission to move to another department, compensation for injury – they had to go through the right channels, but they never believed him. All he had to do was say the word, they averred. I saw how upset he was by such visits, and how stern he looked when he turned away those who tried to bribe him. But I also saw and shared his delight when he could right a wrong and give an underdog the upper hand.

A man in a long coat hovered nearby a little too long, arousing my suspicion. Although I was sure he couldn't be a visitor so early, I hurried to finish dressing. I did not want any distraction today.

By ten o'clock I was boarding the bus from the city centre. I was amazed by how long the ride took. I was sure there hadn't been as many cars on the roads when we had lived here. On the whole, the suburb then had been a pleasant place to live, but now it seemed to have been engulfed by the city. Dust and chemicals were carried here on the wind, so that even the speedily assembled new buildings looked shabby. I strained to see the factory, and spotted Hat Hill, then the outline of the chimney. Though so much had changed, it was still a homecoming. It was not the first time I had come back since I had buried Mother and Xiao Tao, but today I was sure I had done right in making it my loved ones' last resting place. Whatever else happened, Hat Hill would stand for eternity.

I got off the bus and felt the spring sun's warmth on my face; there was no dust, although the wind was blowing. The hill was so close that I could make out the individual graves dotted half-way up. First, though, I had to meet Zhenzhen. We had moved closer to the river, but she had gone further up the hill beside the park, where rows of three-storey apartment blocks had been built for retired factory workers.

She must have seen me coming because she was holding the door open as I panted up the last flight of stairs. 'Zhiying will see us there,' I said, as she glanced behind me. 'He's got a meeting this morning.' I stepped into her flat. 'Cheng Ming?' I asked. Zhenzhen had told me he'd be here to meet us.

She shook her head.

'Not again?'

'He said it would upset him too much.'

I nodded. It wasn't the first time he had changed his mind at the last minute. After the incident at the Bright Light Stadium, he and Zhenzhen had been demoted to menial jobs at the factory, but when Zhiying had become director he had reinstated them. Zhenzhen was a singer once more, which she loved, but Cheng Ming had asked to be transferred to the park. These days, he kept himself to himself – it was only through Zhenzhen that I heard the occasional snippet of news about him. Every Qing Ming, Zhiying and I would invite him to come with us to Lao Gao's grave, but he'd either refuse or promise to come, then fail to turn up. I was pondering this when I noticed the red top Zhenzhen was wearing. 'That's a bit bright for today, isn't it?'

She laughed. 'I put it on for him. It was his favourite. I was wearing it when we first met.'

'At that Beijing conference?' I said. 'Zhiying's still annoyed that Lao Gao wasn't at our wedding.'

She giggled, and the fabric strained – it was too tight for her now, but I didn't point it out. 'If I tell you something else, will you promise not to pass it on to Zhiying?'

'What?'

'For the last two days of the conference, we . . . well, we weren't there.'

'No?'

'I knew I had only two days to convince him to marry me.'

'What did you do to the poor man?'

'I pretended to be homesick for the south and made him take me to the summer palace where we could see the Suzhou Bridge, and then he had to take me to a restaurant that served sweet southern dumplings.' Her cheeks were red.

I took off my shoes and put on the slippers she'd laid out for me. Then I went to the window. To get to it, I had to manoeuvre myself through a maze of pot plants. Each time I visited her she had an addition to her collection. This latest one was a giant with feathery leaves that fanned out to either side. No doubt Cheng Ming had given it to her.

I let my thoughts dwell on him for a moment. The picture I held in my mind of him as a young man contrasted with his now wasted figure. He seemed to have aged more than Zhenzhen – more than any of us. I was used to it now, but when I had first seen him after Lao Gao's death, during the spring festival, his appearance had shocked me. By then Zhiying was working at the library and the worst of our sufferings appeared to be over. The factory had put on a lantern show at the park and we had braved the cold to decipher the riddles that hung on strips of paper beneath the lanterns. We bumped into Zhenzhen, accompanied by a tall, vaguely familiar man. If Zhenzhen hadn't exclaimed, 'Cheng Ming, why don't you say hello to Wenya?' I would never have recognised him. The bright, elegant young man I had once known was now prematurely middle-aged, with a hunted, nervous look. Lao Gao's death had affected him deeply, I thought.

I stepped past the last of the plants to the window. I was aware that Zhenzhen was beside me, but I didn't say anything. On the horizon, near the river, I could see the factory's giant chimneys, smoke puffing out. Below I glimpsed the rows of workshops – built since Zhiying had become director. Further down, near the railway line, I spotted the administration block, also new, where Zhiying would sit in meeting after meeting. Complexes such as this were a common enough sight at the edge of most cities, but Zhenzhen and I shared an attachment to ours. These scenes might not be pretty, and not all of the memories associated with them were pleasant, but this was our place. The East Wind life was the only one I knew. I understood why she wouldn't move elsewhere.

I turned, and my eyes caught something on the wall – the photo I had sent to her with Zhiying when she was briefly imprisoned for singing the Korean folk song, in memory of her husband. The original had been the size of a postcard, but the copy in front of me was three or four times bigger, a little blurred but still vivid.

'I decided to get it blown up,' she said.

'At the town studio?'

She nodded. I shook my head. Lao Gao's name was as yet uncleared and in our town his face was still recognisable. 'The young man at the studio said he liked it,' Zhenzhen said. 'He even said he'd teach me to take photographs one day.'

I pointed at the paper flower Lao Gao wore on the front of his army uniform. 'Who did you say he was?'

'I told him the truth. I said he was my husband, a war hero.'

She embraced me from behind. 'I know – I must be mad. Cheng Ming nearly killed me. You should have seen his face when he saw it! He's still so angry with me that he's refused to come into the flat.' She giggled.

I remembered the day when Zhiying had run home to tell me that Zhenzhen had been released. The testimony of the Korean singer had set her free. Was singing her country's folk songs a crime? she had asked, and Zhenzhen had been bundled out to avoid a diplomatic row. It was a miracle, everyone said. Lao Gao's *mingda* had been of little use to him at the end but it had rubbed off on her: perhaps he was protecting her from beyond the grave.

'I don't understand,' I said. 'Last time I saw you, you said you wanted to get rid of everything that reminded you of Lao Gao – you had to move on.'

She sighed. 'I feel so confused, Wenya. The more I want to be free, the more I miss him.'

The fine lines at the corners of her eyes deepened as she

smiled. She clapped her hands. 'Do you want tea now or afterwards?'

'Afterwards. Zhiying will be waiting for us,' I said.

'Time to go, then.' She winked. 'I'm sure Director Zhiying didn't give me a day off work so that I could be idle. What it's like to have high-level friends, hey?'

We linked arms.

2

It was a soft spring morning but there were sharp exchanges in the lane. A construction van was parked at the entrance, and a crowd of people had gathered. Bicycles were being crushed underfoot, and fists were raised. Men wearing green construction worker's uniforms were being pushed by red-faced residents. Mother's nosy old neighbour was gesticulating to a middle-aged man in a helmet holding a roll of papers.

'As I've said before, you'll all be compensated,' the helmeted man shouted, sounding a little panicked.

'I was born here. How can you compensate me for having to leave my whole life behind?' the old man said.

'Surely it'll be better to live in nice clean new flat than in this dump?' The official gestured at the lane, with disgust.

'I want to die in my own home,' the old man insisted. 'I'm not moving.'

Notices had been pasted along the lane for quite some time, warning of a redevelopment project. I hadn't realised it would happen so soon and sympathised with the residents, but surely it *would* be better to live in a clean modern building? Most of these houses had been built in the 1920s by the Japanese. At this time of the year, flowers grew out of their roofs – a pretty symptom of the damp inside. Mother had aired her bedding on sunny days, and in summer the lane was a rainbow of quilts. When it rained, every container in the kitchen would be pressed into service to catch the drips from the roof.

Theoretically, the houses were factory property, and each leadership had pledged to improve them, but as they were on the edge of the factory complex and there were always more pressing concerns for the leadership, nothing had been done for years.

I was slipping away when the old man saw me. 'Wenya! Wait!' I stopped and he came over to me. 'You see what they're trying to do?'

'Yes.'

'Does Zhiying know about it?'

'I have no idea,' I answered truthfully.

'You know they're doing it in his name? He's the head of the factory now, isn't he?'

I nodded, knowing what would come next.

'And your mother was a resident!' he said accusingly.

A small crowd formed round us.

'Zhiying doesn't take all the decisions. Everything has to go through the committee.' I started backing off.

'Your mother will turn in her grave.' The old man tutted.

In fact, Mother had longed to be out of that slum. She had said many times how much she would like a nice new flat like ours. I struggled free and strode away.

'Tell your husband we won't give up!' the old man bellowed.

I opened Mother's door, went inside and shut it behind me.

Every so often I came alone to Mother's old house. To Zhiying I'd say I needed to check that everything was in order, but really I wanted to think of her alone. It was a long time since she had died, and the house had stood empty since, but I still felt closest to her here. I sniffed, and thought I could still smell Little White, who had died here shortly after Mother. He had outlived my mother and child . . .

All of Mother's furniture had long since been moved to my home. Here, even the walls were bare. The only thing left was the bed, which was too bulky to move. I sighed. The room now reminded me not of Mother in my childhood, but in her later, lonely years. Perhaps it *was* time to move on.

The room grew darker. People were hovering outside the door, waiting for me. Mother's old neighbours. When she had lived here, she was one of many, a hard-working ant like all the others, but now that I was married to the director of the factory, things had changed. I knew what all those crowded outside wanted: to remain in the past.

3

It took her a while to open the door, and when she did I wondered if she was trying to trick me. It was as though I was looking at Zhenzhen as I'd first seen her so many years ago at the ice rink, dancing with Cheng Ming and glancing back at Lao Gao. Her lips were bright red, her eyes dark. She beamed, her white teeth flashing. 'What are you staring at?' she asked.

'What have you done to yourself?' I took the towel she held out to me and wiped the sweat off my face. It was a hot day, and I was always breathless by the time I had climbed up the three flights of stairs to her flat.

She laughed. I smelt a whiff of fragrance. 'Oh, it's only a touch of rouge,' she said. 'I've put on a little makeup.'

Now I was close enough to see the pink dust under the fine hairs on her skin.

'Where did you get it?' I sniffed at the fragrance.

'The entertainment troupe – where else? You forget, I'm still their star.' She smiled at me, then added, 'The only one now.'

I knew she was referring to Cheng Ming. She had been sorry to lose her duet partner, and would often tell me that she missed singing with him. I took the delicate oval jars out of her make-up box. The only other such collection I had seen that resembled this one had been Mother's. We'd burned it after we had witnessed a mass rally in which a woman had been made to dress up in her traditional *qipao*, then had lipstick smudged on her lips. She had been wearing high heels and a pair of old shoes had been hung from her neck by the tied laces – at that time the phrase 'broken shoes' meant 'loose woman'. Things had relaxed a little since then, but still . . .

'You're not going out like that?' I said.

She looked at herself in the mirror. 'Who said anything about going out?'

'You never learn, do you?'

She sank down on the bed beside me. 'I think I'm going mad.'

'Why? What's happened?'

She sighed. 'It's been happening for a long time, the name-calling. I find it hardest when it comes from children. They have no idea what they're saying, they just copy their parents.'

'What sort of things do they say?'

'You can work it out for yourself – they involve Lao Gao's reputation and mine.'

Since his suicide, Lao Gao had been accorded godlike status at the factory and in many parts of the city. To many people, his innocence was proven, and sacred. Officially he was still a traitor, but in many people's hearts he had come to represent all the goodness and nobility that our country had lost. They expected Zhenzhen, his widow, to be purer than pure, his standard-bearer. For a long time after his death that was exactly how she had behaved:

defying the establishment and protesting Lao Gao's innocence at great personal risk. For that she had been applauded, set on a pedestal, but lately . . . Lately rumours had reached my ears and Zhiying's that she had disgraced Lao Gao's good name. I had wanted to talk to her about it, but found it hard to raise the subject. Now, it seemed, I had the perfect opportunity.

'Why would they say such things? Are you seeing someone?'

She peered at me, her face reddening. 'Of course not! How could I? The whole factory's watching me.'

But she protested too quickly which gave me confidence to say, 'Zhenzhen, why shouldn't you see someone? Lao Gao's been dead for a long time now.'

'You have no idea, Wenya. People expect me to be his widow until I die.'

She was right. Nothing in law could stop her, but it would not be easy for Lao Gao's widow to take up with another man. For a moment we looked at each other, full of things we couldn't say.

'You're so brave.' I tried to comfort her.

'No, I'm not. I'm miserable. You don't know what it's like, sleeping in this big bed night after night on my own. I miss him and that makes me want . . .'

For a second or two I was silent. Then I stroked her hair. 'Don't torture yourself. You can't live for ever in the past – nobody can. It's not what Lao Gao would expect. He'd want you to be happy. I know that's what Zhiying would say.' That was a lie. I'd always felt he wasn't as sympathetic as he might be to Zhenzhen's predicament.

'Have you thought of moving?' I asked, after a while.

'I'm not running away from the factory.'

'Talking about moving . . .' I changed the subject, and told her of the plan to demolish all the houses in Mother's lane. 'They all think it's Zhiying's doing – that he makes all the decisions, just like that.' I snapped my fingers.

'They used to come to Lao Gao with their problems and I knew how hard he tried to solve them and how it worried him when he failed. He truly believed he could make a difference.' She looked thoughtful. 'Surely some of them must want to move out? Those old houses aren't very nice to live in, even though they look so quaint and cosy.' Her voice rose as she spoke. 'Tell Zhiying to play up the benefits of the new flats. Once you have a majority, things become easier, although there will always be the odd diehard . . . and who can blame them if they want to hang on to the past, with what few possessions they have?'

She paused and glanced at me quickly, concerned. 'And what about you? How do you feel about it? It'll be sad to see your old home torn down, won't it?'

I thought about it. 'Well,' I began. 'Mother never liked living there – though we were there longer than any-where else. She always told me, wherever we were, that we were only there temporarily and that some day we'd go back to our ancestral home in Shandong, where Con-fucius came from, where her family had a grand house with gardens . . .' I trailed off. Then, after a moment, I added, 'But that's the house I remember her in. Without it . . .'

Suddenly she smiled. 'Do you remember how she looked the first time I called on you and suggested we went out for a walk? Her eyes nearly popped out! But I was the director's wife so she must have felt she couldn't object. And there was that time when you and Zhiying

wanted to be alone and I had to trick her into going out.'
We rolled about on the bed, laughing. She kicked off her
slippers and I caught a flash of ankle.

'I remember that winter when you and Lao Gao first
saw snow.' I giggled. 'We thought you were having a fight!
Mother always said you southerners were more hot-
tempered than us . . .'

We met each other's eyes with sudden understanding.
'You see, Wenya,' she said, her eyes sparkling, 'we'll
remember for each other. All is not lost.' She dabbed her
eyes with a handkerchief. 'I so want to be happy again,' she
said. 'I want to laugh and dance like we used to, Wenya, we
were so poor, but . . . somehow life was full and I remember
always feeling impatient to do things the moment I opened
my eyes. Do things alone, or with Lao Gao, you, Cheng
Ming and Zhiying. There was never enough time. But now
. . . Are we getting old? I feel so dried up.' She glanced at
Lao Gao's smiling face in the photograph, then turned to
study her own in the mirror. An expression spread across it
that I hadn't seen for a long time. I seemed to glimpse her
as she was when I'd first known her, Lao Gao's new wife.
'Enough of the past!' she cried. 'Let's live in the present and
be beautiful. Let me do you.'

First she spread a thin layer of face cream on me, not
the Hundred Blossoms that I used, the only brand sold in
the shops, but something else, from a small pink tin. Then
she dusted my face with powder that smelt like hers – I
recognised the scent as her face hovered close to mine.
Her own makeup had smeared with laughing and there
were dark smudges round her eyes and bright red spots on
her chin. Small beads of sweat gathered on her forehead
as she concentrated on my lips. 'Press them together,' she

said, and I did as she told me. It was like kissing myself. They felt dry, so I licked them. With one hand on my chin, she touched then up with the tip of a finger. A tingle of pleasure radiated from the back of my head to the tip of my nose. Then she turned my face to the mirror and laid her cheek against mine. For a moment we stared at each other's reflections. 'The East Wind first ladies,' she whispered.

I stared at myself with disbelief. I hadn't known I could look so glamorous – and I had enjoyed being made up. It had reminded me of how I felt sometimes when Zhiying touched me.

There was a knock on the door. Quickly, she wiped the rouge, lipstick and powder off my face, then off her own. The scrubbing reddened our cheeks and my heart has thudding, making me feel hysterical. We had forgotten to draw the curtains – had we been spotted?

It was only the postman delivering a parcel.

At home that night, I kissed Zhiying for the first time in a long while. It was as though I still felt the glamour of the lipstick on my mouth, with its seductive power. 'You've been to see Zhenzhen again?' he murmured, as he stepped away from me. Then, seeing me frown, he came closer and held my face. 'I'm sorry, Wenya. You took me by surprise. It's been so long.'

He kissed me back, but didn't notice the smell of the makeup.

I didn't wash my face before I went to bed, and all night I could smell the rouge, the face cream and the powder. The old house would be gone, but I had Zhenzhen to help me keep alive the memories of the past. And perhaps she was right: we should live in the present.

4

I knew from his silence and the number of bowls of rice Zhiying consumed that things had not gone smoothly. After dinner I suggested we had a shower together so that I could rub his back. It had always been a sure way to relax him. But he said he was too tired.

'What's wrong?' I asked, a little dejected. 'Trouble at the construction site? But I thought you'd managed to persuade them!'

When I had told Zhiying what Zhenzhen had suggested he had listened and nodded. A few days later he had come home smiling. 'It worked. The residents' committee agreed to the relocation plan.' That day we toasted his victory and Zhenzhen.

Now he threw himself on to the sofa. 'The committee's agreed, and the residents have too – except that old man who lived next door to your mother. He's resorted to chaining himself to the house.'

'Only one objection, then? That's good news.' I tried to sound encouraging but he smiled ruefully.

'His house stands right in the middle of the site.'

The old man's protest couldn't succeed. A cricket,

however big its legs, trying to stop a car? It was only a matter of time before he was removed.

'Can't you . . .'

He shook his head. 'I won't force him. He's got an unblemished family background – five generations of pure proletarians!' He was exasperated, but his last words made me want to laugh. 'Anyway,' he went on, ' "Even the fearless fear those who do not fear death." He has neither family nor dependants, he's over eighty and he wants to die there.'

I watched Zhiying curiously. 'You admire him, don't you?' I said.

'I envy him,' he whispered. I thought I knew what he meant. Since Zhiying had been factory director we had become somehow less ourselves. For a moment he stared at the floor, deep in thought. I went to him and began to rub his back. 'How's Zhenzhen?' he asked. 'Does she still have that battered old TV?'

'Oh, yes.' I laughed. Last time I was at her flat a queue of children had gathered outside in the corridor, hoping to watch a Yugoslav TV series about guerrillas blowing up German trains. Her sparse sitting room was packed with more, and a boy of about twelve was drawing up a rota, so that every half-hour a group was ushered out and the next came in. Zhenzhen's was the only set in the block. Lao Gao has bought it and she couldn't bear to sell it even though she was hard up. Adults were too shy to ask if they could come in to watch something, but they sent their children along. Among them were some who spread rumours and called her names. Why did she let them in? No wonder there was gossip about her. What the children saw, they told their parents. I wondered what they had said about the large photo of Lao Gao.

'And while we're on the subject of Zhenzhen,' he went on, 'you really must be more careful about those hand-copied books – you know how much trouble I'll be in if you're found out.'

I said nothing. The one I was currently reading lay beside the bed. Many sweaty hands had held it and made some words illegible, especially the bits that described what couples did in bed. Zhenzhen had had no qualms about me borrowing it, but had said I must hide it from anyone else. When I asked where she'd got it, she had smiled mysteriously and said, 'A friend.'

Not all of them were about couples. There were translations of foreign books – thrillers or ghost stories. I'd never read so much in my life or experienced such hunger for books. The outward peace of my life contrasted with my inner yearning for something more, which I could only satisfy by reading. I found it harder and harder to communicate my feelings to Zhiying, who would dismiss what I said as sentimental and bourgeois, or warn me of the consequences of voicing such thoughts. More and more, when he came home from work, he would eat in his office while he read reports and other documents, though sometimes I saw him simply staring into space. We rarely went to bed together: I would make the excuse that I didn't want to disturb him and sleep in another room.

'Wenya?' Zhiying nudged me. As usual, when he sensed he'd upset me, he wanted to make up.

'What?'

'About the books, I didn't say you shouldn't read them. What I meant was . . .'

'That I must read them in secret and not talk about them, because it's not something the wife of a director should do. That's right, isn't it?'

'Well,' he smiled, 'I know I can trust you. It's . . . Zhenzhen who worries me sometimes. There's no stopping that mouth of hers. At her age, she should know better.'

'Why are you so critical of her nowadays? What has she done wrong?' I tried to keep the anger out of my voice.

'Do you really have no idea? She . . . You two have seen so much of each other lately. I thought you must know . . .'

'What she did was her own business,' I said. 'Lao Gao died such a long time ago. Do you want her to be alone for ever?'

'That's not what I meant.'

'What did you mean, then?'

'I'm worried what others might say.'

I stood up and moved away from him. 'Don't hide behind the others – it's you. You don't want to see her happy again, do you? You're as bad as the rest of them! We're in the twentieth century and you want her to be like one of those women who take their dead husband's name placard to bed and count beans to mark the passing of time. Really, Zhiying, can you call yourself Lao Gao's friend yet try to keep his beloved wife a prisoner? He would have wanted her to live!'

'Lao Gao's memory is sacred! I don't begrudge her happiness, and wish her luck with her future. She's entitled to marry again – if she chooses the right man.'

'What business is it of yours who she chooses?'

'Wenya! Of course it's my business. We're Lao Gao's old friends, and we have to make sure she doesn't fall into the wrong hands.'

'What are you saying?'

'Who does she see almost every day?'

'Cheng Ming?'

He nodded slowly.

'But they're old friends!'

Zhiying sneered. 'I'd always suspected it and last week I heard that he was seen coming out of her flat very late at night.'

Zhenzhen and Cheng Ming? 'I'm not seeing any one,' she had protested, yet she had been wearing makeup and her eyes had sparkled.

Cheng Ming and Zhenzhen. Suddenly it sounded right. Why shouldn't they be together? 'What's wrong with him?' I asked.

'He—'

'He was too close to Lao Gao? It would be like her marrying his brother? Is that what you find so hard?'

'No,' he said – too quickly. And now I knew why he was so against it: jealousy.

He sighed. 'What they do is their own business, as you say, but living together without being married is against the law. If there's an official complaint, as director of the factory I'll have to investigate. Can't you see where that would lead?'

Now I knew why they wanted to keep it secret. If the affair became public, they faced condemnation and court proceedings.

'Leave them alone,' I said. Even if they were reported, it was within Zhiying's remit not to pursue them.

'I'll do what I can,' he said, 'but you must warn Zhenzhen of the consequences.'

'I will, but—'

'Make her see sense.'

'I can't tell her how to feel!'

'Please, Wenya, even if I do nothing, people will talk.'

'Zhenzhen's fine,' I said. 'It's you who seem to have the problem.'

We slept apart again and, alone, I carried on arguing with Zhiying. But as time passed, I saw what lay behind our quarrel: the gaping hole between us. Zhenzhen longed for intimacy, while Zhiying and I pushed each other away. The realisation alarmed me, but I chose not to think about it. We argued, then made up. Life carried on.

5

The guard at the factory gate ran out of his office to greet us. Zhiying shook his hand. Now that he was the factory director, we couldn't be waved through: he had to be properly acknowledged. Zhiying hated it. I walked a few steps behind him, and nodded at the guard, who smiled at me. He didn't ask why I was there.

I was quite well known now. I'd discovered this one day when I went into the factory shop and heard whispers at the sweet counter. When I turned the two women had stopped talking but I had caught 'the director's wife'. They had looked at me with deference.

It was not the first time I had accompanied Zhiying on a walk round the factory, but I didn't do it often. I disliked being noticed. But today Zhiying had insisted. He said that as we had different days off, it was the only way he could be sure of seeing me.

The welding workshop was hurrying to meet a deadline, so that was where we headed first. I heard clanging long before we reached it. A strong smell of burning metal made me cover my nose. I dropped my hands to my sides – as director's wife, I shouldn't appear over fastidious. Then, I began to cough. Zhiying shot me a concerned glance.

In the workshop, people in blue overalls, protective gloves and face masks held shields, like metal masks, surrounded by grey smoke. As I watched, a pair took off their masks – they were women, with long plaits tied on top of their heads.

An old man approached, without protective clothing: 'Lao Lin,' Zhiying exclaimed. 'Where are your gloves and mask? You should set an example.'

'I was taking a break.'

'My wife Wenya.' Zhiying introduced me. Then he said, 'How's it going?'

'We reckon we'll be finished by midnight.' The man pointed at the women near us. 'We've brought in extra staff so we're on schedule.'

My shirt was soaked with sweat. How did anyone bear this heat? It was worse even than the scorching sun.

'Lao Lin is our model worker. In welding competitions he wins prize after prize,' Zhiying told me.

'That was a long time ago. Now the young people are catching up,' Lao Lin responded modestly. I wondered how old he was – he looked ancient but was plainly too young to retire.

We stood in front of a blackboard that bore a list of names with little red flags pinned beside them. Zhiying paused to study it.

'I've known Zhiying since he started here,' the old man said to me, then turned to Zhiying: 'How many years ago was that?'

'Can't remember.'

'He didn't mind getting his hands dirty. He left the

design department for a few weeks to get some experience in here.' Lao Lin rubbed his hands, and smiled paternally at Zhiying.

When we left the workshop, Zhiying mopped his forehead and took off his jacket. 'Let's go and cool down somewhere,' he said. 'How about a walk?'

The park was empty, but for an attendant sweeping a path into the distance. We stood at the bridge and looked at the pond, which had almost dried up. The lotus blossoms had died – even the leaves were dry and yellow. At the water's edge thick mud exposed the roots. I remembered lines from a poem Father had taught me:

> A small lotus had only just showed its slender tip,
> but already a dragonfly flew to alight on it.

Next to me, Zhiying sighed. 'I wish Lao Gao was alive,' he said, staring at the pond. 'There are times at the factory, like just now, when I think Lao Gao would have done it differently – he'd have fired everybody up, made them go all out, but I . . .'

'You were just as good. Lao Lin likes you.'

'Perhaps so, but it's my leadership I'm thinking about. I'm always nervous when I go on the walk-about. I keep thinking they're all comparing me with—'

'Not Lao Li?'

'Of course not.' Lao Li's tenure as director had been short-lived, he had been ineffectual, and under him the factory had struggled.

'I'm not so worried about the production side,' he went on. 'I feel out of my depth when it comes to the speeches and political meetings. I'm scared of saying the wrong thing or not saying enough.' I put a hand on his arm, and saw his eyes light up. 'We haven't done things like this for a long time,' he remarked. 'I can't even go to the park with you any more – I feel I'm always being watched. Oh, Wenya, let's—'

'The sun's very strong, even here. Perhaps we should go home,' I said, changing the subject rapidly. The park seemed too small. Our three bedroomed flat was safer – I could disappear into one of the spare rooms and close the door, avoid Zhiying if I wanted to.

'Wenya, stay. What's the matter? Why don't you like being with me any more?'

'What are you talking about?'

He took my hand and faced me.

'Someone's coming,' I whispered, as an old man walked up the bridge.

Zhiying cursed under his breath as the man made his way slowly towards us. As we waited in silence for him to pass, Zhiying glanced at his watch. 'Damn, I'm meant to be at a meeting.'

'Go on,' I said. 'I've got to get back to work too. We'll come again another day.'

When he'd gone, I wandered aimlessly around the park. I had a few hours before I needed to be at the hospital. The park was nearly empty, but for a few grandmothers playing with toddlers. A long time ago, when I was pregnant, I had been here a lot, first with Mother, sometimes alone, and occasionally with Zhiying. I remembered how, on those summer days long ago, he had looked at me and told me I'd 'bloomed'. Now we hardly looked at each other at all – at least, not in that way. Something was wrong and I couldn't pinpoint what it was. But I was wary of him, his impatience, his sneers and criticism. He was no longer the eager young man I had married – and I didn't know what he had become. I wondered what he felt for me. We had a big flat, more than enough to eat, a chauffeur-driven car, prestige. And yet it seemed we lacked so much. In our old life, we had been full of hope for our future together . . .

By the entrance I glimpsed a gardener kneeling on a rough sack, digging a hole. Next to him lay a small tree, its roots wrapped in a plastic bag. I had passed him before I realised his long arms were familiar. Cheng Ming worked in the park . . . I started to walk back as the man straightened.

'So it was you, Cheng Ming,' I exclaimed.

For a second he looked confused. 'Oh, Wenya, it's you!' He smiled and, for a brief moment I glimpsed the old Cheng Ming, elegant, sensitive and quick-witted. He stood up and stretched.

'Let's sit down for a minute,' I said, and pointed at a bench.

He picked up the sack he had been kneeling on, put it carefully over the roots of the tree, then followed me to the bench and sat down. Once again I was struck by how hunted he looked. Perhaps the gossip had got to him. 'There's no need for you to feel so guilty,' I said.

He stared at me, in amazement: 'What do you mean?' The colour drained from his face. He seemed about to run away.

'Don't go,' I said. 'I'm not here to condemn you and Zhenzhen. I saw her last week and we talked.'

'I didn't know. She didn't say . . .'

'She didn't say anything to me, either,' I said. 'I'd

already worked it out.' I paused. I had known them both a long time, but this was a sensitive subject. Yet after my conversation with Zhiying the other night I had no choice. 'I know how she feels about you and how you feel about her,' I began.

'It's my dearest wish to be with her,' he whispered, 'but Zhenzhen's torn. They won't leave her alone.'

'Never mind anyone else. It's the right thing to do. It's what Lao Gao would have wanted. You and I know that,' I told him.

After a long time he spoke again, facing away from me: 'You're so kind, Wenya.'

It wasn't until I was out of the park that I dared to glance back at the solitary figure bending down to the tree. The last time we had been in the park together, he had been Lao Gao's right-hand man, tall and elegant, brushing a blossom off my shoulder. Now he toiled like a common labourer. These were crazy times indeed.

6

If it hadn't been for her voice I wouldn't have known it was her. With her back turned to me, she could have been any of the tired-looking East Wind wives just out of work, come to haggle at the new vegetable market. Rules and regulations forbade it, but the peasants from the countryside had rightly decided that the city folk at this end of the town could afford their produce.

'That stall over there sells them five *fen* cheaper and hers are crisper,' shouted Zhenzhen, holding a bunch of chives. I was used to her odd mix of north, south and Sichuan dialect, but it sounded funny in this context.

'If you can find any fresher than mine, then . . .' I didn't hear the rest of the woman's answer because Zhenzhen had glanced round and seen me. Her hair was swept up in a bun, she had made her shirt-collar stand up, and she wore a red belt, which accentuated her small waist. She nodded at me, then resumed bargaining. 'I'm in a hurry. Let me have it for a couple of *mao* and you'll have yourself a loyal customer for ever. I'll always come to you for chives,' she said, and pressed a note into the woman's hand.

To my surprise she grinned. 'This big sister's very funny,' she said to me good-naturedly, and counted out Zhenzhen's change.

Zhenzhen took it. 'Thank you, sister,' she said, and strode over to me.

'What wind blew you here?' she asked.

She looked weary, her face more lined than I remembered it.

'I want a word with you,' I said.

She nodded. 'I've still got a few things on my list.'

'I'll come with you.'

We went from stall to stall, Zhenzhen haggling over every purchase, just as she had with the first. This was the woman who had scorned my *song xiacao*, but now she had to work hard to make ends meet: she earned little with the entertainment troupe. As we were leaving, a woman approached us. 'Zhenzhen?'

Zhenzhen glanced at her, then nodded.

'Has Lao Gao's paper been processed yet?' said the woman.

'No.'

The woman sighed and touched Zhenzhen's arm. 'You know how we feel. One day the truth will come out.'

'Thank you.' Zhenzhen seemed to be in a hurry to get away, but the woman hadn't finished.

'We're all so proud of you, Zhenzhen. We're all behind you. We'll show them.'

They expected so much of her – and Zhenzhen's face betrayed the strain she felt. She had every right to be happy with Cheng Ming, but she was the widow of no ordinary man. At the crossroads, she glanced about to see if anyone was watching us. I noticed makeup – a flush of pink on her cheek, which looked almost natural, a trace of red on her lips, and faint black smudges on her eyelids.

The room was dark because the curtain was drawn. A strong smell hung in the air, and she rushed to open the window and pull back the curtain. A gust of fresh air blew in, carrying with it a handful of brown leaves from the tree outside.

The bed was unmade, the pillows entwined. On the bedside table, an ashtray overflowed with cigarette stubs. Now I remembered the smell – Hero cigarettes, which I'd smelt at the ice rink on the day Xiao Tao was born.

'Cheng Ming's been here?' I asked.

She paused, then nodded. 'He doesn't come often, these days.'

The portrait of Lao Gao had gone from the wall. I turned to Zhenzhen pointedly.

'I took it down, because it upset Cheng Ming. He said it gave him nightmares.' She blushed.

'It's him I want to talk about,' I said. 'I think you two should get married.'

Her hand froze in mid air, as she reached out for the comb. Keeping her back to me, she began slowly to run it through her hair. 'That would be madness!'

'I know you, Zhenzhen. If you believe in something, you do it. What happened to the courage that made you sing at the Bright Light Stadium?'

7

There had never been a wetter October day, or a more bedraggled bride. It was hard to tell from Zhenzhen's wet face, her long hair stuck to her cheeks, whether tears or rain were dripping down it. The umbrella I held hardly covered her suitcases. It had occurred to me that perhaps the strain had been too much, that after the honeymoon, they might not come back.

She glanced furtively over my shoulder, while Lao Cui waited beside me, his face impassive.

'You'd better go,' I said. Cheng Ming was nowhere to be seen. 'Write when you get there,' I said.

'Thanks, Wenya.' She gripped my hands, her eyes seeming larger than usual, from lack of sleep – and something else. I was full of pity and jealousy. 'I've done the right thing,' she said. 'I'm happy.' She pressed something into my hand. 'Wish me luck.' She took the suitcase nearest to her and disappeared into the carriage. Lao Cui picked up the other two, and followed her.

I noticed only then that she was wearing the red top Lao Gao had liked.

As the train pulled out, Cheng Ming's face was pressed

close to the window, and Zhenzhen was standing behind him, waving. When the train was almost out of sight Lao Cui raised a hand in farewell. I wondered if Zhenzhen could see it. I opened my palm and saw she had given me her flat key. I slipped it into my pocket.

Lao Cui asked where he should drop me and I told him to take me home. Zhiying hadn't wanted to see Cheng Ming and Zhenzhen – he claimed he had a meeting – but he had ordered the car for them. It was partly for their safety – there had been so much hostility to Zhenzhen's remarriage. She had been spat at in the street and someone had thrown a brick at Cheng Ming, grazing his head, as he walked home in the dark one night after work.

'I hope they'll be all right,' I said to Lao Cui. He nodded but said nothing – his discretion had led both Lao Gao and Zhiying to trust him as their driver, but sometimes I wondered if he hid behind a mask. I really wanted to know how he felt about the marriage – I remembered my journey with him shortly after we had heard of the guilty verdict against Lao Gao.

'It's cold for October,' I tried again. A stream of bicycles surrounded us, the familiar evening traffic. Today the comfort of the car felt like a trap. What would Zhenzhen's journey be like, taking a train away from the restrictions of our small town with its morality and gossip? My picture of the south was of the beautiful blossoms, though it was autumn now. It felt as if part of me had left with Zhenzhen, feeling light-hearted and adventurous. Suddenly I was truly happy for her – she had been a widow too long. I only hoped Cheng Ming treated her well.

'Southerners never stay long in the north.' Suddenly Lao Cui spoke.

'Have you been to the south?' I asked.

He peered at me in the rear-view mirror. 'Never. And I've never wanted to go. I'm happy here.'

'But Zhenzhen—'

'She's Lao Gao's wife. She counts as a northerner,' he said, pulled up the car, got out and opened the door for me.

I didn't remind him that Lao Gao had been from Sichuan, hardly a northerner himself.

8

It took me a long time to pluck up courage to go to her flat. Her front door was covered with graffiti – 'Broken shoes' scrawled in black paint. The writing was childish – perhaps a child had done it, one of those who'd watched TV in her front room.

It had been several weeks since Cheng Ming and Zhenzhen had left. I turned the key and opened the door. First I went to the kitchen, found the bucket and a brush, then scrubbed the door until the words had gone.

In the sitting room the air was oppressive and I opened the windows. A cold wind blew in, and I heard fireworks. The town had seemed unusually excited when I was on my way here. New slogans were being pasted up, drums beaten and flags waved. Perhaps it was all part of the National Day celebration – or was it the beginning of yet another 'movement'? The pot plants were huddled together like a miniature forest, a reminder of the man who had taken away my best friend. They were the reason I was here: Zhenzhen had asked me to water them. I touched a giant green leaf on the plant nearest to me. When I'd visited her, Cheng Ming had either just left or was about to arrive, but Zhenzhen had never let me see him there.

I remembered sitting in this room, talking about our losses, our feelings about past and future. Live in the present, we had concluded, as we put on our makeup. Now, she'd made a bold step into the future. Around the room, I saw small additions I hadn't noticed before: an elegant footstool placed by the bed, a small hand mirror lying by a comb, ceramic coat-hangers with floral patterns. I sensed his hand in it. I wouldn't have been surprised to find a flute, and I could imagine its music filling the room.

Her bed – which was made this time – brought memories of the night before she had married him. She had burned incense, and we had sat up late to talk. 'Oh, Wenya, they were such good friends, like brothers. I . . . don't know how I would have survived those days after Lao Gao's death, if it hadn't been for Cheng Ming. And now he's made me feel like a woman again.'

I got up and paced the room. The plants blocked the view from the window. Impatiently I pushed them aside and gazed out into the distance. There was the factory, the only world I knew. Now there were two people fewer in it. They were gone, and the empty room amplified my loneliness.

Back on the bed I closed my eyes: Cheng Ming and Zhenzhen, married. A picture floated into my mind of them holding hands, dancing on the ice rink, Cheng Ming gazing into her eyes . . . Mine flew open. He had loved her from the start. The way he had smiled at her – I had seen it again at their wedding as he had bowed with her. It was the look of a man who'd finally got what he wanted.

I had no idea how he had kept it secret for so long. Back then we hadn't been looking, but had Lao Gao sensed it?

Had Zhenzhen suspected? She had spent so much time alone with Cheng Ming but I had detected no hint of anything between them. She had thought of no one else while Lao Gao was alive, I was sure. Their love had been powerful enough to bridge the age gap and survive political movements – even his death.

Deep down, she must have known, but somehow she had blocked it out. You tend to see what you want to see – and she had seen a devoted brother. I wondered when she had allowed herself to notice the love in Cheng Ming's eyes.

I looked at the empty wall where Lao Gao's photo had been. It was lying beside the bed, rolled up. It must have been hard for Cheng Ming to look at it and lie next to the woman who had been Lao Gao's wife. No wonder he had looked so tortured at the wedding.

Abruptly I sat up. I didn't want to think any more. I knew I must bury my suspicions deep inside me and talk to no one, least of all Zhiying. They were married now, the wood had already been made into boats. I slid off the bed and opened the big wardrobe by the TV. Her long coats were hung neatly, scarves draped round the hangers, and the dresses she had worn as the first wife at East Wind. I spotted the yellow summer dress she had worn when she found me at the pond. I pushed it further back into the wardrobe and as I did so another dress fell off its hanger. In retrieving it, I felt a bundle – a cloth bag tied with ribbon. Curious, I opened it. Baby clothes and shoes.

I put it away and shut the wardrobe door. They were not Xiao Tao's, as I had first feared, but brand new. A baby. That must have been the push she needed. She was carrying Cheng Ming's child.

9

I accompanied Zhiying to the lane.

'Be gentle,' Zhiying ordered an official in a helmet. I had never heard him sound so authoritative before. 'If anything happens to him, I'll hold you responsible,' he said.

The man spoke anxiously into a walkie-talkie. Crowds were watching, people from the lanes who now wanted clean houses. A group of four strong young men went inside and carried out the old man; he barely struggled. Then a digger approached the only house left in the vast area of rubble. One of the four walls had already come down, and it took no time to destroy the others.

The old man was put into a white van. I saw doctors wearing white hospital gowns, a stretcher and medicine bottles.

'You prepared it well,' I told Zhiying, and held his eyes. There was sadness in them – this was not the look of a man who had triumphed. I turned back to the growing mound of rubble: a once familiar street had become wilderness. Zhiying whispered to the man with the walkie-talkie, then waved a hand. A whistle was blown.

Construction workers, who had been waiting behind a yellow line, thronged on to the site and I even heard a few people clap. 'Let's go,' Zhiying said, holding the car door for me. Lao Cui started the engine.

'You go. I'll walk back.'

The workers, who had appeared full of energy, had slowed down. They didn't seem to notice me as I picked my way through the rubble. Perhaps they were used to former residents coming back to see what was happening. I wore Zhiying's thick coat, but still the cold seeped into me, making me shiver. It was hard to believe that this was the row of houses through whose windows I had tried to peep as a teenager. This lane had been so full of my youthful dreams. I began to search for objects that had been left behind: children's shoes, ribbons, a broken pot, old newspapers, half a wooden spoon. There was little to find: people had taken whatever they could still use. We had eventually removed Mother's bed, so there would be nothing of hers near where her house had stood.

Suddenly I was frightened – a little girl who'd lost her way home. But this time I had no home to return to: my past life had been wiped out. As I wandered in the ruins, the only comfort I drew was from the image of a woman walking into the future in the sunny south without a backward glance. I wished I could be like her.

10

For the third time Lao Cui knocked on the car window, and for the third time I shook my head. Mass rallies terrified me, even this one – the rally to rehabilitate Lao Gao's memory, led by my husband. Once bitten by a snake, one feared the appearance of a rope for ten years. Experience had made me fearful of big fanfares.

In our hearts we'd never doubted Lao Gao's innocence, and for a while now Zhiying, who had access to confidential documents from above, had said things were changing. There had been shake-ups in the central leadership, and many former cadres had been reinstated in the positions they had held before the chaos of the so-called Cultural Revolution. Soon it seemed obvious that revolutionary cadres such as Lao Gao would not be the only beneficiaries of these welcome new policies: they would extend also to many of those classified as 'class enemies of the people' and 'rightists'. Zhiying and his colleagues had written numerous letters appealing for Lao Gao's conviction to be quashed to the provincial and central governments, and now it had happened.

I stayed in the car which was parked outside the

assembly hall, and wound down the window so that I could hear what Zhiying said. It was December and the biting wind hinted at colder days to come. Still, the atmosphere was warm: flags were waving and drums sounded, as they often did now.

It had started on the day I had gone to Zhenzhen's house, a celebration of the 'new era', as everyone described it. That day, I had feared a new 'movement' – but when I had said as much to Zhiying he had told me I was behind the times.

'Comrades, workers of the East Wind truck factory.' It was Zhiying's voice. He sounded confident, but I could tell from the speed of his delivery that he was far from calm.

'Today is the twentieth anniversary of the birth of our factory. Many of you present were there at the very beginning, putting a spade into the earth to dig its foundations, shedding the first drops of sweat in its construction. Together, through our labours with our hands and our brains, we have made East Wind one of the key heavy industries of our country, the pride of our people.'

I felt a tingle at the back of my neck. I never knew Zhiying was so powerful a speaker. Perhaps he was emulating Lao Gao. I peered at the faces around me, their eyes fixed admiringly on my husband. They looked so different from the young men I had seen on that first night when Lao Gao spoke. Then their faces had been full of hope. Now they bore the scars of disillusionment . . .

'We owe what we've achieved today to numerous individuals, whose collective efforts have ensured that the name East Wind has become well known throughout the country. But to one particular person we owe an even greater debt. Many of us here knew him from the day we arrived in the factory. He fought bravely for our country during the war against the American invaders. In peacetime, not content to rest on his achievements, he came to settle in this poor but proud part of the northeast, far away from the land of rice and fish he had come from. He brought us friendship, leadership, courage and much more. It is down to him that we have what we have today: the nursery, the school, the hospital, the workers' park, the workers' palace, and the famed East Wind entertainment troupe. Our lives would not have been the same without this warm-hearted and energetic man, who devoted all his life to East Wind. He is comrade Gao Yutang. Our hero Lao Gao.'

My throat tightened when he said Lao Gao's name.

When he spoke again I could tell he wasn't looking at his notes. 'But we have lived through an extraordinary time, when even such a man could be accused of treachery, and driven to kill himself. The factory lost a great leader, the country a devoted son and I a dear friend. I'm proud to say that Lao Gao helped me personally and I'm sorry that I did not have time to repay him. I will never have that opportunity . . .'

He couldn't finish the sentence. My eyes were brimming with tears now. Lao Gao's public persona had intrigued me when I first met him but his generosity and warmth would make him live in me for ever. It was the private Lao Gao, the husband and friend, I missed most. This praise had come too late.

Zhiying continued: 'Those were crazy times. There was a Gao Yutang reactionary clique, they said, and arrested not just our hero but his friends and colleagues, too. All were denied justice. Here are the names of those who

were persecuted to death. Yu Linlin, Zhang Hong, Li
Liying, Wang Xiang, Zheng Daowen, Hao Xingyi . . .

'Now let us pay our respects to the deceased with a
minute's silence.'

As we lowered our heads all that could be heard was
crying and a few flags flapping in the breeze. It was
unsettling to hear names called out in a mass rally. Only
recently such a list would have been followed by harsh
slogans and brutal denunciations. I wondered if I would
ever shake off my fear. I knew I should be thinking of our
good fortune, but all I could contemplate was how much
we had lost, not only the lives but the dreams of our
youth. I had lost my innocence, too, and trusted no one.

11

'A freezing pond reflects the shadow of a crane,
Cold moon buries the souls of the blossoms . . .'

I murmured the poem to myself, but Zhiying insisted that I repeat it aloud. Laughing, he threw a stone into the water, breaking the smooth surface. He turned to me, eyes twinkling, and said, 'What was that? Who is it by?'

'I can't remember – it just came to me. Let me think . . .' But I saw from his eyes that he wasn't really interested.

Another night of celebration. Zhiying was drunk again, and still high on his speech – for which he had been widely congratulated. People kept coming up to shake his hand and reminisce. For once he sounded casual and warm as he chatted with old friends. I had watched him laugh, sigh and nod, and seemed to glimpse the youthful Zhiying I had once known. When he had suggested a late-evening walk in the park he had spoken with a natural assurance I had long missed.

'Wenya, darling.'

'What?'

He reached for my hand and pulled me to him. 'Are you happy?'

I nodded. It was expected – in any case, I wasn't unhappy.

'Finally, the bad days are over.' He sighed, and raised his head. '"Running dog of Lao Gao, stinking intellectual", ha! Now see who's laughing!' His loud voice echoed in the quiet park. As I watched him pacing across the bridge, it occurred to me how different we were. Public recognition was important to him – far more so than I had known – and I was private, perhaps too much so. I should try harder to meet him half-way.

He was back with me, standing close. 'Zhiying . . .' I reached out a hand to stroke his neck, still scarred from the rope with the placard. We deserved this, I thought suddenly. The bad old days were truly over. We would no longer live in fear of insult and abuse. As he stroked my face, I felt a twinge of pleasure shoot through my body.

'I've sent a telegram to Zhenzhen and Cheng Ming,' he said softly. 'She'll be back soon.'

'Still on her honeymoon . . .' I said, half to myself.

Zhiying leaned forward, his face close to mine. 'Wenya, look at me.'

I turned to face him.

'Shall we try for another?'

I returned his kiss almost as passionately as he kissed me. From beyond his head I glimpsed the moon, and the line of the poem I'd quoted ran through my mind again. This time, I remembered, it had been composed by two lonely women in the classic novel *The Dream of the Red Mansion*. Why was I thinking of such sad words at a time of romantic reunion? I clasped Zhiying tighter to me to dispel the sudden sense of fear. We have each other again, I thought. Long may it last.

12

I stood back to check the angle of the portrait and wondered briefly if Zhenzhen would want it on the wall. How much of the past would she wish to remember in celebrating Lao Gao's rehabilitation? Now she would grieve anew, with the painful knowledge that her new husband had driven the first to his death.

Cheng Ming had turned in Lao Gao.

I had seen how Zhiying looked when he held up the incriminating letter, in Cheng Ming's handwriting, that accused Lao Gao of treachery during the Korean war. New regulations had given him access to old files, which was how he had discovered it. How could Cheng Ming have done such a thing?

In later years, when we had heard other stories of betrayal, we were less shocked. Worse things had happened: brothers had turned on brothers, children had denounced their parents, wives betrayed husbands. But when this had happened openly, reconciliation was easier. A stab in the back was harder to forgive.

Of course, the times were partly to blame: only in a time of paranoia and suspicion would an accusation like

Cheng Ming's be acted upon. He wasn't evil – or, at least, he hadn't been. Could he have envisaged the consequences of what he had done? He wouldn't have wanted Lao Gao dead, surely. Disgraced, humiliated, perhaps – if that meant Zhenzhen might transfer her affection to him. But the lower Lao Gao had fallen, the more steadfast Zhenzhen had been.

Then Lao Gao had killed himself, which must have been when Cheng Ming had repented. He ceased to pursue Zhenzhen and started to look after her. That was when she had grown fond of him. But how could he sleep at night, knowing that his betrayal had led to the death of the man she loved? That hunted look. I was only surprised that he hadn't gone mad.

She'd be back tomorrow – she would sleep on this bed and breathe in the peculiar damp scent of the plants. I contemplated throwing them away – surely she wouldn't want to be reminded of Cheng Ming? News of her imminent return had created a stir: there had been a sharp division of opinion in the factory. She married a despicable traitor, one small but vehement minority had hissed. She should never be allowed anywhere near the factory again; she had been Lao Gao's wife, shouted the others, equally passionate, and had played a huge part in making East Wind the success it was. When Zhiying relayed this to me, I realised how touched he was by such a strong show of feeling. Lao Gao was still alive in people's hearts, he said, and as his friends, it was our duty to look after Zhenzhen when she returned to us. There had been calls in the factory for Cheng Ming's blood, but Zhiying felt that exposure of what he had done was punishment enough. He was anxious not to hurt Zhenzhen even more.

What saddened me most about Cheng Ming's betrayal was that it had tarnished my memories of a golden friendship. So many things in my life had failed, or were broken, but until now I had had those innocent times with which to console myself. No longer.

13

Though she had been adamant on the telephone that she did not want to see anyone other than me and Zhiying, a small crowd in blue East Wind uniforms clustered at one end of the platform. Perhaps Lao Cui had told them of her return date, although he insisted he had not. The station was full anyway, of people waiting to pick up their relatives from the last train before the Spring Festival. The East Wind crowd consisted mainly of middle-aged men and women, one holding a black-and-white portrait of Lao Gao adorned with white paper flowers. A few curious passengers hovered, pointing at the portrait, but the sombre atmosphere discouraged them from approaching. I exchanged a glance with Zhiying, unsure of how she would take this show. I understood her wish to keep her return low key, but we had all overlooked the power Lao Gao's name still held. The air, heavy with snow, was filled with the acrid smell of fireworks. Children walked past, jabbering excitedly. Suddenly I felt joyful. I had imagined I would spend this Spring Festival alone, with Zhiying visiting factory families as usual, but now I would be with Zhenzhen.

She was nearly the last to get off. I saw the familiar smile when she first spotted us, but it froze when she caught sight of the East Wind crowd.

'Zhenzhen,' I whispered, 'you're among friends – they're only here to welcome you.'

She glanced at Lao Gao's portrait, then shook her head, her face pale. It was too much for her. 'Tell them all she's ill,' I said to Zhiying. 'She can meet them later.' Then, to Lao Cui: 'Take us home.'

I had left the lights on when we went out, for although it had been only four o'clock, it was already dark. But the curtain wasn't drawn so when we were in we stood at the window to watch the twinkling lights of ships on the river. The fog had fast descended outside, blurring the lights into a soft glow. The warmth of the flat was welcome after the cold outside.

Beside me, Zhenzhen sighed. 'It's good to be back. I've missed being properly cold!'

She sat chatting with Zhiying and Lao Cui while I cooked a simple dish of noodles. We would have a feast of dumplings later. Now she needed to eat and rest. We could make the dumplings after she had woken – the fireworks were sure to disturb her.

After dinner Zhiying and Lao Cui went off to visit the families of workers who had to stay overnight at the factory – in the tradition of East Wind leaders that Lao Gao had set. He would not be back until after midnight.

I took Zhenzhen to one of the spare rooms, and urged her to lie down. Time passed slowly. I straightened the tablecloth and noticed stains I had missed when I last washed it. The window seemed murky and a chair was facing the wrong way. As I walked about putting things right, I knew somehow that deep down all was well. I wanted Zhenzhen to sleep, but I couldn't wait for her to wake up so that we could talk as we made our dumplings. There was so much to catch up on.

Suddenly I noticed how quiet everything was outside. I rushed to the window. At last it was snowing. I heard Zhenzhen stirring in her room and ran to her.

She was sitting on the bed, her arms round her knees, watching the glistening white flakes. When I went in she turned to me and said, 'I need to confess something, Wenya.'

'Tell me.'

'That day at the pond when Cheng Ming beckoned me to him. I never told you what he said.'

I waited. Whatever he had said, it didn't matter any more.

'He said he wanted to marry me.'

I watched her in silence.

'I told him that as long as Lao Gao lived it was out of the question. And I told him I never wanted to see him again.' She glanced away. 'I never saw him again until the day Lao Gao died.' She paused again.

'Zhenzhen . . .' I said softly.

'I couldn't bear to tell you and Zhiying before – if it hadn't been for Cheng Ming, Xiao Tao and Lao Gao might both still be alive. I've been so stupid.'

I wasn't going to dwell on the past or punish her now for what he had done then. I put a hand on her forehead.

'Lie down, Zhenzhen.'

'I'm fine.'

'You look awful.'

'I had a miscarriage.'

I reached for her hands. I knew how much she had wanted a child. She was gazing at the snow again, her thoughts far away. Snow is auspicious: it heralds a good year, or so they say.

Part IV:
The Factory, Early 1990s

1

'Mummy! Auntie Zhen!' Shanshan glanced back at us and shrieked with joy and disbelief. Lao Cui poked his head out of the window and smiled. 'Mind the thistles,' he said, as Shanshan ran towards the pond, her feet bare. It had been many years since I had last been here, but it felt like only yesterday.

'Watch out!' Zhenzhen went towards her, but I grabbed her arm. 'It's all right, remember? She can swim.' For the past year or so, Zhenzhen had been teaching her every week in the city pool. We watched as Shanshan stopped at the water's edge, her pink dress a vivid contrast to the emerald water. Then she turned and waved. 'Auntie Zhen! Let's dive in.'

'For a swim? In March? Are you mad?' I exclaimed.

But Shanshan shrugged her shoulders. 'So what? I feel hot, and Auntie Zhen and I packed our swimming costumes!' I turned to give Zhenzhen a mock-angry look.

Shanshan had come into our lives when Zhiying and I had given up hope of conceiving again. Even when I was nearly five months pregnant, I wasn't really aware of it – when no period came, I had thought I was going through the menopause. Shanshan had been delivered by Caesarean, and I had been incapacitated for quite a while – Zhenzhen had looked after me and the baby. This was how she had bonded with Shanshan. In those early days, when I was still recovering from the operation, she probably spent more time with my daughter than I did.

I walked to the water. Perhaps I shouldn't have suggested this trip – perhaps I had underestimated the power of the past. The seven years since Shanshan's birth had made me lax and greedy for more happiness. I had thought, rightly or wrongly, that unless I could face the pond again, I would never regain the contentment I had experienced after Xiao Tao was born. Then, I had known no fear.

A hand took mine – Zhenzhen's. Wordlessly she pointed to Shanshan, whose smile seemed to sweep away my doubts like a summer breeze. Of course this was the right thing to do – if not for me, then for Zhenzhen. She needed to know that she was not only forgiven but that I was grateful for all she had done for me. 'Auntie Zhen is coming,' I called to my daughter. 'Just wait.'

I heard them giggling after they had told Lao Cui to turn his back so that they could change. As they jumped in, drops of warm water splashed over me. Suddenly I felt as though a constriction within me had loosened. The bad spell of the pond had relinquished its power over me.

I made my way back to the jeep, which was parked by a tree. Lao Cui was unloading the picnic. I bent down to pick up the drinks box, but he stopped me. 'No, Wenya, your back.'

'Oh, it's all right.'

He put a finger to his lips. 'I promised Zhiying I'd look after you.'

'I can't just sit here – and, anyway, it's been all right lately.'

He took the box from me. 'My mother used to say that any ailment you get when you're pregnant you keep for life. I bet you weren't careful enough when you were carrying Shanshan. Remember, you're not a twenty-year-old. Call yourself a doctor?'

Only old friends could talk to me in that tone, and I obeyed Lao Cui as if he was my older brother. He wasn't getting any younger. In fact, Zhiying had said he'd already reached retirement age, although he wasn't prepared to give up yet. I was glad that Zhiying had kept him on as one of his chauffeurs when the two factories – East Wind and the former Red Flag engine factory – had merged. Zhiying had been appointed director of both.

I'd had trouble with my back when I was pregnant with Shanshan and, indeed, had never recovered properly. On bad days I had to stay in bed. I had been unable to lift my baby, a constant sorrow to me in the early days of her life. Zhenzhen had been my arms and legs.

Shortly after Shanshan was born I had asked to be transferred to the East Wind factory clinic – the workload was lighter and I could drive there each day with Zhiying, rather than struggle to catch the bus. I saw Lao Cui almost every day.

Finally, when everything had been unpacked, we collapsed on to the grass.

'We're all getting old.' Lao Cui sighed.

'Not you,' I said. 'Or her.' I pointed at Zhenzhen.

Lao Cui grinned. 'If only Lao Gao could have lived to see this . . .'

Zhenzhen and Shanshan emerged from the water.

'Mummy, why didn't you come in?' Shanshan's slippery wet arms were round me as I put a tin of Coca-Cola into her hand.

'I don't like the water,' I said and, when she looked disappointed, added, 'but I can swim – ask Auntie Zhen.'

'She can – but not as well as you.' Zhenzhen winked.

Shanshan's black eyes darted from me to Zhenzhen, then back to me. 'Are you two best friends?'

'I suppose so,' I said.

'Even better than sisters?'

'Much!' Lao Cui answered.

Shanshan seemed pleased with this – she hugged me tight. 'I wish I had a sister, Mummy. Or even a brother.' She cocked her head. 'I think I'd rather have a sister.'

I dropped the plastic cup I was holding. There was an awkward silence. Lao Cui rose. 'I'm going to set up the stove. Any orders?'

Shanshan got the first roasted sweetcorn and ate it with her head in my lap and her feet on Zhenzhen's legs. 'Is this a nice birthday treat?' I asked.

She nodded and sat up. 'But I wish Daddy was with us. Why does he go away so much?'

'Because he's an important man,' Lao Cui replied.

'How long will he be in America this time?'

'He'll be back soon,' I told her.

It was the longest time he'd been away. For some reason, the visa had taken for ever to arrive. He had nearly given up hope when it finally came. Suddenly everyone went mad: suits were ordered, meetings scheduled. I hardly saw him in the weeks leading up to the trip. At the railway station I had waved at a husband whom, once again, I hardly recognised. It seemed that each time he went away something changed in him before he left. He was dressed so smartly, in a western suit and carrying a new briefcase; the white hairs creeping among the black enhanced his distinguished appearance. I had been full of things to say to him, but the crowd had drowned my words. In the end, I couldn't get near him so his last wave, intended for me, was obscured by an over-enthusiastic colleague, who followed the train as it left the station. Lao Cui was right: Zhiying was an important man . . . so important that he barely had time for his family.

In the depth of the wood we could hear someone moving. Lao Cui stood up. An old man with a basket on his back came out of the trees, and was as startled to see us as we were to see him. 'Hello, Uncle.' Lao Cui greeted him quickly, so as not to alarm him. As the man approached I saw that he was staring at the drink in Shanshan's hand. 'Would you like to try it?' I asked him and handed him a can of Coca-Cola.

'Thank you, madam.' He took it from me, evidently puzzled. Shanshan, sharp-eyed, opened it for him. The hiss made him step back.

'It's all right, Uncle,' I assured him.

'Are you from the town?' he asked.

I nodded, and pointed to the pond. 'It's so peaceful here.'

He frowned. 'So you haven't heard, then.'

'Heard what?'

'That they're going to mine this part of the hill.'

'What?' Zhenzhen had been dozing and sat up.

'Yes, they're going to find gold. The plan has already been drawn.'

'When was this agreed?' Zhenzhen asked.

283

'Oh, a few months ago.'

For a moment neither of us spoke.

Then Lao Cui said, 'I suppose you or your family will be able to find jobs at the mine?'

The man shook his head. 'I'm too old for mining, and I have only a daughter who's ill. To tell you the truth, this will finish us. We'll lose what little land we have.'

'But you can't let it happen!' Zhenzhen said.

'What can we do? It's been approved by the district officials.'

'You shouldn't give up.' Zhenzhen was angry now. 'We'll help you put a stop to this so-called development.'

Shanshan was fumbling in the old man's basket. 'What's this for?' She drew out some herbs and sniffed.

'That's for bright eyes.' He smiled.

'And this?'

'Mending broken bones.'

'And these are pretty.' She held out a bunch of red blossoms.

'They're really useful. They stop bleeding.'

'Are you sure?'

He nodded.

'So if I cut myself all I would have to do is . . .'

'Dry these flowers, pound then into a paste and put it on the wound. Your mummy could do it for you.'

'You're a magic herb man!' Shanshan cried.

For some reason, this exchange had made me uneasy: I disliked talk of illness in front of Shanshan. She had always been a delicate girl, and she had had her fair share of colds and flu. I went to the edge of the water and tried to ignore them. So we might lose the pond . . .

The episode did nothing to dampen Shanshan's spirits.

That night, we had noodles with eggs and tomatoes – her favourite dish. Then we placed candles on the fancy western cake that Zhenzhen had bought from the city's new cake shop, with 'Happy 7th Birthday' iced on the top.

Zhenzhen stayed until Shanshan had gone to sleep, helping me tidy up. She seemed preoccupied and I discovered why as she was leaving. With her hand on the door, she said, 'We must tell her about Xiao Tao. It's time.'

Taken by surprise, I couldn't speak.

'If you won't, I will,' she said firmly, and left.

2

There was a hesitant knock at the door.

I opened it to find my old colleague Ying outside. 'Well, well! It's good to see you! come in,' I said. Since my transfer to the factory clinic I hadn't seen much of her, apart from the occasional chance meeting in town when I was always in a hurry.

'Wenya – look at you! You're getting nicely fat and round.' She was uncharacteristically chatty. She wore a fashionable top, and more makeup than she needed.

'You haven't changed a bit,' I said, even though I was sure her wrinkles had deepened. As Zhiying's wife, though, I had learned to be diplomatic.

Ying inched in, eyeing my sitting room enviously. 'They told me you'd moved to a palace, and now I see why.'

I glanced round the room uneasily. We had moved in after Zhiying's promotion to director of the joint venture – the apartment was on three levels with four bedrooms and two bathrooms. Also, it was even closer to the river than the last one had been. 'How did you find me?' I asked, guarded now.

She laughed. 'Well, it wasn't hard. I just asked, "Where does the first lady of East Wind live?"'

I laughed too. 'Would you like some tea?'

'I won't stay long, so no, thank you.'

'Do, for old times' sake,' I insisted.

'All right, then,' she agreed.

Silence fell between us as we sipped our tea, so I stood up and fetched a photo of Shanshan. Ying seized it. 'This is Shanshan? What a beautiful child she is. She's five, six?' Her smile was genuine.

'Seven last week,' I replied.

'Such a nice age,' she said.

I remembered that she had a daughter too. 'How about yours? What's she doing now?' I couldn't remember the girl's age.

She sighed. 'Well, that's what I'm here about. You see, there's nobody else I can turn to . . .'

Those were the words that 'visitors' always used before they asked a favour. In the earlier days they had been addressed mostly to Zhiying, but now they turned to me as well.

'Of course we'll do whatever we can,' I said, as I had to so many before her.

'I'm not a good mother.' She sighed again.

I was growing impatient. In the past she had been straightforward and direct. 'Please, just tell me what the problem is.'

Finally I understood what she wanted. Her daughter, who had married an East Wind boy last year, was still waiting for the flat to which all newlyweds had the right. It should have been given to them at the time of the wedding, but for some reason it had not. I promised I'd mention it to Zhiying. 'Is that all?' I asked.

She told me that the girl had once fallen in love with a bad character and nearly killed herself. Her new love had saved her, but without a roof over their heads, they couldn't consummate their marriage. She was Ying's only child and it hadn't been easy to bring her up alone . . .

My impatience must have shown because she stopped, reached into her bag and drew out something wrapped in newspaper. 'Here's a little something . . . I don't know what you like nowadays . . .'

It was a jade bracelet, not the fine kind but a darker, heavier green with brown impurities. Zhenzhen and I had scorned such when we came across them in a street market. If it hadn't been for Ying's nervous look and the careful packaging, I'd have thought it an insult. But I realised, from the care with which she handled it, that it must have been expensive – at least, for her.

'I'm sorry it's so little . . .' she was watching me closely '. . . and I know I shouldn't have come to you, but you're the only person I know with high-level connections . . .'

I rewrapped the bracelet and put it back into her hand. She stood up, looking anxious. I took her hands. 'I can't promise anything, but I'll do my best.'

'Please take it – or I shall feel—'

'No. I don't wear bracelets.' It wasn't true, and I knew she would see it straight away – I was wearing one that Zhenzhen had given me. 'Listen, believe me when I say I'll do my best. You can cook me a nice meal as a thank-you afterwards, if you like. I'd much prefer that to a bracelet.'

I saw from her awkward smile that she still only half believed me. At the door I put a hand on her shoulders.

'Back in the famine you did so much to help me and I've never returned your kindness. Do you think I'd let you suffer now? Besides, what has happened to your daughter is wrong, and she should have a home. Now do you believe me?'

She shook my hands, so overcome that she couldn't speak. But after she'd gone, I stood at the window to watch her walk away. I was filled with trepidation. Something in the way she had smiled troubled me. I closed my eyes and remembered the stern look she had given me when she ordered me to drink the soya milk when we were working at Peach Blossom Village.

That look had been far more sincere than her smile.

3

Shanshan said she liked the cemetery. She said it was peaceful and that she remembered the few times I'd taken her there when she was younger to pay her respects to my mother. Today at her behest we went first to Mother's grave.

We were one of the first families to arrive for Qing Ming. It was cool and cloudy – it had rained the day before. To my surprise, she picked out Mother's grave from hundreds of identical ones. When I asked her how she knew it, she pointed at the pines in the woods nearby and said that she remembered the scent of the tree from our visit. Together we dusted the tombstone and swept the grave, Shanshan with a look of concentration on her face. Then she turned to Zhenzhen, who had carried the basket of food. 'Can we give Granny the dumplings now?' she asked. Zhenzhen let her lay out the plate of twelve. Then we stood in front of the grave and bowed, Shanshan closing her eyes and murmuring to herself.

We followed Zhenzhen to Lao Gao's grave, at the top of the hill. With the recent rain, the grass had grown rampantly; Shanshan pulled it out and tossed it into the woods while Zhenzhen and I gazed down at the view. It was clear now that the city government had allowed the expanding paper mill to cut down the trees that had stood in the way. Though it was foggy we could see as far as the Korean side of the river, and the new high-rise flats on the Chinese side, half shrouded in fog. We were unable to make out the factory, but we knew the landscape so well that we could work out where it was. Since the merger it had taken over almost half of the city, with all the new workshops, living accommodation and offices.

Zhenzhen bent down to Shanshan. 'There is another grave we must visit now.'

'Whose?' She was still busy tidying Lao Gao's.

'This way.' Zhenzhen held her hand and I followed them down the hill. It wasn't far. Suddenly I was panicking. Would Shanshan be upset by this revelation? But I was most concerned by how it would affect her relationship with Zhenzhen.

We met other families on the way and for a while Shanshan was distracted by the array of offerings people had brought: paper cows, paper flowers, paper cars and funny-looking buildings whose names we couldn't make out. Shanshan asked what would happen to all the paper. Wouldn't it make the cemetery untidy? We told her it would be taken away and burned in a big furnace.

A family was busy sweeping the grave next to Xiao Tao's, and Zhenzhen paused. I saw that she was hoping they might finish soon and go away, but they lingered. The woman kept peering at us and tried to catch Zhenzhen's eye.

'Why are we here?' Shanshan asked, and tried to read the words on the tombstone: 'Liang Xiao . . . What does it say?'

'Tao,' Zhenzhen said. 'Liang Xiao Tao.' She bent down and pointed at the word. 'Tao means "waves".'

'Liang Xiao Tao.' Shanshan looked up. 'Who's he?'

Zhenzhen peered impatiently at the other family, who were still hovering. Then she said, 'He is your older brother.' Her voice shook.

I took Shanshan's hand. 'Now you're old enough for us to tell you that Xiao Tao died in an accident,' I said.

It was hard to say it. I saw wonder and bewilderment in Shanshan's eyes.

'I had a brother? Why didn't you tell me before?'

'Well . . . I thought you might be sad,' I stuttered. 'He drowned . . .'

'Why? Couldn't he swim?'

'He was too young to learn . . .'

'I can swim,' she exclaimed. 'I won't drown, will I?'

'No.' I clasped her to me.

'You have to be ever so careful with water. Auntie Zhenzhen told me so. I'm always careful, aren't I?'

I tried again. 'When he drowned—'

But Shanshan wasn't interested in the detail, she just wanted to know more about Xiao Tao. 'Did he look like me? Did he like puzzles?' she asked eagerly.

I gave up.

'He – did look a bit like you,' Zhenzhen said, with a smile, and tears in her eyes – it was exactly what she had said when she first saw Shanshan.

'But he couldn't play with puzzles because he was too little. He liked the sun, though, and the wind, being out-doors. Auntie Zhenzhen and I used to take him out for walks,' I said.

Zhenzhen squeezed my hand.

Shanshan glanced from one to the other of us. 'Poor Mummy. You must have been so sad.'

It was then that the woman hovering next to us caught Zhenzhen's eye. 'Forgive me, but are you Zhenzhen?'

Still preoccupied with our little drama, Zhenzhen nodded absentmindedly. The woman shook her hand. 'You probably don't remember me but we met once at the city entertainment competition.'

Recognition spread across Zhenzhen's face. 'Oh, yes, I do! You're Xiao Jin, who played the piano for the city electricity bureau.'

'Yes!'

'That must be – what? Fifteen years ago?'

'More like seventeen.'

'What are you doing now?' Zhenzhen asked.

'I teach the piano – and it pays well. So many rich kids wanting to learn! Come,' Xiao Jin said, 'I'll introduce you to my family.'

Shanshan was still holding my hand firmly and when I glanced down at her. I saw she was still anxious about me. 'I'm all right now,' I said. 'I was very sad at first, and I still miss him, but now I have you I'm much happier.'

She dropped my hand and started to tidy Xiao Tao's grave. She had accepted his death so easily. Now, I thought, I can talk about him without anxiety. Perhaps I could even enjoy coming here with her.

'Let's go,' I said, as Zhenzhen said goodbye to the other family. Shanshan ran back to Xiao Tao's grave. There she whispered to the stone. When she came back I asked her what she'd said.

'Just "goodbye" to my brother,' she said.

I walked down the hill with a light heart and step.

Finally, I had put something difficult to rest. Zhenzhen, though, was pale and preoccupied. I tugged at her sleeve. When she turned to me, the look on her face stopped me in my tracks. 'What's the matter? You don't look well.'

'He's back, Wenya,' she whispered.

'Who?'

'Cheng Ming.'

It seemed that the past would not leave us alone, after all.

4

I stood at the station in the heat of the midday sun, surrounded by crowds of people wanting to welcome Zhiying back. Before I had spoken a sentence to him he was snatched away to shake hands with senior municipal leaders. Then we were swept off to a banquet at which I had to sit next to the mayor's wife and make small-talk. Zhiying looked at me as he talked about his trip. I tried to imagine the height of the skyscrapers and the different-coloured people walking in the streets of New York, but I felt detached from what I was hearing. His secretary, the efficient Xiao Wu, made sure I had enough to eat. I tried to ignore her. It wasn't until she had appeared alongside Zhiying at the door of the carriage that I realised she had gone to the States with him – usually he took his male secretary for business meetings. Xiao Wu was a social secretary. I searched Zhiying's eyes, full of questions, but unable to ask them so publicly. Once or twice Zhiying stood up and walked round the table toasting everyone; as he passed me, he squeezed my hand when he thought no one was watching, but that was all the contact we had until the banquet ended in mid-afternoon.

Even when we were together, in the back seat of the car, I couldn't touch him because Lao Cui was there.

'Daddy!' Shanshan ran to greet Zhiying as soon as the door opened. 'I missed you so much.'

Zhiying hugged her and beamed at me. It was the first time we had acknowledged each other properly since he had returned. I had missed him, but I didn't know how to show it – we had been apart for too long. 'Let Daddy rest,' I said to Shanshan, who was hanging round his neck like a monkey, and to Zhiying: 'Then, perhaps . . . Are you going to the factory today?'

Zhiying glanced to Lao Cui, who was waiting at the door. 'Well, I do have a meeting later on . . .'

Lao Cui put in: 'Zhiying, you really should rest at home. Everyone will understand.'

'Then I shall stay.' Zhiying said quickly.

As soon as Lao Cui had gone, Shanshan grabbed her father and demanded 'my presents'. Holding hands, the pair went into the sitting room where his suitcases had been placed. I went to the kitchen but left the door open – I wanted to hear their conversation. Since Shanshan had been born, everybody had commented on how much more talkative Zhiying had become. I loved to hear him play and chat with her when he got home from work.

'These are for drawing . . .' murmured Zhiying, and there were squeals of delight. I heard 'school' many times and wondered if she was talking about her imminent start at the factory primary. She had been excited and nervous at the prospect, as had I.

I sighed, and surveyed the bare kitchen. I hadn't expected him to stay. Quickly I picked up my purse and went out, closing the door softly behind me.

The market was bulging with summer vegetables and I bought Zhiying's favourites: spinach, aubergine, tomatoes and peppers. I was in such hurry I forgot to haggle, and bought more than I could carry. It took me nearly half an hour to walk the short distance home, as I stopped often to rest my back. As a young girl passed me I thought once again of Xiao Wu. I wanted to ask Zhiying about her, but would he think I was being intrusive? Perhaps there was a good reason he had had to take her along. A sharp pain shot down my side and I leaned against a wall to recover.

Zhiying opened the door. 'Why didn't you say you were going shopping?' he snapped. 'How many times have I told you not to carry heavy things?' He carried the bags into the kitchen.

That night he cooked dinner as I lay flat on the floor.

Later, after Shanshan had gone to sleep, we sat in our bedroom.

'You told Shanshan about Xiao Tao,' he said quietly. I could hear the hurt in his voice.

I straightened my back, which hurt. 'She's seven and starting school soon. It's time she knew the truth about her family.'

'You should have consulted me.'

'But you're never here! Even when you're not abroad, you're home too late for that.'

'I'm busy at work – is that a crime?'

'Zhiying, I was only trying to do what was right.'

'What did you say to her?'

'That he'd drowned in an accident.'

'Really? Is that all?'

I nodded. He seemed relieved. He must have thought I blamed him as well as the Gaos for our baby's death – and that I'd said so to Shanshan. How could he imagine I'd be so nasty?

'But what prompted you to tell her now?'

'We went to the pond,' I said flatly.

'The pond?'

'Lao Cui took us – it was Shanshan's birthday treat. Another that you missed.'

'I'm sorry, Wenya, I've been too . . . quick. I'm tired – forgive me.' He took my hand. 'We're all right, aren't we?' he murmured.

Later, while we undressed, he said, 'You didn't ask about my trip.'

'Tell me.' Of course I wanted to know, and what he had said at the banquet, in front of everyone else, didn't count. I wanted to hear not just the facts, but how he had felt when he saw this or that, and whether he had thought of me.

He scratched his head and laughed. 'Where shall I start?' Then his eyes lit up. 'I've brought you a present.' He padded into the sitting room.

When he came back he handed me an oval bottle with fancy foreign writing. 'Perfume?'

'Yes, it's called Paris.'

'Paris? But you went to America.'

'Oh, they sell everything there – it's the real thing, you know.' He took off the lid, sprayed some on me, then closed his eyes and breathed in.

Somehow I felt as if he was inhaling the scent of another person. I didn't like the smell. He used to bring me scarves, dresses, craft pieces, things that I could touch and hold. The scent seemed impersonal. He bent to kiss me and I kissed him back, but inside I was cold still. A thought struck me. Did his social secretary smell of that scent?

'Is your back still hurting?' he asked.

The simple question made me want to cry.

'I slept on the plane and now I'm wide awake,' he said. 'How's Zhenzhen?'

'Fine. She's got a giant cactus, it's really ugly, but she loves it.'

He laughed quietly. 'It's nice to be home – in New York it was so hot.'

Then I remembered I had news for him. 'Cheng Ming's back.'

'Cheng Ming?' He sat up.

'It's true. They say he's a multi-millionaire now, an entrepreneur.'

'Does Zhenzhen know?'

'She told me.'

'Extraordinary,' Zhiying murmured. 'You'd have thought he'd want to keep as far away as possible from this part of the world after what he did.'

It *was* curious that Cheng Ming had come back. What had happened had been a long time ago, though the pain he'd caused was still vivid. I had not been able to find out from Zhenzhen what else she knew, or how she felt about his return.

Before we fell asleep I told Zhiying about Ying's daughter.

'I'll do it if you'll do something for me,' he said, after a short pause.

'What do you mean?'

301

'Get some help in the house. We can afford it and I don't want you wearing yourself out.'

'I can cope.'

'But today—'

'Today I learned my lesson,' I said.

5

When Zhenzhen and I arrived, a small cluster of parents was already waiting outside the school to collect their children. I smiled briefly to them. Everyone knew me, because I was Zhiying's wife, but I didn't necessarily know them. I was as nervous as they were – Shanshan's first day had been a long one for me.

When the bell rang the children thronged out, like bees from a hive, and the buzz was such that we couldn't see Shanshan. It was she who spotted us. She ran towards us, the ribbon in her hair fluttering.

'What did you learn today?' Zhenzhen asked, but Shanshan had turned to a woman carrying a large brush. In her other hand she held a pencil case – Shanshan had dropped it in her hurry to find us. Something about the woman's eyes . . . I had seen her before, but where? Shanshan was trying to thrust some papers into my hand. I took them: registration, payment and health-check forms. I put them in my handbag.

'This is Auntie Yun, who cleans our classroom,' she told me.

'Yun?' I repeated.

The woman moved closer. 'So it is you, Dr Wenya. I'd wondered – Shanshan is so like you.'

It was Yun from Peach Blossom Village. Of course! She was older and thinner, but her eyes hadn't changed – deep pools that drew me in. 'It's nearly twenty years since Yun and I last met,' I told Zhenzhen.

'Dr Wenya saved my mother's life.' Yun shook Zhenzhen's hand.

Now Shanshan was telling her new classmates excitedly that her mummy had saved Auntie Yun's.

'How long have you worked here?' There were so many questions I wanted to ask but Zhenzhen had a better idea.

'Why don't we all go home and have tea? Are you free, Sister Yun?'

Yun hesitated. 'Well, I have three more rooms to do here and after that I have to clean two houses.' She paused, and added apologetically, 'And then I have to catch the last bus back to the suburb, where I rent a bed.'

'Do you live alone now?' Zhenzhen asked.

Yun nodded.

'Well,' Zhenzhen winked at me, 'we can help you find another job.'

'You're the boss.' I grinned.

'Good,' Zhenzhen said, and to Yun: 'Don't worry about the houses. We'll help you finish off here, and after that, we'll go to Wenya's house. We can telephone the other people to tell them you can't come any more.'

'But—' Yun looked confused.

'Leave it to me,' Zhenzhen said bossily. 'Wouldn't you rather clean Wenya's house? She's a director's wife now so she can afford to pay you.'

'Is that true?' Yun was plainly amazed.

'If you'd like to come and stay, you're very welcome. As for cleaning the house . . .'

She hugged me. 'Oh, Dr Wenya, thank you so much. I'd love to stay with you and I'll work for you for nothing.'

6

Zhiying, Shanshan, Zhenzhen and I had shown Yun the kitchen, the bathroom and the bedrooms. 'This is even bigger than the biggest house I've cleaned!' Yun exclaimed.

Zhiying did not seem to mind when we turned up with Yun – after all, it had been his idea that I should find someone to help me at home. And I think he, like me, was pleased to see one of the spare rooms filled. When I had first moved in, I hadn't liked the envy, even hostility, of some visitors when they'd seen the flat. I'd felt uncomfortable to have so much space when their homes were so cramped.

Zhiying's mobile rang. The speed with which he answered it made me frown – it was as if he had been expecting a call. He spoke briefly, then said to me, 'It's Xiao Wu. I have to go back to the factory.' I was used to him being called away, but his evident relief to be going out was irritating. He called on his way out that he'd send Lao Cui to go and collect Yun's belongings.

Soon Zhenzhen, Yun, Shanshan and I had congregated on Zhiying's and my bed. It was the first time it had seemed too small. Yun saw the photo of Xiao Tao on my dressing-table and pointed. 'Is that Shanshan?'

'No, that's my brother, Xiao Tao,' Shanshan told her.

'Xiao Tao?'

'He's dead,' Shanshan told her. 'He drowned in a pond.'

One of the first things Yun had asked me was how my children were, so she knew that what Shanshan was saying must be true. What she knew, and Shanshan didn't, was that he had died in my absence. For a moment Yun's eyes met mine. She had told me earlier that she hadn't found her daughter – but she was still looking. We had reconnected through the loss of our children.

That night, when Zhenzhen had gone home and Shanshan and Zhiying were in bed, Yun filled me in on everything that had happened to her. Later, in my dreams I was with her when she had been thrown off the train for having the wrong ticket, when she queued for leftover soup at a restaurant, when she saw the night lights of the city for the first time.

She had worked at a brick factory for nearly ten years – she had found her husband there soon after her arrival in the city. When he had died in a car crash she had moved on, doing casual work, searching all the time for her lost little girl . . .

I woke up to the pattering of rain and felt for Zhiying, but his side of the bed was empty. He had left for work. There was a knock on the door and Yun's smiling face appeared. She was wearing a new-looking blue top, but her eyes were red and puffy.

'What happened?' I said.

Briefly it seemed that she hadn't understood what I meant. Then she caught sight of her face in the mirror.

'Sister Wenya,' she said, and came towards me. She turned my face to the mirror and I saw that my eyes, too, were red.

'I dreamed of the children,' I said.

'So did I.'

7

'This way, Auntie. Slowly.'

When I had arrived at Ying's daughter's flat I had found two young people waiting for me at the bottom of the stairs, with a torch. It was drizzling. As we climbed the stairs – the lifts had been installed but were not yet functioning – I apologised for Zhiying's absence, and explained that he had had to take Shanshan to the hospital for the pre-school health check. It was a lie, of course – Zhenzhen was with her. Zhiying had chosen not to come – he didn't want to be seen taking bribes, even in the form of a thank-you meal. 'Don't be silly,' I had said. 'You're giving housing to those in need, doing your job.' But he had shaken his head.

When we reached the flat, I told the couple that Mother and I had known the lane well.

'It's a shame she never lived in a flat like this,' said Ying's daughter, kindly, and I glanced at the new curtains, the white walls, still smelling of paint, the colour TV draped with a velvet cover, the fridge, the huge chest of drawers and the large mirror. Compared to what Zhiying and I had had, newly married couples were well kitted out.

Our short tour of the flat finished – it was very small with only one bedroom. When the child arrived, they would realise how tiny it was. But for now it would do. I raised my wine glass: 'To your lovely new home,' I said, and saw that the girl was pregnant. They must have consummated their marriage, after all.

Ying put food on my plate. 'Eat. Try the pepper – I cooked it myself. Do you think the beef is tender enough? I bought it at the peasant market. Do you still not like lamb? Taste it – it isn't like lamb at all, is it? If you deep fry it like this the funny smell goes.'

'A guest will follow the will of the host,' as the saying goes. I laughed and picked up my chopsticks again.

Dessert was toffee apple, which Ying brought in from the kitchen. I told her it was my favourite.

'I know – that's why I made it. You always liked apples.'

'Your mother and I go back years, you know,' I said to the daughter.

Ying sighed. 'When we went to Peach Blossom Village, we weren't much older than these two.'

'Talking of Peach Blossom Village . . .' I told her of my chance meeting with Yun.

The young couple listened with wide eyes as if we were telling stories from another world. But soon their eyes glazed – it was understandable, I thought. They had no idea of what it had been like in those days. When I looked at the new flat and the table full of food, even I found it hard to believe that we had once starved, and that some, like Yun, had been desperate enough to give away their children. I saw from her expression that Ying had had the same thought.

By the time we had finished the toffee apples Ying and

I were back on our old, close footing. We promised each other we'd try harder to see each other. As I stood up to leave, my back twinged and I winced. Ying's daughter held my arm to steady me and Ying explained that I had been in pain since my pregnancy.

'But you have a lovely daughter,' the young woman said. 'I'm sure it's all worth it.'

'Worth it? She's the most beautiful child. Wenya, let's have a toast,' Ying said, her face red, a little drunk. 'A lovely daughter, and a rich husband who adores you. How does it feel to be so lucky?'

I lowered my eyes. I supposed I was lucky. Shanshan was my pride and joy and Zhiying was successful . . . but Ying did not know the true state of my marriage.

Ying took my silence the wrong way: 'Don't be modest! Zhiying's got such a reputation for being fair and just, you don't find such men any more, not in this day and age!' I could only nod. It was true there were many corrupt officials around, but Zhiying was not one of them.

When I set out it was still raining. Ying offered to come with me, but I declined. I hadn't far to go, I insisted. The truth was that I wanted to walk alone. After my hosts had disappeared inside, I stood at the entrance to their compound, trying to work out where I was in the old lane. The twelve-storey building was on the site of mother's old house, but I did not want to tell them that. But I couldn't concentrate: I kept thinking of the young couple, their astonishment when Ying and I had recalled the past. They were untroubled by the fear we had known and had only the future to look forward to.

We lived in two different worlds. Ying and I would forever be looking backwards; the past was a heavy burden that we were reluctant to let go, however tempting it seemed. I had helped Ying in return for the care she had shown me all those years ago. And the old affection was still there. But as I walked away, I felt uneasy: I didn't blame her for coming to me for help – in her shoes I'd have done the same – but was it right that I had the power now to give away something that wasn't mine to give? All I'd had to do was talk to Zhiying, and although it was true that the pair were entitled to a flat, as stated in the factory charter, dozens of other newly married couples were in the same situation. They wouldn't get a flat quickly because they didn't know me. And I had just learned that after the couple had lived in the flat for ten years, they could buy it from the factory at a discount. Quite a little investment! I couldn't have refused Ying – I lived by the maxim 'The debt of a drop of water should be repaid with a flowing fountain,' and she deserved my help. Yet I still didn't feel altogether comfortable with what I had done – even though I had broken no rules.

The past was not a place to visit lightly.

8

The hot tea burned my lips. When Zhenzhen had rung to say she needed to talk to me at her house, I'd had a feeling I knew what the conversation would be about. Ever since we had discovered that Cheng Ming had come back from the south, I had been on edge. Zhenzhen hadn't said much, but I knew she was upset about it. He could have been in the city for any number of reasons, but I wasn't naïve enough to believe that his return had nothing to do with Zhenzhen. I put my cup down. 'Has he been in touch?' I asked.

She shook her head. 'He wouldn't dare.'

'But he knows where you are?'

'I suppose so. He's rich. The woman I met at the cemetery told me he had an apartment in the Grand Riveria hotel.'

'What line of business is he in?'

'Property development, among other things.' Suddenly she laughed. 'Can you believe it? Cheng Ming, a businessman!'

Lao Gao had once said of him, 'I'm so proud of the lad. If he puts his mind to something, he can do it. Anything –

you show him something once and he'll do it better than you can.' He could play the flute, talk about poetry, and make money too. He had brains, a keen sense of opportunity, and was certainly not averse to risk-taking. Why had he come back now? I knew he had tried to contact Zhenzhen a few times after her return from the south. She had thrown away his letters unread, and as far as she was concerned, he might as well be dead.

There had been no other man in her life. She had been a devoted auntie to Shanshan – a second mother, a better one than I – and a sister to me. I could go without seeing Zhiying for months when he was travelling, but if I didn't see Zhenzhen for one day I felt something missing. I'd never doubted her friendship, after all that we'd been through.

But now, as I watched her pace up and down, I was worried. A lotus root may snap but its fibres stay joined. Was it so easy for her to erase all those memories, to be free of her attachment to him? She had once risked every-thing for Cheng Ming – she had carried his child – and what he had done to her first husband was despicable, but perhaps she had softened. Perhaps she wanted to see him.

'What if he's come to ask for forgiveness?' I said slowly. She went very pale, and turned her face to Lao Gao's portrait on the wall above me. It had faded and the edges were yellowed. Death leaves such a mark on us. Shanshan's birth had healed my grief for Xiao Tao, but when people asked me how many children I had, it was hard to tell them I had only one. Yet I couldn't bear to say, 'Two,' because then I had to explain what had happened to the other. Sometimes Zhenzhen was with me when the subject came up and I saw my agony on her face.

'If Lao Gao hadn't died, perhaps I might have been able to forgive him,' she said quietly. 'But Wenya, I know he didn't come for that, I just know it.'

'Whatever happens, don't be afraid,' I said. 'You've got us.'

9

The banquet was held in the big and noisy Sea Food City restaurant. As Zhiying introduced each guest to me, my face muscles strained to continue smiling. The stiff suit I wore was uncomfortable in the cool, damp room – the air-conditioning was switched on but I still perspired. As official banquets went, this wasn't the worst. Apart from the three officials from the Provincial Economic Bureau, who were directly responsible for the factory, I was surrounded by people I knew: Zhenzhen, who sat opposite, Zhiying, his secretary Xiao Wu, two workshop heads and a man from Sales. As usual, we were there with one aim: to cultivate the officials so that they would make things easier for the factory. I understood from Zhiying that they were there for the annual inspection and to determine the factory's quotas for next year.

As the merged new company had gone from strength to strength, the quotas had been set higher and higher. It would be all right if things went well, but some years, like the year before last when there had been a steel shortage, production was down and the quotas were not reached. Workers complained at cuts in bonuses, and if it had not been for the reserves, Zhiying's leadership would have been in serious trouble. Now they played cat-and-mouse with the Provincial Economic Bureau: they would deliberately produce less than they could for the year so that the next quotas were set lower. But the bureau had caught wind of this and had come to investigate. They had been in the factory for a week now and the purpose of this banquet was to leave them with a good impression of the factory and an awareness of the problems facing it, which might result in low production figures. I knew that, for the factory's sake, Zhiying had no choice but to do this yet I still felt as if we were cheating. Some day, I feared, he would be caught.

The table was covered with rich food in fine china, barely touched. However many such formal banquets I went to, and however sophisticated the dishes, I could never eat much. Perhaps the splendour of the gold and red decorations inhibited me, or the four young waitresses in red silk who watched my every move. Possibly it was the sheer amount of food: the eyes feasted and the stomach felt full.

I caught snippets of conversations between Zhenzhen and the bureau chief, a thin bespectacled man. From his appearance I gathered he was a southerner. '. . . and sweet osmanthus wine to go with it,' he was enthusing. 'They belong together. The strong fragrance of the wine somehow offsets the earthy flavour of the river crabs . . . but as for the sea crabs . . .'

He picked at a piece of crab on his plate, which had been alive about half an hour ago – we had taken him to the tank where they were kept and he had selected those he liked the look of. 'I must say, for sea crab, though, this tastes quite decent. I like the ginger paste with it.'

'Have some more wine.' Xiao Wu tried to pour some into the man's cup, but Zhenzhen stopped her.

'Wait. Why don't we have some osmanthus wine to compare?' She rose and called for the waitress, who brought a bottle. The man sipped, nodded and smiled. Then he leaned back and sighed. 'It makes you want to do this every day, doesn't it? Local wine and freshly caught crab. Alas, once one retires, nowadays, life isn't so rosy.'

Zhenzhen smiled. 'Why retire? Lao Zhang, you have a bright future. I heard on the grapevine that the Central Bureau beckons.'

'Oh, no, no – nonsense. I'm one of the oldest in the Provincial Bureau – I've even planned my retirement party!'

'You have a southern accent, Lao Zhang. May I ask where you're from?'

'Yong Zhou.'

'Really? Which part?'

'Gusu district originally. Why?'

'You're a fellow countryman!' Suddenly Zhenzhen's accent switched into the soft tone I hadn't heard for a long time. It was only when she talked like this that I was reminded she was not from our part of the country. 'I was born there,' she said, 'and stayed until I was five when I moved with my parents to Cloud Town.'

Zhiying and I exchanged a glance. We watched their animated faces and knew that all was well, though it was a struggle to follow their conversation as the accent became stronger and their speech faster.

'Lao Zhang was sent here during the Cultural Revolution, as a disgraced rightist. He married a local girl and stayed,' Zhenzhen told us in our own accent.

Lao Zhang also switched to Mandarin, which we could more easily understand. 'I've just realised who Zhenzhen is! I met Lao Gao twenty-five – no, twenty-seven years ago, at the Party school in the countryside. We two "bad elements" were in the same so-called "cowshed", Lao Gao and I, and I stole some sweetcorn from a nearby field, which I shared with him. Oh, it was so good.' His eyes passed over the food in front of him. 'Food was so delicious back then.'

Zhenzhen counted on her fingers. 'It must have been when the investigation started, when Lao Gao was first accused of being a traitor.'

The man nodded thoughtfully. 'How tragically it turned out. What a great loss to us all.'

Zhenzhen looked him in the eyes. 'And what made you a rightist?'

Lao Zhang took off his glasses, blew on them and began to clean the lenses with the tablecloth. 'It was something silly I said during a meeting about Chairman Mao not being perfect. It wouldn't seem like much now that we know he was no god, but then . . .' He smiled at Zhenzhen, as if they were old friends. 'We were naïve, weren't we? These days, it's hard to imagine anyone suffering as we did over mere words. But what price "principles" or "ideals" now? Now only money talks.'

Without trying, Zhenzhen had won the factory a useful ally and a firm friend in the Provincial Economic Bureau. The wining and dining had helped our cause, but nothing could match the bond of a shared hardship. From then on, we felt confident Lao Zhang was on our side. Towards the end of the meal, I no longer felt we were networking for

Zhiying's business, we were reminiscing. Idealism had been the essence of our generation – we had lived and died for our principles, and were united in confusion and disappointment at what was happening now. Though we had benefited as much as many others had from the economic reforms, we found the increasing gap between rich and poor unsettling. Back then everybody had been poor. Perhaps that was why the sale of state industries to individuals was the most bitter pill to swallow. A handful of people were making huge fortunes at the expense of many, which went against everything we had believed in and worked for since we were young.

Dish after dish was brought in as we talked. At banquets, the food only stopped coming when a guest protested and said he had had enough. Usually he had to insist several times. But we allowed Lao Zhang to do so just once – we considered him one of us, and I saw that the feeling was reciprocated. Finally able to relax, I noticed a dish that had escaped my attention, a green vegetable. I tasted it. Underneath the oyster sauce, garlic and sesame oil, I could taste bitterness. It was *song xiacao*, the plant Mother had once treasured. I raised some on my chopsticks and showed it to Zhenzhen.

'I wondered when you'd notice it,' she said.

She told me that it was all the rage now, with coarse brown flour and sweetcorn paste. All these foods we associated with the famine were considered healthy, after the scares about chemicals and hormones in the food we ate now. 'You don't eat out much, do you?' She laughed and turned to Lao Zhang to tell him about *song xiacao*.

Lao Zhang hung back as his colleagues left. While we waited for Lao Cui and the other drivers to fetch the cars, he said to Zhiying, 'Don't worry about the quotas. I understand your situation, and you were right to be conservative in your estimates. I don't just speak for myself, I know the others share this view. However . . .' He looked around to make sure no one was eavesdropping.

'What is it?' Zhiying asked.

'A powerful entrepreneur wants to buy your factory.'

'Our factory?'

Lao Zhang nodded. 'I don't know who it is, but he's sent people to lobby for it, spreading rumours that the factory is making losses. You should be careful with your figures – don't give him the opportunity to strike you. A few industries have fallen into private hands recently but it would be a shame to see Lao Gao's East Wind taken over.'

Before he got in Lao Zhang waved. Zhenzhen waved back, then whispered, 'So, someone's plotting to buy East Wind.'

I wasn't convinced. The threat seemed unreal: East Wind was the biggest factory in the province, a key state unit. It had survived so much and had gone from strength to strength since the merger. How could anything happen to it now?

But when Zhiying came back to us his eyebrows were knitted – clearly he took Lao Zhang's warning seriously. He turned to Xiao Wu and murmured, 'Get that file . . . with the sales figures we agreed at the workshop heads' meeting, the reorganisation pamphlets and the ISCM papers. Deliver them to me tonight. I want to look at them again.'

Their eyes locked, and I saw only a moment's hesitation

as she replied, 'I'll go now.' She turned to hail a taxi, smiling briefly at me and Zhenzhen. It was as though a wall had been erected to seal them away from me – even though she drove away and Zhiying stood next to me. Panicking, I clasped his arm.

10

As we left the town hall the traffic stalled. When we hadn't moved for nearly ten minutes Lao Cui switched off the engine and got out to investigate. I exchanged a glance with Zhenzhen. 'You were good just now,' I said to her.

'It didn't work, I know it.'

We had just come from a meeting with the mayor to hand over our petition about the pond and the redevelopment plan. Zhenzhen had argued our case eloquently, using her charm and status as the widow of a war hero to its maximum advantage. It hadn't been hard for us to gain an audience with the mayor, whom I had met at several banquets. He had promised to 'look into it'. But, like Zhenzhen, I wasn't convinced. I had been Zhiying's wife for too long not to recognise the official way of dealing with things. He hadn't given me the impression of someone who would fight for our cause.

The car ahead began to move as Lao Cui ran back. Wiping sweat off his face, he started the engine.

'What's up? Another demonstration?' Zhenzhen asked.

'Road works.'

Zhenzhen looked relieved. There had been so many demonstrations lately. Just the other day, when we had taken Lao Zhang and his colleagues to the station at the end of their visit, we had seen the police clearing away around thirty people with banners, that read 'We want justice' and 'Long live socialism!'

We had driven on but it was hard to ignore the fact that they were East Wind employees – they all wore the East Wind uniform. Lao Zhang, mindful of Zhiying's embarrassment, had begun to talk about his upcoming trip to Europe, but this did little to dispel our shock and anxiety. I had spotted a man beside an upturned traffic cone and recognised him as the old welder with whom I had had a brief conversation on a walk-about with Zhiying. Shouldn't he have retired long ago? What was he doing among the protestors? East Wind's retired workers were looked after better than any others around here – or, at least, that was our reputation. Last time I'd seen him, at the workshop, he had looked no younger, but his back had been straight and his laugh hearty, full of pride. It was difficult to reconcile that image with the beaten old man in front of me, forlorn and lost. I wondered how many more of the people I had seen that day were in the crowd.

That short drive past the former East Wind workers had felt like a long trek. When the officials had departed on the train, Lao Cui, sensitive to our feelings, had taken a different, longer route home. I was grateful, but couldn't bring myself to thank him for his consideration – it was too embarrassing to acknowledge the fact that we were no longer popular. Although no one could see us through the car's smoked glass, we couldn't miss their stares of accusation, which penetrated us like bullets.

Zhiying had sat buried in paperwork, and it was then that I had realised my impression of East Wind's impregnability was false. Never mind the outside bidder, the cracks had appeared from within.

Lao Cui's voice had dragged me out of my reverie. 'They can't afford to be ill, you know. They beg – they have to! They go to the rubbish bins outside the big hotels. I tell you, it's like it was in the old days, before the liberation. Can you believe it?'

'Who has to beg?' I cut in.

Lao Cui didn't answer, but Zhenzhen whispered, 'The laid-off workers.'

Mother was the only person I had known who had begged, and that was decades ago. Despite the revolution, our sweat and blood, a new underclass had emerged. It was a chilling thought. And it did not bode well for the future of the factory. Why were the welfare benefits inadequate? Why couldn't the factory provide for its workers when it had done so well? Recently Zhiying had been asking himself and his close colleagues these difficult questions, but today was the first time they had struck me so forcefully.

We arrived outside our flat. I got out of the car and waved to Zhenzhen: Lao Cui was to drive her back to the factory. 'Don't despair,' Zhenzhen said to me, 'we'll fight to the end.'

As I turned for the door, Lao Cui leaned out: 'I nearly forgot. Zhiying asked me to tell you he's not coming home for dinner tonight. He . . . they have another meeting.'

He sounded apologetic. It wasn't the first time he had passed me such a message, but his hesitation bothered me. I lingered outside the building, watching the lit room in my flat: how warm and cosy it looked, with Shanshan sitting in a chair, Yun at her side, pointing at something she was reading. Any passer- by would have admired it, but would they notice the absence of her parents? I couldn't remember the last time Zhiying had eaten with us.

11

'Whoever it was,' Zhiying said, 'he knew the factory well.'

We were in his study, and Zhiying sat in his usual armchair, a cold cup of tea on the table. His face was unshaven, his eyes bloodshot as he looked at Zhenzhen, who sat on the sofa opposite.

'Are you sure about this?' Zhenzhen asked.

Zhiying nodded. 'Lao Cui heard them chatting about it in the car after our committee meeting. And, you know, of all the members, Lishan was the most ambitious and influential. If he was persuaded, a significant number would be swayed.'

I knew Lishan. A short, stout man of about fifty, he was the chief accountant at the factory and one of the two deputy managers. Clever and ambitious, he was the only one of the five committee members who was not from Lao Gao's old circle. From him the factory had gained a well-run accounting system and reliable cash-flow, but he was not emotionally tied to East Wind as the rest of the committee members were. The mysterious private bidder had apparently been working on him – Zhiying was only

331

guessing but the clues were in the snippets of conversations Lao Cui had reported. Lishan had been overheard boasting about the position he would hold if he could persuade the other committee members to sell the factory to the unknown individual, who, according to Lishan, had already bought other factories and companies in town.

Things had moved so fast. It seemed only yesterday that Lao Zhang, from the Provincial Economic Bureau, had hinted to us of the threat to East Wind.

Now Zhenzhen was saying, 'We need to have another committee meeting and a show-down. Lishan has to be told to ask himself where his loyalty lies. They can't force us to sell. East Wind is making profit – nobody can dispute that. It would be scandalous to give away a successful factory.'

She sounded decisive, but I saw from her eyes that she was not as confident as her words suggested.

After a while Zhiying said, 'You're right, but I fear it might not be as simple as that. Lishan has access to all the factory's figures. It won't be hard, if he puts his mind to it, to produce a different set that contradicts those we've agreed on.'

They exchanged a concerned look. 'We'll have to watch him closely,' Zhenzhen said.

'And is there anything that needs taking care of at grassroots level?' Zhiying asked.

Slowly I raised my hand. 'Lao Zhu's wife's been here three times while you were out.'

Zhiying frowned. 'I thought I told you she was to be discouraged from visiting.'

'You never told me she had cancer.'

'That's irrelevant. Rules are rules. I can't give Lao Zhu

more money just because his wife's sick. She was never an East Wind employee. It wouldn't be fair to the other laid-off workers.'

I was hurt by his bluntness. The soft-spoken woman had been the least obtrusive of my visitors. I didn't let her knock twice when I saw her tired face through the keyhole. She hadn't come shouting that she'd got cancer. After I'd seen how pale and thin she was, I'd made enquiries and discovered the truth.

'I hadn't realised East Wind had come to this – unable to help a family in need. Or is it just not willing?' I said coldly.

Zhiying played with his pen. 'I've offered him compensation.'

I knew that. Lao Zhu's wife had returned the money Zhiying had given them from his own pocket – we could easily have spent on one meal the amount they'd got from the factory. 'It isn't money they want, but a job for one of her sons. She said they didn't want to be beggars.'

'They nearly are beggars. I saw Lao Zhu hovering around the factory vegetable yards picking up cabbage leaves,' Zhenzhen whispered.

'East Wind,' I sneered. 'The mighty factory that can't even feed its workers.'

The pen flew out of Zhiying's hand as he stood up. 'The welfare system has changed, and we can't do what we did before. Wenya, don't you live in this world? We can't just employ anybody who wants a job and we have to get rid of inefficient workers – that's the way things are now. I don't like it, but it has to be done. Would you rather lose a limb or risk losing your life?'

'When the lips went, the teeth felt cold! Don't you feel

anything for them? I'm sure they don't want your pity. They want you to care, like a proper leader – like Lao Gao!' I blurted out. I understood his dilemma, but his harshness was unbearable.

My words seemed to have struck home. Zhiying stared at me, speechless.

Zhenzhen stepped in. 'I'm sure Lao Gao would have done the same. You have to do unpopular things sometimes. Wenya, don't be so hard on Zhiying.'

In the quiet that followed, we heard giggles and singing from the next room, where Shanshan had been sitting patiently for Yun to plait her hair. Though she would scream if I so much as touched it, she had sat like a quiet little cat for Yun.

'We must preserve the factory at all costs,' Zhiying muttered.

I knew what he meant: the factory was a way of life – our life. The school, the hospital, the old workers' palace: to us, this was the world. It was unthinkable that it could be taken away.

12

On the wall opposite his comfortable leather chair, in which I sat, photographs hung of Zhiying with visiting officials. Some names I knew, others I'd seen on TV during the national news. On the other side of the wall there were certificates and awards: National Model Worker, National Model Industrialist, the Provincial Medal for the Advancement of Industry, silver medals for improvement of the environment . . . The chair had a knob that adjusted its height – I turned it so that I could see out of the window, a panoramic view of the factory. I felt proud of Zhiying's achievements, and of East Wind. But when my eyes returned to the room, my spirits were lowered – I couldn't remember the last time Zhiying had brought me here, and, I didn't like its new, showy style: the big black leather chair, the giant flower vase with the tall orchid, the blownup photos . . . This wasn't the Zhiying I knew. And there was a feminine touch to it all, which I knew to be the work of his social secretary.

Xiao Wu helped Zhiying draft speeches, prepared reports and filled his diary. He was happy with her but I hardly knew her, even though she was responsible for our personal affairs. She seldom came to our house, but she often accompanied Zhiying to banquets and meetings. One of her most important assets was that she could drink like a man, a useful attribute when dealing with clients. Zhiying was not a natural drinker, and an unofficial duty of an aide like Xiao Wu was to drink on behalf of the boss so that he could be clear-headed in subsequent negotiations. I recalled an evening on which Zhiying had come home late from a banquet. Although he was leaning on Lao Cui when I opened the door, I had the distinct feeling that the fresh-looking girl was really supporting him. She smiled and handed me Zhiying's briefcase, but then she left with barely a word. Long after I had helped him to bed, I lay awake, trying to remember what she had been wearing.

Now I heard the clip-clop of high heels coming along the corridor and straightened in the chair. A light knock, a beaming smile. It was her. 'Zhiying is at an important meeting and his mobile phone is switched off,' she said, sounding professional. 'Would you like more tea?' Her smile was cool, her posture stiff. She held a blue folder, which she smoothed as she talked.

'Won't you sit down?' I asked, in an attempt to be friendly.

She sat on the chair opposite me. Looking into her youthful eyes, I was lost for words.

The phone rang. We both reached out and she withdrew reluctantly as I touched the handset. I picked it up. 'Sorry to have kept you waiting, darling.' Zhiying's voice. How had he known I was waiting when Xiao Wu had said his phone was switched off?

The girl stirred uneasily.

'Darling?'

I didn't answer. Somehow, although he always called me 'darling', I knew that the endearment hadn't been meant for me.

'Hello – who's that? Where is Xiao Wu?' His voice was suspicious.

I put the phone down. 'It's for you,' I said, and rose.

As I went to the door I heard Xiao Wu calling behind me, 'Teacher Wenya, Teacher Wenya—'

Ignoring the security guards I strode out of the gate as if I had a purpose. But once I was through it, I wandered aimlessly until I saw the park.

I paused at the gate to look at Lao Gao's beautiful calligraphy, now obscured by a crane in a nearby construction site, like a giant hand blocking the view. Where was I? What was happening? I felt suddenly very tired, and tears flooded my eyes. There was only one person I could turn to.

13

'Mummy, why aren't you home?' Shanshan's voice prompted fresh tears. Zhenzhen had brought me a bowl of noodles in bed. I nodded gratefully.

'Shanshan, I need to sort something out before I come home. I miss you.'

'Daddy said . . .'

I couldn't hear the rest – she must have turned away to talk to Zhiying. Then I heard his voice: 'Wenya?'

I passed the phone to Zhenzhen.

'Zhiying? It's Zhenzhen,' she said. She listened to him for some time, nodding and occasionally saying, 'Yes.' 'Well, I'll talk to her,' she finished, and hung up.

For a moment she said nothing. Then: 'I'm to tell you it wasn't what you think . . .'

'He called her "darling".' My voice wavered and I felt weak; I was glad I was sitting on the bed.

Zhenzhen sat beside me, but she didn't attempt conversation. I wolfed down the noodles, and I wanted more.

Through the open window we could hear people outside – the night market in the street below was in full swing, the smells of food and cigarettes wafting up to us. Zhenzhen's street had once been an oasis compared to mine, in which new hotels and dubious-looking massage parlours had sprung up, despite protests from the residents. Until recently Zhenzhen had been used to peaceful nights. Not any more. Ever since the people on the ground floor had discovered they could convert their flats into shops now that they owned them, there were new commercial enterprises almost every time I visited. The municipal government had rules against such practices, but with so many workers laid-off, Zhiying and his colleagues had tended to turn a blind eye to former workers making money to support themselves.

A loud cry in a heavy northern accent floated up to us. 'You used to laugh at our accent,' I said.

'I grew fonder of this place than I wanted to.' She sighed. 'Soon I'll have lived here longer than I did in Cloud Town where I grew up. That's something, isn't it?'

A ripple of laughter surged up from below. Zhenzhen's eyes twinkled. 'You'd think they'd have nothing to laugh about, being laid off from work. You see them during the day, always complaining – things are so expensive, we have nothing to live on – yet still they laugh . . .'

As the night drew on, the noise increased. The food would be rudimentary – home-cooked dumplings, noodles, chicken or meat roasted on a stick over a slow fire. Factory politics were discussed, complaints aired. I thought I heard one or two voices I recognised. Would they talk about Zhiying and me? It was the oldest story in the book – middle-aged man falling in love with a younger woman.

Amid the laughter and jokes, I could hear distant music – it sounded like a flute . . .

Further into the night, when the market had closed and the building was quiet, I remembered the flute I had heard earlier. I wondered if Cheng Ming still played. Since his return, I had often thought of the old days and wondered what had been going on in his mind. It was hard to *really* know someone. After everything we had been through I had thought I knew Zhiying inside out. Now I was not so sure. I tossed and turned, full of things I wanted to say to Zhenzhen.

'You want to talk?' she whispered

'I thought you were asleep,' I said.

She sat up. 'I was giving you some space.'

'I've been thinking,' I was surprised by how clear my mind was at this hour, 'about betrayal.'

She kept quiet.

'He called her "darling". That's what he calls me. I can't tell you how I felt to hear him use that word, thinking I was her. It was as if all our years together were a dream, and I'd woken up.'

Zhenzhen repeated slowly: 'Betrayal.'

'Betrayal,' I said. 'I could forgive anything but that.'

It was his old self, the young man I had married, whom Zhiying had betrayed.

14

I stayed with Zhenzhen for a week, and did not leave her flat for fear of bumping into people I knew. On the third day, after a lot of hesitation, I rang home at a time when I knew both Zhiying and Shanshan would be out, hoping to chat to Yun – I knew she would be looking after Shanshan well. The phone rang and rang, but nobody answered it. I toyed with the idea of stealing back, to check that Shanshan was really all right, but the though of bumping into Zhiying stopped me. For the rest of the week, I busied myself with Zhenzhen's plants, or tidying her bed, but Xiao Wu's face would suddenly appear and I would hear Zhiying's voice calling her 'darling', and feel a sharp pain in my chest. Eventually I had to flee Zhenzhen's flat. I took a basket with me – I would buy her vegetables, I decided, and cook for us tonight.

I didn't look sideways as I stepped out. The news of Zhiying's and my separation would be all over the factory by now. Many of the people here had been laid off, but they would know others who still worked there. I held my head high and made for the market.

The peasant girl serving me with tomatoes was red-

343

cheeked, smiling and attentive. When she leaned to tip them into my basket her strong forearms and smooth hands caught my eye. Then I saw my tired, wrinkled face reflected in her scales. I was an old woman. Suddenly my legs crumpled and I fell, dropping the basket of vegetables. The girl rushed to my side and helped me up. 'Auntie,' she said, 'you're not well. Come and sit down.'

She placed me on a little stool surrounded by tomatoes, aubergines and peppers, smelling of earthy goodness. Out of nowhere she produced a cup of hot water, and made me drink it. When I looked up, her big black eyes were filled with concern: 'My back,' I said.

'My mother has the same problem. You shouldn't be trying to carry all this. Where do you live, Auntie? Perhaps I can help you.'

I didn't want her to know where Zhenzhen's house was. 'It's not far, and I feel better now.' I gulped the hot water and stood up. She walked with me to the market entrance, then waved me off.

In the midday sun I returned slowly to Zhenzhen's flat. She wouldn't be back for lunch, but I'd cook myself something simple and prepare a more elaborate meal for later. The girl's kindness stayed with me and, for the first time since I discovered her intimacy with Zhiying, I saw Xiao Wu in a different light. She was such a child – I couldn't hate her. It must be so easy to take advantage of a young girl who worked for you, who looked up to you. I wondered what lies Zhiying had told her – all those nights I'd waited up for him, only to be told that he was delayed at yet another meeting. Maybe it hadn't been like that . . .

Nearer to the building I spotted a familiar car, Lao Cui

standing next to it, apparently searching for something.

A dark figure crossed my path, nearly knocking me down. 'Wenya.' It was Zhiying. He tried to take the basket of vegetables from me.

'Get off!' I shouted. Our scuffle drew attention – passers-by stopped to watch.

'Wenya, come home with me,' Zhiying begged, in a whisper.

I took back the basket and started to walk fast, dodging him when he caught up.

'I'm so sorry,' he said, as he trotted next to me, but I ignored him. It was only a few more steps to Zhenzhen's building. I felt for the key in my pocket.

'Shanshan misses you. She's ill – she's got a temperature,' he spoke first. 'She cries all the time.'

I stopped and glared at him. 'Lin Zhiying, if you're so concerned about your daughter, you wouldn't have behaved as you did. Now, let me pass. I don't wish to see you ever again.'

'Please, Wenya, let me explain.' He caught my hand and his touch made me flinch. I started to run. Breathless, I reached the building and looked back. He hadn't moved.

15

After we'd had dinner I begged Zhenzhen to come for a walk. My head felt as if it was going to burst. She led me in and out of the maze of snack bars and crowds to the path that led up Hat Hill. She had wanted to go to the park, but I had insisted on the hill. 'Wouldn't the river do?' she asked.

'We might bump into him. And not the park,' I said. 'I can't bear to see anyone. I don't want to explain.'

She sighed and we carried on. The moon was bright and Hat Hill stood out clearly. For a long time neither of us spoke and the sound of our footsteps rang out on the path. I breathed in the scent of the wood, grass and blossom, so soothing after such a traumatic day.

'Did Zhiying contact you again?' Zhenzhen asked. I had told her of how he had waylaid me that day.

I shook my head.

'He came to the office—'

'I don't want to hear about him!'

But Zhenzhen went on, 'He's worried about Shanshan.'

'He's using her to get to me.'

'Poor child.'

347

I bit my lip and quickened my pace. I had only left my daughter overnight once before, when I was on an emergency call. Poor Shanshan – she must be so miserable and I longed to hold her. Suddenly nothing else mattered – I had to go to her. But . . . to see her meant seeing him. I wasn't ready for that.

Zhenzhen said softly, 'You can't avoid Zhiying for ever, Wenya. You have to talk to him.'

'What is there to talk about? Besides, it's not just . . . this, it's other things too. We've grown so far apart.'

As we approached the top of the path we could hear a loud, dull thudding and the earth beneath our feet shook. I followed the brightness that lit the top of the hill. As we reached the summit, I saw where the sound had come from: down in the valley, part of the hill had been cut away. Spotlights shone on the workers, and a gigantic digger was burrowing into the ground, hissing and groaning like a bad-tempered beast.

'The pond . . .' I watched, horror-stricken, and turned to Zhenzhen. The look on her face told me this was not news to her.

'I'm surprised you didn't hear the pounding this last week,' she said.

I had been preoccupied with other thoughts. 'How long has it been going on?'

'It doesn't matter now, Wenya. I've got over it and you'll have to. We'll look the other way.' She held my elbows and turned me to face the river.

It was the umpteenth time we had been up there, but perhaps the first night visit. As always, I searched for the factory but the bright lights by the river obscured it. That would never have happened during the day, when the chimneys would have marked it out. For a brief, mad moment I fancied that the factory had disappeared, like Mother's house and the pond. As if she'd read my mind, Zhenzhen pointed out the neon-lit factory sign by the border bridge. My sense of relief was brief as once again I felt the pain of Zhiying's betrayal and closed my eyes.

'Wenya, I've been thinking . . . this last week . . .'

'What?'

'Oh, nothing much.' She waved a hand. 'It's just . . . Perhaps I'm getting old, but I'm thinking of going home to the south.'

'For good?'

For a moment she said nothing, as if she was trying to make up her mind. Then she burst out laughing. 'Of course not, silly girl! My home is here, with you and Shanshan.'

'You won't go by yourself. I'll come with you.'

'I was about to suggest exactly that and . . . I've had this fantasy for a long time! We'll take a holiday and I'll show you all my favourite places. I'll be your guide. I've been waiting for the right time to mention it . . .'

I asked her what she would show me.

Her eyes brightened. 'Oh, the famous West Lake, the moon framed by the gap in the bridge, the restaurants serving osmanthus wine and river crabs, the willows on the edge of the lake, and you must smell the sweet scent of gardenia at night . . .'

I had been to the south a few times with Zhiying but had never enjoyed it. He had been on business and was always in meetings. The places we'd visited, though beautiful, were always crowded and hot. But it would be different going with Zhenzhen . . .

'Most of all, I want to show you Cloud Town and the river on the outskirts where I often swam. I miss it so much. I've told you about it, haven't I? That was where I learned to swim with the other children. The water was so clear you could dive in and come back up with a fish in your hand. We used to have competitions to see who could catch the most.'

I imagined her as a little girl, slim, dark, slippery in the water, holding a wriggling fish triumphantly. She'd told me her father had been a fisherman, and that her parents, both dead now, had brought her up on a boat.

'I miss water, especially now. I thought I'd better go there and have a last swim before I'm too old.'

'You know who'd like to take a dip with you?'

She nodded. 'Shanshan would love it. The pond was good, but nothing beats a river where you can catch fish!'

I slept well that night, dreaming of the journey we would take together. When I woke the phone was ringing. As I picked it up I saw the note Zhenzhen had left: 'Gone to work. Talk when I'm back.'

'Is that you, Wenya?' It was Zhiying. I was about to hang up when he shouted, 'It's Shanshan. Her temperature won't go down.'

Was this a trick to bring me home?

16

Shanshan was overjoyed to see me. 'Mummy,' she sobbed, as she buried her face in my shoulder. She looked pale, and her forehead felt hot, but she was not as ill as I'd feared. I should have known Zhiying was using her as bait to get me to see him – but I was so glad to be with Shanshan.

Zhiying came up to me. 'They've taken a blood sample,' he said, trying to smile, 'and we're waiting for the result.'

As soon as we had it, I decided, I would take Shanshan to Zhenzhen's and he could go home on his own. I was focused on the future now, and I wanted time away from him to decide what I should do.

'Shanshan was very brave, weren't you?' he tried again, and Shanshan raised her arm to show me the plaster that hid the mark of the needle.

I held her to me and whispered, 'Would you like to come and stay with me and Auntie Zhenzhen for a few days? Just the three of us?'

Her eyes lit up, but dimmed when she glanced at Zhiying. 'What about—'

Before she could finish the door to the consultant's

room opened. A nurse came out, then went to Shanshan. 'Little friend,' she said, 'your parents need to see the doctor for a minute. Would you like to come with me and watch some cartoons? We've got *The Monkey King*.'

Shanshan looked up at me for permission. I smiled at the nurse. 'There must be some misunderstanding. She's had a routine blood test and we're waiting—'

The nurse interrupted: 'I know. The doctor has the result. He's waiting for you through there.' She pointed at the door she'd left ajar.

Zhiying and I went into the office. Suddenly I felt cold.

'Sorry it's taken so long, but we wanted to make sure,' the young doctor began.

I stepped past Zhiying. 'I'm a doctor, too. Please tell me what's happening.'

He handed me the piece of paper he was holding. 'The blood tests result – see for yourself.'

I took it from him.

'What does it say?' Zhiying asked.

I studied the piece of paper and didn't answer. The doctor spoke: 'There's been a mix-up. Her condition should have been spotted during the pre-school health check . . .'

He went on talking but I felt as though I wasn't there. She had always been prone to colds and fevers. A cut took a long time to heal. But this couldn't be true. I leaned on the desk for support.

'. . . Of course I'm not saying that all is lost.' The doctor was still talking. 'There's a lot we can do and some new technological developments will probably make a big difference.'

'Please, Doctor, I'm still confused. What's wrong with

my daughter? Can you tell me?' Zhiying had stood up.

The young man looked at me, then at Zhiying. 'I'm afraid your daughter has leukaemia.'

17

Two weeks later, Shanshan started to haemorrhage and had a blood transfusion. Zhiying, Zhenzhen and I took turns to be with her at the hospital. At one point a nurse told me there was a spare bed in the next room. I thanked her but didn't stir. I couldn't leave Shanshan, even for a moment. I held her hand close and felt the heat of her little body.

I bent to smooth her damp hair, and wiped away the thin sheen of sweat on her forehead. I wished I could go on singing, as I had all day, but my voice was hoarse. Dear heaven, blessed ancestors, Mother who now must live in heaven, give me one more chance.

A hand touched mine. 'Let me take over,' Zhiying begged. It seemed that his hair had turned white overnight. I got up and dragged myself to the washroom to bathe my eyes in cold water and splash my face. When I went back I sat opposite Zhiying, and tried not to look at him.

'Wenya,' he said, 'please let me explain.'

'If it's about you and Xiao Wu I don't wish to hear,' I said quietly. I wanted only for Shanshan to be cured.

'It's about us.'

I rose to fetch the Thermos from the table by the window.

'I . . . liked you the first time I set eyes on you, when you came into our class. Do you remember? You walked in wearing a purple fur coat and looked so pretty. The teacher introduced you and I thought how appropriate the name Wenya was: elegant. Your shoes were a bit big and you tried to hide your feet.'

The coat had belonged to an aunt, and Mother had cut it down for me. The shoes, which I had been ashamed to wear, had been a cousin's. I remembered those details, but hadn't noticed the pair of eyes that had scrutinised me so closely. I had felt nervous starting at my third school of that term: Father had just died, and Mother had had to move house again.

I started to pour water into a cup. Why was he bringing up the past? I let him talk and kept my eyes on Shanshan.

'You weren't interested in me – you ignored me if I spoke to you. The only proper conversation we had was when we stood in front of our class list, which showed our marks. You asked me what I'd got and when I told you, you said, "Well done." I thought at last that I could be your friend.'

The water was hot and I burned my tongue.

'Then I was sent to Harbin. At a word from you I would have turned down the offer, but you only asked when I'd be leaving. I was heartbroken, thinking you'd never be interested in me. Why should you? I was too ordinary, not remarkable in any way.

'But I missed you all the time I was in Harbin and that was when I knew I had to have you. I wondered about writing to you, and eventually I did. Distance gave me courage, and I wrote things I could never say to you in person. I'm glad you never saw those letters – they would definitely have frightened you off. I wouldn't have had a chance!' He gave a short laugh.

'Luckily they never arrived. You'd moved house again. After four years away, when I'd heard nothing from you, I was desperate to come back. And I met you in the street . . . You looked so beautiful. You smiled and gave me your hand and even said yes when I asked you out. You had no idea how happy you made me. I felt so lucky. And the night you became my wife was the happiest of my life.'

The night I became his wife. Our wedding night? For me, the night I became his wife was the night on which Xiao Tao had been conceived.

'Yes, you made me the happiest man alive. Nothing mattered, so long as I had you.'

He bent to check Shanshan, then straightened. 'But something happened after Xiao Tao died. You were only half alive. I wanted and tried to get the old Wenya back, but something in you had died and our marriage withered. You didn't care about me, I thought, and I wondered if you ever had.

'Do you remember the night when I . . . when we made love despite your grief? I felt I'd forced myself on you. It was after that night that I realised you'd never felt for me what I felt for you. The love that had sustained me didn't exist.'

What was he talking about?

'There was a time when you were very depressed, and nearly . . . suicidal, Wenya. I felt the same. What had I to live for?'

His tone was calm, but his words shocked me. He had never worn his heart on his sleeve. The night he forced himself on me? I remembered it as the night I had sought comfort from him. Had I ever been in love with him? Now I looked into his eyes. Love: that word drove me mad. It appeared in books and we heard it on the radio and TV all the time: one loved the country, the factory, the Party. But even when we had been at our closest, we had never uttered it between us. Love was not associated with one's partner. Suddenly I felt as if my whole world had been turned upside-down.

His mouth twisted and he looked as if he was about to cry. 'Strange, isn't it, how one thing led to another? Zhenzhen persuaded me I had to live, if not for me then for you and for her. She said we were her family, and that if one of us died, we would all die. We had to survive and help each other. She bullied me into agreeing with her. That was what kept me going – the thought that you and she needed me. But it was so hard when *you* wanted to die.'

I finished the water and stared into the empty cup.

'But gradually you gained strength,' he went on. 'After we moved to our new flat, there was a time when we . . . when you gave me hope of a new beginning.'

The duty nurse came in to check Shanshan, efficient and smiling. Zhiying's eyes followed her as she closed the door behind her. He turned back to me. 'Then, thank heavens, came Shanshan, our treasure.'

He shouldn't be saying such things in front of our daughter, I thought. I stood up and went across to the window.

Zhiying spoke again, 'Life has been good. We have a

beautiful home, enough money to live well, I'm happy with my job and we're well respected. I know I should be content. But I've never had your full attention, and after Shanshan's birth, you just threw yourself into being a mother. I suppose I felt ... I don't blame you, but suddenly someone seemed to admire me, and I was flattered.'

Anger, fresh and poignant, rose in me. I could have slapped him, but I held back. I hadn't felt so strongly about Zhiying for a long, long time. I hated him.

'These last few nights, I've been thinking hard, and the terror of losing you was so strong that I couldn't sleep, couldn't eat. It was as if we were back in the old days, and I realised I couldn't live without you, that my life would be worthless, a void. Wenya, can you try to understand and have pity on me? For Shanshan's sake?'

'For Shanshan's sake?' My voice trembled. 'If you'd thought of her you'd never have done this. Xiao Wu is only twenty-two! You're old enough to be her father – how could you?' I flung my cup at him. It hit his cheek, dropped on to the floor and shattered.

The night nurse strode in. 'Sorry, I slipped,' I said, and asked her to fetch a broom. Zhiying covered his cheek with his hand and moved to a corner of the room, pretending to look at a chart.

The quick footsteps that echoed along the corridor didn't sound like the nurse's – she had a steady but well-paced stride. As I had guessed, when the door was pushed open, Zhenzhen came in, holding a big pot with a lid. She put it down. 'Come on, you two. Yun made this for you – have it while it's fresh.'

When the nurse came in with the broom, Zhenzhen

said, 'I'll tidy up.' The other woman stared at her briefly, then left.

We ate in silence, standing on opposite sides of the room. Zhenzhen sat with Shanshan, holding her hand, head bent. After a while she looked up at Zhiying, then at me. She got to her feet to switch off the light the nurse had turned on as she came into the room. 'The moon is lovely tonight,' she said.

18

Shanshan was prone to infection and had to stay in hospital. She bled and bruised easily. A bone marrow transplant was her only chance of survival. The operation, plus aftercare, would cost a lot of money.

'Have some green bean soup, Wenya,' Yun whispered timidly, and put a bowl on the table for me. The air conditioning was on, but sweat was pouring off me. 'Thank you, I'm not hungry.'

'You must eat. Green bean soup will cool you. Both you and Brother Zhiying are kind people. The heavens will look upon you favourably . . .'

How irritating well-meaning people could be, I thought.

Zhenzhen intervened: 'It's all right, Yun, you go. I'll make sure Wenya eats.'

But Yun lingered. 'Sister Wenya.'

'Yes?' My impatience showed in my voice.

'Here are some "feelings" of my own. Please take them.' She took out a bundle tied up with a handkerchief. Zhenzhen unwrapped a jumble of paper notes and coins. 'My w-wages,' Yun stuttered. 'I never need to spend anything as you let me sleep and eat here and I – thought . . . it was for when I find my daughter . . . but now – please take it. I'll be offended if – you don't . . .'

I pulled her to me. She had a heart of gold, but a cleaner's wage wouldn't pay for the operation.

Gently Zhenzhen took Yun from me, then picked up the handkerchief and put it into my hand. 'Take it, Wenya.' She turned to Yun. 'Wenya needs to rest. Why don't you go and get some vegetables from the market?'

Finally, she was gone. But the quiet made me jumpy. Zhiying was with Shanshan – we took turns at the hospital now. I didn't know whether I should look forward to his call or not. The clock was ticking and we needed to find two hundred thousand *yuan* to pay for the operation and after care. When the doctor had told us we were shocked. It was an astronomical amount. 'But aren't you a chief executive?' asked the young doctor.

'East Wind is a state industry,' Zhiying said, and the doctor nodded – it was well known that there was a huge discrepancy between pay in the state and private sectors, and the gulf was widening. Many, including Zhiying, felt it was unfair: they saw the vast difference between the wealth they'd generated and the amount they took home. We were not greedy, but it was at times like this that we felt a sense of injustice. Although the factory would contribute to medical fees, it could offer only a fraction of the cost of the operation. We had some savings, but nowhere near as much as we needed. The costs mounted with every day that Shanshan spent in hospital.

'I wish Zhiying was a *dakuan*,' I whispered to myself. A 'big sum' was a rich business man.

'He doesn't need to be, Wenya. I've had an idea, but I'll

only tell you when you've finished eating,' said Zhenzhen.

A flame of hope ignited within me, and I ate the soup. I'd thought Zhiying and I had already considered everything.

'I'm going to see Cheng Ming,' she said.

'You can't!'

'Of course I can. He has money. Lots of it.'

'But you're not going to . . . sleep with him?'

She laughed. 'Of course not. I'll make him do as I say, though – somehow. You'll see.'

Gently I shook my head. Was she mad? How could she be so naïve?

'He's still quite keen on me. I didn't tell you, but last week he sent me a letter, asking to see me,' she said. She was a young-looking fifty-year-old but . . . if he'd said he wanted her back, it could be for any number of reasons.

She nodded. 'I know I'm not seventeen any more, but he said he's missed me and I have a feeling from his letter . . . One doesn't easily forget one's old loves.'

Love? That word again. It made me tremble. But, looking at her, I knew it was useless to argue. 'All right. Let's say he still cares about you and wants you back, how would he be persuaded to part with a large sum of money to someone against whom he probably bears a grudge? Are you going to tell him why we need it?'

'I'll think of something, Wenya – you forget the things people do when they're in love.' Her eyes had taken on a strange intensity, which made me both fearful and excited.

'It's the only thing we can do, and we have to do it fast. In fact, it's no use you objecting because I've already told him. I'm seeing him tonight. Where's your makeup?'

We sat in front of my large dressing-table, which now resembled a makeup counter in a department store. I helped her to put some on.

But when I looked into the mirror I saw the faces of two old women. We were trying to trap a man, and even if he deserved worse it was beneath us to do it. Zhenzhen didn't seem to share my concern. As she applied some lipstick, she smiled to herself, then at me.

I leaned out of the window and watched her disappear into the distance. The sky was dark and low. A thunderstorm was coming.

19

She came back during the storm, her makeup smudged. She stared at the floor and I went to get her a drink of water from the kitchen.

When I returned to her she was shaking. 'He agreed to give us the money,' she said.

I was astounded. Her demeanor had told me the opposite. 'What?'

'On condition,' she went on, 'that Zhiying declares the factory bankrupt and sells it cheaply to him.' Her face was ashen. 'Wenya, he's the secret bidder for East Wind.'

We stared at each other, speechless. Zhenzhen stood up abruptly and circled the small table in the kitchen.

'I don't know why I didn't smash his head in. He said he wants to teach Zhiying a lesson, not you and me – he was always fond of us. Oh, I could kill that man!' She began to sob and fell into my arms as if she was a child. 'He fooled me at first – he made me believe that – that he did still care for me. Oh, I hate him! I hate him!' She was nearly hysterical and I held her tight. It was for Shanshan that she had suffered this humiliation.

'Zhenzhen, I will never forget what you've done for us—'

But it was as if she hadn't heard me. 'I'm so angry – why didn't I *make* him give me the money? Why couldn't I?'

'Zhenzhen, look at me.' I held her face. 'Did you tell him why we needed it?'

'I wasn't going to but . . . he seemed reasonable at first and I thought it might move him . . . I shouldn't have done.'

'Why?'

'As soon as I mentioned it was for Zhiying's child, he turned into another person. He gave such a strange laugh that it makes me shiver to think of it.'

'But . . .' I was slow to understand.

'He's never got over the miscarriage I had – he always believed it was an abortion, that I'd got rid of it deliberately, with encouragement from you and Zhiying. It's Zhiying he blames.'

An image appeared of Cheng Ming and Zhiying when I had first seen them together, so many years ago, at the factory living quarters. Even then they had not been the best of friends, but I knew they were both good men. How had youthful rivalry escalated to this ugly clash, in which Shanshan had to suffer for our crimes?

'He said he'd get East Wind sooner or later anyway, but if Zhiying declares it bankrupt now, it'll make things quicker and easier.'

'Give East Wind away?' I murmured. Zhiying would rather sell himself! How could we destroy the one thing that bound us all together, the one thing that had made us who we were? On the other hand, how could we watch our daughter die?

'Wenya, what shall we do?' Zhenzhen whispered. As I paced the room she followed me, for once looking lost and confused. It was this that calmed me.

'Zhiying would never agree to sign over the factory, would he?' she said.

'I'll make him,' I said.

20

Zhiying winced.

'Zhenzhen tried her best,' I said. It occurred to me then that we were discussing a sensitive issue, but Yun's door was shut. Anyway, even if the window was wide open and the whole world was listening I would have said what I had to say. I was beyond caring.

'That's impossible,' Zhiying said. I stared at him, unblinking. He averted his eyes. 'There must be something else we can do.'

All last night, while I waited for Zhiying to come home, I had gone through the options and come to the conclusion that the only way to secure the amount of money we needed quickly was to do what Cheng Ming had asked. But my resolve lasted only until I set my eyes on the piles of envelopes on the table – from East Wind workers and colleagues. I used to dread the sight of envelopes – they meant bribes – but I was proud and moved to see these: all sorts of people had dropped by, people we'd done favours for and those we'd never thought were friends. Hardly a day passed without a knock at the door, and the postman was kept busy. Some letters had come from other provinces. My heart sank. How could we let all these people down? Then I pictured Shanshan, so pale and ill, so brave. She didn't understand what was happening to her, but she knew she was ill. I couldn't bear to see her suffer. And however generous people were, by the time we had enough to pay for the operation, Shanshan would be dead. The long dark days after Xiao Tao's death haunted me. Eventually the prospect of losing another child forced me to make up my mind. For Shanshan's sake, I would persuade Zhiying to do what Cheng Ming – no, what *I* wanted him to do. Wiping my tears away, I spoke to him in the calmest voice I could manage.

'It's the trend now – you told me so. The state industries are being taken over. Didn't you say there was some new policy about encouraging private enterprise?' I asked.

He glared at me. 'That's for ailing industries. Ours is going from strength to strength.'

'The other day you said it was easy to manipulate figures if you put your mind to it. Why don't you do that?'

'I can't believe you're saying this. You talk as if you don't care about the factory.'

'You know I do, but our child is dying! The factory can't breathe!'

'I'm responsible for three thousand lives! How many will lose their jobs and homes? Have you thought about that? Wenya, the factory is our life and theirs!'

I stood by the window. After a long time I turned to him. 'It's your life, not mine. Not any more.'

He strode over to me. 'You know what you're asking, don't you?'

'Cheng Ming said quite a few of your senior managers

had already been persuaded.' Zhenzhen had seemed shocked when she relayed to me what Cheng Ming had said. Lishan was not the only one he had been working on.

'If they want people to spit on them and curse their names in years to come, that's their problem.'

'There won't be any years to come for Shanshan, if we don't do this.'

'Wenya,' he said, 'I can't believe this – only three weeks ago we were prepared to fight to our last breath for the factory, and now you want me to hand it over to a man I despise.'

'Can't you see we have no *choice*?'

'I'd give my life for her, I would, but I can't bear to have our names blackened. And even if we save her, what will she have to live for, with disgraced parents?'

'I don't care what people think of us. Our names are tarnished anyway. How much worse could it be?' I whispered.

He turned very pale. 'Wenya, you hate me, don't you? You'll never forgive me for Xiao Wu.'

Trembling, my hand touched something on the table. I glanced down. It was one of Shanshan's teddy bears. I held it to my chest. 'If you agree to this, I will.'

21

After the intense heat outside, the air-conditioning made me shiver. Though both ends of the day were cool now, the midday sun seemed hotter than it did on the hottest summer days. The private dining room was discreet, the windows veiled, admitting only blurred views of the river. In contrast to the noisy karaoke music in most restaurants Zhiying took me to, here the music was restrained: soft, traditional harp and flute. The four of us sat around a huge round table. I glanced quickly to Zhiying and Zhenzhen, who was staring out of the window, and set my eyes on Cheng Ming, who sat opposite me. Before he arrived, I thought I wouldn't recognise him, but I did almost immediately. He wore a traditional white shirt with a stand-up collar. It was pure silk, and at first glance he had the gentle gestures of a *t'ai chi* master: the fine wrinkles and the deep-set eyes from which a strange light shone spoke of wisdom and experience. He'd lost the hunted look of old and was poised and smooth, a man at ease with himself and the world. It had been a long time.

He raised a hand, and a waitress materialised as if by

magic. Perhaps she had been crouching behind the velvet curtains in the corner of the room. I'd had no idea she was there. He whispered to her and she nodded, then left. A stream of waitresses came in with a big plate of cold meat, four small bowls of rice and four plates of prettily arranged vegetables. It was by no means a banquet, rather an ordinary meal beautifully presented. He extended a hand. 'Let's eat first, then talk business.'

Zhiying ate angrily and noisily, as if he was starving. Once in a while Cheng Ming paused to peer at him, frowning with disapproval. I thought he was hoping Zhiying would look up, which he never did. Finally, Zhiying put down his chopsticks. He stared at Cheng Ming as if he planned to eat him alive. But now Cheng Ming chose not to meet his eyes and instead raised his hand. In a matter of seconds, the waitresses had cleared the table. 'Don't come unless we call,' Cheng Ming said softly. The last nodded and closed the door behind her.

Cheng Ming swung his chair round and gazed at the view. 'The river never stops.' He swung back suddenly, and laughed. 'But we grow older.'

At this he glanced quickly at Zhenzhen with an ambiguous look. Her face turned crimson. Bastard, I said to myself, but managed not to show my fury. Cheng Ming continued, 'What a reunion this is. When was the last time we all met – ten years ago? Or longer? Wenya,' he smiled at me, 'you've hardly changed.'

I shuddered. I remembered his face above mine on that New Year's Eve when I was pregnant with Xiao Tao. He had made a pass at me – the wife of a colleague, a friend. He had been drunk so I'd excused him and never told Zhiying. But today he was sober, and we were all in his power. Because of our daughter, we had to beg money from him – a man who had hurt us all.

I smiled back. 'You flatter me, Cheng Ming. We change slowly, but it seems you are very much in tune with the times. You always were.'

His smile remained but he said nothing.

Zhiying was trembling, his fist clenching, relaxing and clenching again. 'Don't waste time. Let's talk money,' he said, without looking at Cheng Ming.

Cheng Ming nodded. As I watched him, I realised that perhaps for him this was simply another deal.

'Money isn't the issue,' he said lightly. 'Tell me about your lives. We haven't seen each other for so long.'

'There's nothing to say,' Zhiying said. 'If it hadn't been for Shanshan, I wouldn't be sitting anywhere near you.'

'Oh dear,' said Cheng Ming, as if he was surprised. 'Not even for old times' sake?'

'Don't tempt me,' Zhiying snapped, and I glared at him. However strongly he felt, I didn't want him to antagonise Cheng Ming, whose soft voice frightened me more than Zhiying's outbursts.

Zhenzhen remained quiet, staring straight past us at the floor.

'Let's talk about the present then,' said Cheng Ming. 'I heard Zhiying has found himself a nice little secretary . . .'

'You—' Zhiying sprang up and made as if to hit him.

But Cheng Ming didn't budge. 'Zhiying, it's no secret, and I'm not going to criticise you. It's a rare chief executive indeed in today's world who doesn't have a "companion". I'm neither surprised nor scandalised.'

The room was so quiet we could hear each other breathing. I was overcome with disgust, not only for the sneering Cheng Ming but for Zhiying and myself.

Suddenly Cheng Ming became brisk. He reached down and drew a thick wad of papers out of a briefcase. 'To business,' he said.

Zhiying signed the documents, which declared the factory bankrupt, based on figures worked out by Lishan. Armed with them, Cheng Ming would be able to bid for it – and he would get it: he'd bribed the provincial leaders to grant their approval so that no other bidder would stand a chance. It was eerily quick and matter-of-fact. Indeed, the other committee members had already signed. Now Zhiying's name joined theirs. On the last paper, Zhiying glanced at me, as if for reassurance. I nodded. The corner of his mouth twisted and he scribbled his name without glancing at the paper.

Cheng Ming took the papers. 'Now,' he rose, 'to the bank for the transfer. Will you come with me, Zhenzhen? You promised you would.'

He extended a hand to her, and she stood up slowly. She shivered, almost imperceptibly, then grasped the hand. There was a strange twinkle in her eyes. Was she all right? I nearly touched her forehead. She was only going to the bank with him, but I felt as if she was leaving us for ever, as I had when she had gone with him to the south. With a sense of foreboding I reached for her free hand. It was icy cold.

'Why are you taking her?' Zhiying asked.

'Well, let's just say we have unfinished business to resolve. She left me stranded last time. Don't worry – I won't harm her.' Cheng Ming laughed, and pulled her closer to him.

'He's right,' Zhenzhen said softly, and looked up at him,

a strange smile spreading across her face. She let go of my hand. 'You two go to Shanshan and wait for the good news.'

I was struck by what a handsome pair they still made.

'Swine,' Zhiying whispered, as they swept past us.

Cheng Ming stopped, then came slowly back to us wearing a sarcastic smile. 'I've only betrayed one person,' he said, 'yet you call me a swine. You have betrayed an entire factory – as well as your family. What do you call yourself?'

They left.

We stood by the window. A boat was crossing the river, its sails high as if in triumph. On the wide boulevard, traffic flowed past. There was no sound, and the scene seemed remote. It dawned on me then that life would never be the same again.

22

Outside, the heat clung to us, while the hustle and bustle around us was a shock – life went on. We'd just done the unthinkable. Would Cheng Ming complete the deal? Would Zhenzhen be all right? Cheng Ming had assured us the tracks were covered, that Lishan's figures were so well worked out that nothing could go wrong. But although I knew it was in his own interests that Zhiying should not be found out, I was frightened. We had made a pact with the devil. I had forced Zhiying to betray his principles. State industries had been sold previously to private individuals, but only ailing ones. If it was discovered that East Wind had been sold through bribery while it was making a handsome profit, he'd go to jail.

The sunlight made me feel faint. I watched Zhiying stare at the crowds and realised I no longer hated him – instead I pitied him. A minute later, he said, 'It's hot – let me take you to a bath-house.'

I followed him along the riverfront until he stopped in front of a huge glass-fronted building. I had walked past it several times before and had always been interested in what went on inside. The posters outside advertised massage and traditional Chinese medical treatments for all sorts of ailments, but the smartly dressed people going in and coming out had always made me feel it was forbidden to me.

Zhiying seemed to know it well. He nodded at the scantily dressed receptionist, then led me up a carpeted staircase to the second floor, where we walked past rooms, from which strong fragrances wafted, with curious classical names: Leisure Scholar Pavilion, Red Sleeves Holding the Candles, Moon Veranda. On either side of each door were pinned couplets from traditional poems. He stopped in front of a room called Pool of Fallen Blossoms and opened the door. A large bathtub stood in the middle of the room, filled with steaming water. A sofa-bed stood at either side. Zhiying unbuttoned my shirt. At first I protested. 'Why is it so dark?' but he didn't answer. He continued to undress me, then himself.

The room had a hypnotic effect on me. I succumbed to the allure of the scent and the inviting look of the bath. The water was the perfect temperature. I lay down in it next to him. Sweat poured out of me, I felt drowsy and sank into a daydream.

I was back at the pond on a hot day . . . Everyone was there: Lao Gao, Zhiying, Cheng Ming and Xiao Tao. Zhenzhen? There she was, about to dive in. I turned to Zhiying but something was worrying me. I glanced over my shoulder. Zhenzhen hadn't emerged from the water. Why not? I strained to see her but she was gone. I spun round and discovered that Zhiying and Xiao Tao had disappeared, too . . .

'Come in.'

The knock at the door and Zhiying's voice jerked me

back to reality. At first I thought they were attendants – in the darkness all I could see was two girls holding towels. But as they came near I saw that they were wearing bikinis. 'What is this?' I asked Zhiying.

'Wenya,' he said, 'let them give you a rub. This is a treat. I meant to bring you here a long time ago but . . . It might be hard at first, but try to enjoy it.'

I stood up, not caring that I was naked in front of two strangers. 'Get out!' I screamed. 'Get out and don't come back! Go and find something else to do! You're too young to work here!'

They were out of the door in no time.

As soon as the door was shut I hissed at Zhiying, 'You call this a *treat*?' I went to the window, pulled at the curtains and tried to open it. The lock was rusty. It was clear that nobody had opened it for a long time. But anger gave me strength and I managed to twist it open. A gust of wind blew in from the river, cool and refreshing. I stood in front of it, eyes closed, arms wide open. When I turned back, Zhiying was standing in the middle of the room, bewildered. 'I'll give you a treat,' I murmured. 'Turn to the wall and put your hands on it,' I told him. He did so. I grabbed a hand towel and started to scrub his back. At the base of his neck I found the scar from when he had been persecuted about Lao Gao. I used to bathe the sore red skin with hot damp towels. My hands trembled: though it was bruised, aged, and stained by another woman's touch, I knew his body better than I did my own.

I scrubbed his arms, neck and waist, then his legs . . . The rhythmic work was satisfying. Years ago, when we had first married, there was no bathroom in our flat, and this was how we washed – scrubbing and rubbing each other's back. We'd hardly ever done so after we had moved to the luxury flat. His skin grew pink, and red patches appeared but he didn't stir. When I had finished I marched him to the shower, which I'd seen just as the girls were leaving. I turned it full on and made him stand there. His shoulders heaved as he sobbed, the water pouring down him.

Exhausted, I let the towel drop. A strong feeling, of protection and possession, took hold of me. My hands trembled with the urge to slap him and hold him close. I stood there until a sharp pain stabbed me and I sank on to the wet floor. 'My back,' I managed to say between spasms.

Wet from the shower, Zhiying helped me to a sofa-bed where I lay flat. He knelt in front of me. 'Wenya, are you all right?'

After a long time I sighed. 'Better,' I murmured.

'Listen to me,' he said. He swallowed, as if he was trying to make up his mind about something. From where I lay, I could see the lines on his face. I saw, too, a red fingermark on his shoulder where I'd scrubbed him.

'Now you know about my . . . other life,' he said slowly.

'You call this a life?'

He watched me with sad eyes. 'They're not prostitutes, but massage girls. I come here often for work with customers . . .' He lowered his eyes. 'I want you to know me – this new me. You might not like it, but I owe you the truth.'

I liked his voice, low and earnest, a voice I used to know well.

'Sometimes I think there are two Zhiyings, the Zhiying that remains truthful to you, to the past, and the Zhiying who lives in an exciting new world that sometimes disgusts me. All those years of hardship we suffered – isn't it right that we should enjoy life a little? Big wrists like Cheng Ming have all the things money can buy. I have no money, but I do have power. Isn't that mine to use? And if I don't, people around me—'

'Don't talk about other people.'

'About me and Xiao Wu,' he continued. 'Don't hate her, blame me. I took advantage of her youth. She reminded me of you when we first met. That may be a bad excuse, but it's the truth.'

The pain in my back was receding. Now the curtain was pulled back I could see the room clearly – the stains on the carpet. It wasn't as luxurious and clean as I'd thought. So this was part of Zhiying's new life: dirt behind a glittering façade. Tears of humiliation flowed, tears of disgust and pity. How had my pure, idealistic man changed so much?

I struggled to my feet. Through the window I glimpsed the high-rise flats by the riverfront, festooned with for-sale signs. Many blocks were still being built. I shuddered. What right had I to condemn him? Had I not enjoyed the privileges of being an East Wind first lady? I had helped to corrupt Zhiying, by making him favour Ying, my old friend. I had made him the criminal he now was, forcing him to sell the factory against his principles. Zhiying was not the only one who had been corrupted. I had been, too.

I glanced back to him still kneeling beside the sofa-bed, looking straight at me. 'Wenya, I'm sorry. I never wanted to hurt you.'

I began to get dressed, the pain in my back slowing me. Zhiying had put on his clothes quickly and helped me with my shoes. Holding my elbow, he helped me down the stairs.

Outside the bath-house, he gave me an unexpected grin. 'That was a good rub.' As the clock at the town hall struck, I took the hand he held out to me. It had been brave of him to take me into his world, and he was right: I had been repelled by it, but I wanted to know more.

'Wenya, Xiao Wu said she loved me. Nobody's ever said that to me before, not my parents, not you. There was something about that word . . .' He gazed into the distance. 'It's the curse of our generation that we never learned to say it. But it doesn't mean we don't feel it. It's just a word . . .'

'No, it isn't. I wish I'd said it to you.'

He looked at me expectantly, and I knew what he was waiting for, but I still couldn't say it. It felt too intimate, too soon.

His eyes dimmed. After a while he murmured, 'But will you say you forgive me? Tomorrow might be too late.'

'I forgive you.'

23

Zhiying's mobile phone rang while we were in a cafe. 'It's Zhenzhen,' he whispered.

I grabbed it from him. 'Zhenzhen, are you all right?'

'I'm fine. I've got good news. The money's in the bank – I saw Cheng Ming make the transfer. And I've got the papers Zhiying signed. I got them back from Cheng Ming. Meet me at the Long Life bar by the river.'

She sounded rushed and far away. I put it down to the background noise – as if she was washing something. I heard water. 'She's done it! The money's in! And she's got the papers!'

'What papers?'

'The ones you signed – she's got them back from Cheng Ming. You're all right now!'

'I don't believe it!' A glimmer of hope came into Zhiying's eyes.

'Zhenzhen's got the papers back from Cheng Ming.'

'But why did he give them to her?'

'She says to meet her in the bar by the river. Let's hurry.' I wanted to see the papers for myself, but I was more prepared than Zhiying to believe Zhenzhen.

We hailed a taxi. It was a short drive but it seemed to take a long time, made even longer by the heavy rush-hour traffic. We studied the buildings that had erupted everywhere. When we had first moved here, ours had been the tallest, newest building, but now it was dwarfed by even taller, and newer ones. Rich people lived here, and sometimes we had been fooled into thinking we were like them. What was two-hundred thousand *yuan* to a wealthy man like Cheng Ming? But to us it was a life-saving sum – and people like Yun would work all their lives and never see anywhere near that amount. Still, nearly a quarter of a million *yuan* was waiting for us in the bank, taken from an evil, wealthy man, and Shanshan would get better. At the thought of my daughter I was suddenly seized by emotion: I hadn't seen her all day, apart from a snatched, five-minute visit on the way to the meeting with Cheng Ming. Normally Zhiying or I would be at her bedside, day or night. Now we had the money, now we were so close to being able to save her, I wanted nothing to go wrong.

I turned to Zhiying; why was his face so pale? Half in affection and half in frustration, I wrapped my arms round him. 'Something isn't right,' he whispered. 'I can't believe it's so easy. I fear for Zhenzhen – hurry,' he yelled at the driver.

I paused to read the sign for the bar: 'Long Life Noodle, Eat Here for Eternal Life.' For some reason it checked my sense of jubilation.

I searched for Zhenzhen and saw her sitting at a table with a cup of white wine in front of her. The only other customers were two peasant couples at the table furthest from the counter, where the owner, a middle-aged man in a white apron, was chopping raw meat. As we arrived Zhenzhen tapped a pile of papers at her elbow.

Zhiying sat down and flipped through them. He flinched at the sight of his signature, along with those of the other committee members. But he didn't dwell on them for long. He was focused on Zhenzhen, whose face was red with wine. 'How did you get these, Zhenzhen? Did he . . . do anything to you?'

'No. And he can't do anything to me – not any more,' she said.

'What do you mean?' Zhiying asked.

'You don't need to know. Just go – you've no time to lose. Go and tell them we've got the money and they can operate,' Zhenzhen said.

'But . . .'

'Go now, Zhiying. Don't you trust Sister Zhenzhen? I've got a few things to tell Wenya, and then we'll be done. Women's matters,' she added, when Zhiying lingered.

I had no idea why but, like Zhenzhen, I was suddenly overwhelmed with the urge to get Zhiying out of the way. I grabbed the papers and handed them to him.

'Zhenzhen—'

'Go, quickly.' We hurried him out.

I waited for Zhenzhen to finish her drink, but she seemed in no hurry, although the hand that held the cup trembled. I pretended not to have seen. The man behind the counter held the chopper high above his head, then smashed it down on a lamb joint and hacked at it with uncanny precision. His sleeves and apron were spattered with blood and a few flies buzzed round him, impatient to feed. The peasant couples left. I turned to Zhenzhen – and I saw the red spots on her torn white shirt.

'Zhenzhen—'

She put a finger to her lips. 'It's hot, isn't it?' she said, helping me up.

The restaurant man took the large note she'd pressed into his hand, looking puzzled. We didn't wait for the change.

Outside, it was getting dark and I followed her, my feet light and unsteady, as if I was drunk, too.

24

Night fell and mist rose, half obscuring the river and the bridge that connected China with Korea. Time seemed suspended, as if there would be no tomorrow.

'We workers are powerful. Every day we toil hard.
Our faces shine, our sweat pours – for what?
For the liberation of the world.
We are the new masters, we can change the world . . .'

Zhenzhen's voice rang out drunkenly in the still night. I joined her halfway through, wanting to laugh, but instead my throat tightened. I steered us to the street, where taxis streamed past. 'I'll take you home,' I said. 'You need to rest.'

'Home?' She looked at me as if she was confused, then shook her head. 'No, Wenya, I don't want to go home.'

I was determined that she should go home and rest. 'Come on . . .' I grabbed her and raised a finger. A taxi cruising on the other side of the road screeched to a halt and stopped, then drove across to us. Zhenzhen struggled. 'I'm not going home, Wenya.'

The taxi was in front of us, the driver hooting impatiently.

'Come on!'

'No, Wenya, I can't.'

I dismissed the driver who spat and screeched off. 'Tell me what really happened.'

Slowly she raised both her hands and stared at them, then glanced down at her white shirt with the red stains. 'He's gone.'

'Zhenzhen!'

'We're safe now – I made sure of it. We're safe from him for ever.'

I felt the blood drain from my face, as a chill spread through me. 'Zhenzhen . . .'

A shrill sound. My mobile phone. I pulled it out of my pocket. 'Wenya?' It was Zhiying.

'What is it?'

'It's Shanshan. There's a problem with her spleen – she's bleeding internally. They want to operate now; it's an emergency. Come now.' He hung up.

'You must go,' Zhenzhen whispered.

'I'm not leaving you, Zhenzhen. Come with me to Zhiying – we'll think of something. He'll know someone. Go to the south. I'll come with you.' I talked and thought fast.

She nodded vaguely but kept her eyes on the river. 'To the south . . .'

'But for now, come with me to the hospital.'

She hesitated for a second. 'No. You go to Shanshan. I'll walk here by the river to clear my head. I'll join you later.'

A taxi drove by and stopped a little ahead.

'Come now, Zhenzhen.'

'Later. I need to see the river first. I must think.'

The driver beeped. Zhenzhen pulled me towards it and pushed me in. 'Go, Wenya. You lost Xiao Tao. You don't want to lose Shanshan too. Go now. Give her a kiss from me.' She turned to the driver. 'City hospital, quick.'

The last I saw of my sister Zhenzhen, she was walking towards the river, her back to me.

25

For three days Shanshan struggled between life and death. For three days Zhiying and I stayed with her, praying that she would pull through, and recover sufficiently to undergo the bone marrow transplant. I called Zhenzhen's mobile constantly, but got no reply. Zhiying went to her flat and searched in all the usual places, but couldn't find her. We feared the worst, but comforted ourselves that she might have gone south, or even further.

On the fourth day, when Zhiying came back from a quick visit to the factory he told me Lishan, one of the other signatories, had been arrested. I realised Zhiying might be in danger. Could anyone else have witnessed Zhiying signing the papers the other day? Would Lishan incriminate Zhiying? I was anxious, but Zhiying remained calm. That night, when the ward grew quiet, Zhiying made a strong pot of tea, as he had these last three nights, and sat next to me by Shanshan's bed. We talked and talked, and sometimes we just held hands, saying nothing. We wondered where Zhenzhen might be. When Zhiying spoke of consequences, I did not stop him: I knew that he was preparing for the worst, and that he was trying to prepare me, too. We had attempted a crime, and we knew that, somehow, we would have to pay.

'All I want is to see Shanshan smile again,' said Zhiying.

I managed to sleep that night, and when I woke up the next morning, the sound of birdsong filled me with hope. Somehow, I knew Shanshan would come back to me. Zhiying left to go to the washroom. When he had gone, I leaned to check on Shanshan; I thought I could see a little pink in her cheek. Once, in my childhood, I had watched for a seed I'd planted to grow. I had stood for nearly a whole afternoon willing it to burst out of the soil. It didn't. Many days later, when I'd forgotten about it, I'd come home to find a green shoot. Patience was all I had now.

Zhiying came back from the washroom. 'Wake up, Shanshan,' he whispered, squatting beside her, holding her hand. Gently he held it to his forehead.

I heard heavy footsteps in the corridor, followed by doors opening and closing. They stopped just outside our door.

Zhiying glanced up, his face pale but calm. 'Be good,' he mouthed to me, and gazed once more at Shanshan, still fast asleep. Then, before I could speak, the door was pushed open.

A team of green-uniformed police thronged in, headed by a man with a pair of handcuffs. 'Lin Zhiying, follow us,' he said.

As he was led away, I stretched my hands towards Zhiying. 'For only one day of being a couple you owe each other a debt of affection for a hundred days.' The old saying flashed into my mind. How many days of affection would that make now that we had been married for thirty-odd years?

I listened to the last echoes of his footsteps as he left the building and to the car as it drove away. Then I glanced down, to see Shanshan opening her eyes. 'Mummy,' she said with a smile.

Epilogue

Half of the city was engrossed in the trial. There were demonstrations for and against Zhiying, which the police had to disperse. After the guilty verdict, his supporters rioted, and were quelled again by the police. Zhiying, with three colleagues, was sentenced to ten years' imprisonment for accepting bribes.

It had taken them two days to discover Cheng Ming's body, with a stab wound to his chest. A few weeks later a fisherman who lived downstream found Zhenzhen's.

Zhiying's prison was not far from Peach Blossom Village, where Yun had lived. After Shanshan had been discharged from hospital, I moved with Yun to the countryside nearby, and nursed Shanshan back to health. From there we paid monthly visits to Zhiying. One autumn day, when we were with him, he slipped suddenly off his chair and died of a heart-attack. He was in the third year of his imprisonment. After we had buried him on Hat Hill, with Mother, Xiao Tao, Lao Gao and Zhenzhen, Shanshan and I emigrated to Australia. I wanted Shanshan to be near the best treatment money could buy in case she should have a relapse. Also, I needed to be out of China: where we had lived with Yun, nobody had known who we were, but I couldn't be sure that this would be so for long. I had resolved to tell her of all that had happened on her eighteenth birthday, but not before: the weight of three lives would be too heavy for those slender young shoulders to bear.

I lived under a false name and made a living by offering Chinese massage and cleaning. Shanshan did well at school and even made the swimming team. Sometimes, as I watched her, I thought I could see the shadow of Zhenzhen with her.

Some days I managed to forget all that had happened in the far-off land of my birth. But one day, in the street, I thought I saw a ghost – a face I had once known so well: Father's on the day he had left me and Mother all those years ago. Coincidence? I followed the man as he went about his shopping. But he resembled Father not only in appearance but in his gestures – even the way in which his gaze shot absently through a crowd. Finally I could bear it no longer. I stopped him in the street.

'Do you know Zhou Chen?' I asked, in Chinese, and saw his eyes twinkle.

'Why do you ask?' He was Chinese, but his accent was odd.

'Zhou Chen was my father, and you look like him,' I said.

'Your father?' he said sharply.

'Yes.'

'My father was also called Zhou Chen.'

'Zhou Chen from north-east China?'

He nodded.

'Zhou Chen who played the flute and joined the KMT?'

He grabbed my hand. 'You must be Wenya! Father's only daughter!' he said. 'I'm your half-brother, Wenjie, from Taiwan. Father always talked about you.'

My father hadn't been killed during the retreat to Taiwan. He had survived, settled there and as the gulf between the mainland and Taiwan widened, gave up on ever being reunited with his family and married a woman from Shandong who had borne him two sons. My half-brothers said that Father often talked about his mainland family. He had died at the age of seventy-four.

Exile was easier to bear after I had found my family. My half-brothers were settled in Australia, and Shanshan grew fond of her cousins. They were always curious to hear about our life in China, but I could never bear to describe all that we'd been through. They had not lived there through the movements and persecutions, so how could they appreciate the sacrifice, passion and compromise? Would they judge our standard of living, our concept of beauty, our interpretation of truth harshly? Would they say that we loved too little and hated too much? Would they condemn me for not loving my husband when he was good and innocent, or for having grown to love him after he had hurt us? Would they understand why I had now forgiven everyone, including Cheng Ming? Would they wonder, as I did sometimes, whether things might have been different had I known that Father was still alive? Would I have idolised him as I had? Would I have felt so drawn to Cheng Ming? Would I still have married Zhiying? Would Xiao Tao still be alive?

It wasn't long before Shanshan rebelled against my protectiveness: I was so at odds with the morals and beliefs of our new country. But I kept trying: she was all I had. She alone could wash away the pain and sadness.

When Shanshan went to university I felt free. I often took myself to the coast and walked along the shoreline, the waves lapping at my feet, reminding me of my past on the other side of the ocean. Sometimes I would remember what Zhiying had said to me, during the long night before he was arrested, when we had sat up talking: 'I have always admired women like you, your mother and Zhenzhen. When you believe in something you stick to it, no matter what. We men are cowards, and when we betray, which we do, you must remember it is through weakness, not malice.'

Author's Note

I have an aversion to politics, and yet I've written a book which seems to be full of political terms, almost too much so for my own liking. Let me explain.

A quick glance at the key dates that follow this note will tell you that China has had its fair share of political movements. In mid-sixties' China where I grew up, politics was the most important subject at school. This meant studying the history of the Chinese Communist Party, Marxist philosophy and current affairs – the latter involved studying and understanding the essence of the numerous movements launched by the government through the editorials of the *People's Daily* newspaper. Naturally these lessons did not appeal to teenagers.

Real life was also full of politics and its consequences: a neighbour killed a man during the violent clashes in the earlier days of the Cultural Revolution; my own grandfather was termed a 'rightist' and was humiliated and then exiled to the countryside – this had a rippling effect on his children, who faced varying degrees of prejudice. Having publicly denounced a beloved teacher at school, I was scolded and shunned by my wise grandmother. Telling her the teacher herself had invited this criticism confused me even more . . .

That was when I decided politics was both boring and dangerous, and that I wanted nothing to do with it.

As I grew older, however, my elders' attitude to this period fascinated me. I found, for example, that my mother, who suffered because of her father's status, vacillated between wanting to talk all the time and declaring that she never wanted to remember the past.

Now I understand this apparent contradiction. It was a painful past, but it also defined the youth of my parents' generation. Their experience embraced real idealism and simple confusion as well as oppression and violence; happiness and generosity as well as pain and turmoil. For them, politics were intensely personal. In writing this novel, I have concentrated on the latter dimension: the emotional and physical price this generation had to pay as a result of the numerous upheavals and political movements they lived through. I don't blame them for wanting to forget the past, but it is my hope that their courage and endurance, and above all, their individuality, will never be forgotten.

All this I hope helps to explain the liberties I've taken with dates: I start the book on a spring day in the 1960s, with a courting couple at the height of the Great Leap Forward, their hope for their own future entwined with the country's hope for a new, better China – only for it to be dashed by the combined blow of the years of famine and the withdrawal of economic help from the Soviet Union, one of 'New China's' few international allies at that time. Young and positive as they were, this disappointment only made them eager and more passionate in their beliefs. Historically the height of the 'Great Leap Forward' is 1958; by 1960 it was subsiding. The famine years were 1960–1963 and the Soviet Union withdrew its technical experts in 1960. In other words, to make a dramatic scene, I've placed the Great Leap Forward slightly later in time.

Not all 'movements' of the period are mentioned here, I have avoided referring to those that are not relevant to the development of my characters. At the end of the book, I have taken a slight liberty with the mobile phone, which although not unheard of in China in the early 1990s, was certainly not ubiquitous. I hope, though, that readers will agree that this technology has been one of the defining experiences of the last fifteen years or so.

At the other end of the technological spectrum, the bark, leaves and blossoms of pagoda trees are edible and were a food source during the famine years, but *song xiacao* is my own invention.

In other words, what is most important as one tries to build up a portrait of these years, is not dry facts and dates, but the lasting emotional impact they have on the lives of those who lived through them. What I hope I've achieved is an evocation of the atmosphere of the period, true to the spirit of the times.

Liu Hong
March 2007

A Brief Outline of Key Dates

1912	End of last feudal dynasty and establishment of the Republic of China under the Nationalists
1937–1945	Japan invades China – Sino-Japanese war
1945–1949	Civil war between the Communists and Nationalists
1949	Communist victory in civil war resulting in establishment of the People's Republic of China
1950–1953	Korean War – Chinese army helps North Korean Communists fight South Korea and US army
1957	Anti-rightist movement
1958–1962	The Great Leap Forward
1960	Soviet Union withdraws financial help from China
1960–1963	Famine
1966–1976	Cultural Revolution
1976	Death of Mao Zedong
1989	Tiananmen Square massacre – peaceful

	pro-democracy demonstration violently suppressed by government forces
Late 1980s	Economic reform started by Deng Xiaoping
Mid-1990s	Large-scale privatisation of state industries begins

Acknowledgements

I thank my parents and parents-in-law. From Dandong and Chalk Farm, they came in our hours of greatest need and never wavered in their love and support. Their numerous English stews and Chinese stir fries nourished the body and warmed the heart, while many reminiscences of the past and heated discussions provided rich sources of information and inspiration. I thank my husband Jonky for being the central pillar of my existence. As well as being the most hands-on, adoring daddy, he is instrumental in helping me to find my voice in this new, adopted language. I am grateful for the understanding and patience of our girls when Mummy had to disappear into session after session of writing her 'stories'. I hope they will learn to love them as they grow older.

As ever, I benefited hugely from the generosity and wisdom of my agent Jessica Woollard, editor Mary-Anne Harrington and copy-editor Hazel Orme, as well as from the professionalism of Alice Shepherd and Leah Woodburn at Headline Review. Susie Jolly, whose judgment and comments I increasingly rely on, helped to shape the novel for the better. In reading through the manuscript, Zoe Wardley made razor-sharp observations with her keen doctor's eyes, but gave her advice with the lightest of touches. I thank Ross Hulbert, my publicist, for his infectious enthusiasm. In sharing with me her tremendous insight into, and knowledge of, contemporary Chinese society, Xinran Xue has made me feel both truly humble and well supported. Thank you also to Kirsten, Linda, Rachel, Ruth and Sue, other mums who, along with many others, offered encouragement as well as practical help. I have drawn great strength from their much-valued friendship.